A SIMPLE CASE OF SEDUCTION

ADELE CLEE

This is a work of fiction. All names, characters, places and incidents are products of the author's imagination. All characters are fictitious and any resemblance to real persons, living or dead, is purely coincidental.

A Simple Case of Seduction
Copyright © 2017 Adele Clee
All rights reserved.
ISBN-13: 978-0-9955705-3-5

The Mysterious Miss Flint (excerpt)
Copyright © 2017 Adele Clee
All rights reserved.

Cover designed by **Jay Aheer**

Books by Adele Clee

To Save a Sinner

A Curse of the Heart

What Every Lord Wants

The Secret To Your Surrender

A Simple Case of Seduction

Anything for Love Series

What You Desire

What You Propose

What You Deserve

What You Promised

The Brotherhood Series

Lost to the Night

Slave to the Night

Abandoned to the Night

Lured to the Night

Lost Ladies of London

The Mysterious Miss Flint

The Deceptive Lady Darby

The Scandalous Lady Sandford

The Daring Miss Darcy

CHAPTER 1

THE THICK SMOKE WAFTED THROUGH THE TURKISH-INSPIRED bedchamber. The heavy scent of spice and strange tobacco clawed at the back of Daniel Thorpe's throat. He waved his hand in front of his face in a bid to breathe clean air, resisted the urge to cough and splutter. The sound of raucous laughter, coupled with the satisfied grunts of other patrons in the rooms adjacent, made it impossible to listen to his inner voice.

The ebony-haired woman sat on her knees and gestured to the bed. "Are you going to stand there all night? Do you not like what you see?"

Daniel shook his head and tried to focus on her bare breasts, hoping to rouse a sliver of enthusiasm.

What the hell was wrong with him?

Many times he had sated his lust in a similar way. Many times he had buried himself deep inside a woman, thrust long and hard to eradicate the image of Daphne Chambers.

But the time spent in Mrs Chambers' company these last two weeks had taken its toll. The widow's alluring essence had penetrated his skin, seeped into his blood. Whenever his mind was

1

quiet, he could hear the seductive lilt of her voice, the sound like a siren's song singing to his most primal of needs.

Bloody hell!

Had he not learnt anything over the years?

Like a fool, he believed his forged armour strong enough to withstand her attack. But he failed to appreciate the power of her mystical presence.

"Damn it all." The bitter words burst from his lips.

In response to his sudden outburst, the naked woman crept across the red satin sheet like a panther stalking its prey. She grabbed the waistband of his breeches and tried to pull him closer to the bed. "Nerves is it? Do you want a helpin' hand?"

Masculine pride forced him to take hold of her chin, claim her lips and thrust his tongue into her mouth. The act did nothing to ease the deep sense of longing filling his chest. It did nothing to flame his desire, to banish the ghosts of the past.

He broke on a curse. "Damnation. I must leave."

"Leave? Leave!" The woman palmed her breasts as though he had failed to appreciate their magnificence. "I've never had a man leave once he's paid."

"Keep the money," Daniel snapped. "My decision bears no reflection on your ability to please. I have pressing business elsewhere."

"That's all well for you to say. What if other men hear you left without so much as a grunt or groan?" She gathered the sheet to cover her modesty though the action conveyed contempt as opposed to bashfulness.

Daniel dragged his hand down his face. He took his coat from the chair and shrugged into it. "Here." Taking two sovereigns from his pocket, he threw them onto the bed. "They should ease your concerns."

Without another word, he strode from the room and descended the stairs as if late for an appointment. As always, his carriage was waiting outside. The streets were not safe for a man of his profession although a fight would ease the deep-rooted need clawing within. One man, or even two, would not prove to be a problem for someone skilled with his fists. But those intent on revenge often used dishonourable methods to achieve their goal.

"New Bond Street," he called to his coachman, Murphy.

"Aye, sir. Same place as last night?"

The innocent question caused anger to flare. Why could he not stay away? Why could he not push Mrs Chambers from his thoughts and be done with it?

"Indeed," he said, knowing he would not sleep until dawn, until certain no one entered Madame Fontaine's shop uninvited. "The fog has lifted. I shall need you to wait a little further along the street tonight."

Murphy nodded. "Right you are, sir."

Daniel climbed into the carriage, threw himself back into the seat and buried his head in his hands. The rhythmical rocking of his conveyance did little to soothe his irate mood.

Although loath to admit it, Daphne Chambers was an accomplished enquiry agent. So why did she insist on living above the modiste shop? Why did she not understand the importance of privacy? Why was she so damn stubborn?

If only he had been outside Madame Fontaine's on the night the thief entered the premises. The matter would have been dealt with swiftly. And he would not be consumed with the need to protect the one woman he desperately wanted to avoid. The thought of Mrs Chambers waking to find the rogue in her home caused his heart to thump wildly in his chest.

Why would she not accept that London was a dangerous place for a lady on her own?

The carriage rumbled to a halt outside Brown's pawnbrokers. From this location, he had a perfect view of the modiste shop. Yet what he saw hit him like a whip to the face. The wooden board covering the large front window had not been there last night. Curiosity burned. Anger flared. He suppressed the urge to pound the door and demand to know the reason behind this recent addition. But then an argument would ensue, and Mrs Chambers would shoo him away as one did a mangy dog.

With hours to wait until dawn, he folded his arms across his chest and settled down to keep watch. Few people walked the streets at such an early hour of the morning. Every noise—the clip of shoes on the pavement, the closing of a sash—captured his attention.

When a carriage rattled up and stopped outside Madame Fontaine's, the blood rushed through Daniel's veins so rapidly he could not sit still. Without thought, he pulled the pistol from the box under his seat, opened the door and vaulted down.

Rounding the suspicious vehicle, he saw a figure lingering in the doorway. The gentleman's top hat sat askew. His blue velvet coat was crumpled and creased. He stood but a foot from the door, his hands hidden from view.

"What business do you have here?" Daniel's blunt tone did not rouse a response.

The gentleman burped, wobbled, but did not turn around.

"Show me your damn hands," Daniel insisted, "else you'll feel a lead ball in your back."

"W-what?" The man attempted to swing around but lost his balance and ended up in a heap on the ground. "Can a man not take a piss in peace?" He blinked, his eyes growing wide as he noted the barrel of a pistol aimed at his head. "I … I … don't shoot." With one hand raised he scrambled to his feet.

Daniel's gaze drifted to the wet patch on the wall, and to the thin stream trickling towards the gutter. "You have ten seconds to return to your carriage and be on your way. The streets are unsafe at night. Should your bladder prove weak in future, I suggest you carry a pot beneath your seat." Gripping the pistol with one hand, Daniel removed his watch and flicked open the lid. "Now you have five seconds."

Clutching his top hat to his head the gentleman scurried to his vehicle, and the conveyance charged away.

Left alone at Madame Fontaine's door, Daniel contemplated knocking. But what would he say? Mrs Chambers would berate him for his interference.

With a disgruntled sigh and pistol in hand, Daniel returned to his carriage.

A long, lonely hour passed.

Sleep beckoned.

But his heavy lids sprang open at the sudden sliver of light in the upstairs window. He saw her then—Mrs Chambers. She peered out onto the street before closing the drapes.

In the dark confines of the small space, his mind concocted a host of images to account for her movements. He imagined her undressing slowly, sliding in between crisp white sheets, her ebony hair splayed across the pillow. In his fanciful musings, she appeared vulnerable. She needed him—wanted him. Rather than hear her clipped words, he heard the sweet moans of pleasure.

Bloody hell!

He should have taken the wench at the brothel when he had the chance.

Movement in the upstairs window caught his attention. Once again, she glanced out onto the street. With the absence of any light in the room beyond, he could not tell if she wore a dress or nightclothes. Not that it mattered.

Minutes passed.

The drapes twitched.

Damn.

He considered leaving.

A shadow appeared in the doorway. The shapely figure lingered, glanced left and right before striding across the road towards him. As always, the lady presented an amusing contradiction. The pelisse buttoned up to her throat was so opposed to her black hair draped seductively over one shoulder.

She ground to a halt at the door of his carriage and rapped twice on the glass.

With a muttered curse he lowered the window. "Good evening, Mrs Chambers."

"Evening? I think you'll find it is almost morning, Mr Thorpe. And this is the third night in a row that you have sat outside my door."

Daniel cleared his throat, purely because he did not know what to say.

She raised a brow. "Now, either you're in desperate need of funds and cannot wait for Mr Brown to open his shop, or you're intent on snooping."

"Snooping? Madam, snooping is the pastime of a gossip or a debutante with her eye on a suitor."

"Then pray tell me why you're here, Mr Thorpe."

What was he supposed to say? That he felt responsible for her. That in securing her safety he hoped for a night when she did not monopolise his dreams.

"I heard about the theft."

She seemed surprised. "And you thought I might have use of your investigative services?"

"Do you need my services?" Perhaps he'd gone about this the wrong way. Perhaps the best way to keep the woman safe was to work alongside her. With any luck, he would grow tired of her company.

Her bottom lip trembled. To disguise it, she wrapped her arms across her chest and shivered. "That depends on your fee."

A black cloud descended to darken his mood. Did she think so little of him? "For you, I would waive my fee and any expenses incurred. A lady must feel safe in her home."

Fear flashed in her eyes. It hit him like a barbed arrow to his heart. So much for his blasted armour.

"As much as I hate to admit it, I would value your opinion," Mrs Chambers said.

"Sometimes you can be too close to a case to think objectively."

He inclined his head in agreement. "Then tell me when and where we should meet, and I shall do my utmost to attend."

"There is no time like the present." She gestured to the house behind her. "I find I cannot sleep and so, if you have no prior engagement, you are welcome to come inside."

Daniel swallowed. To sit next to her on the sofa and relax in her private residence would create a level of intimacy best avoided. A heart hardened to all emotion brought a sense of peace. Would time spent in her company disturb his equilibrium, force him to address feelings long since buried?

Suppressing a sigh, he inclined his head. "Do you have something strong to drink?"

"I have brandy, Mr Thorpe. It often helps after a difficult case."

No case had ever taxed him to that extent. But working with Daphne Chambers would test his resolve, lead him to question his sanity. "Then I accept your hospitality," he said, despite grave reservations. "And you may tell me all about the pressing problem keeping you awake at night."

CHAPTER 2

RECKLESS WAS A WORD OFTEN USED TO DESCRIBE A WOMAN PAID
to pry into other people's affairs. Tonight, foolish and desperate
were accurate descriptions of Daphne's character, too. Why else
would she invite Mr Thorpe into her home? Why else would an
independent woman agree to his offer of assistance?

A shiver raced through Daphne's body at the thought of
Thorpe's commanding figure swamping her private space.

Time spent in Mr Thorpe's company proved exhausting.
Disapproval was an expression he wore to intimidate. As a
consequence, Daphne was always armed, always alert and ready
to challenge his critical opinion. Yet despite her initial anger at
finding him camped outside Madame Fontaine's shop, his presence brought her peace. Indeed, as he followed her into the
narrow hallway, his confident aura enveloped her like a cloak of
invincibility.

With a gentleman like Thorpe at one's side, what would a
lady have to fear?

"I assume Madame Fontaine is in bed?" Thorpe's question
disturbed her reverie.

Daphne stopped on the second stair leading up to her rooms.

Even from her elevated position, Thorpe was still an inch taller. "Betsy rises at five each morning and works until her eyes ache from squinting in the candlelight. At this hour, a bull on the rampage would struggle to wake her."

Thorpe frowned. "Betsy? Did the woman not train in Paris?"

"Paris? What a lazy assumption. Do you not scrutinise the background of every person you snoop on?" Daphne couldn't help but tease him. "As a skilled enquiry agent surely you know she hails from Spitalfields and learnt her trade with the Huguenot silk weavers."

Thorpe's intense gaze bored into her. "Why would I know that when I am not here to spy on the modiste?"

"So you admit you are here to snoop on me."

"Snooping is a woman's hobby," he said with some disdain. "Spying is a man's profession."

"So you're here purely in a professional capacity?" she said, knowing that he no longer considered her a friend. Thorpe had no friends—other than Mr Bostock.

A dark shadow passed over his face. With his mouth hidden behind the full beard, she imagined his lips drawn thin. "I am here out of concern for a colleague. You may make of it what you will."

Daphne sighed. The next hour would be long and painful. At least he'd not made a derogatory comment about a woman working. Had that been the case, she'd have thrown him out, which would have been a foolish thing to do under the circumstances.

"Whatever the reason, I am grateful to have someone to talk to." Daphne turned and climbed the stairs. Fear was the last emotion he would see swimming in her eyes.

The trudge of heavy footsteps confirmed he was following. Daphne led him into the small parlour, a place clean and comfortable yet sparse. One sweeping glance around the room and she knew Thorpe's mind was engaged in making an assessment.

"Pray, take a seat." Daphne waved to the chair next to the hearth. "I can light a fire if you're cold."

"That won't be necessary. I have a strong constitution. Nights spent trawling the streets thickens the blood."

His narrow gaze travelled down the front of her pelisse and lingered on the sturdy brown boots. A man with an eye for detail would note the lack of stockings. With the hour being late, one did not need Aristotle's grasp of logic to know she wore nothing but a nightgown beneath the coat.

The absence of his greatcoat proved intriguing. Thorpe wore it as a priest did a ceremonial robe. It was a symbol of his work, acted as a means to hide his weapons. The heavy garment conveyed a sense of strength and mystery necessary when dealing with scoundrels.

"Yet you have not been walking the streets tonight, Mr Thorpe." She inhaled the exotic scent of incense, cheap perfume, and some strange tobacco that lingered in the surrounding air. Despite her skill in deduction, any woman would know where he had been. "Is it true what they say?"

"About what?"

"That one must have a cold heart to bed a whore."

Despite his blank expression, the muscle in his cheek twitched. "One must have a cold heart and an empty mind. The latter is the reason I left before seeking satisfaction."

His honesty was refreshing. The comment held a wealth of information that would keep her awake for hours. "Thankfully, there are many ways to achieve fulfilment," she said, though couldn't imagine his dark eyes ever glowing with desire. "Your work has always brought contentment."

"At the risk of sounding patronising, they are entirely different needs."

Daphne moved to the side table and pulled the stopper from the decanter. As soon as he heard the clink of crystal, he would know her fingers trembled. "I understand passion, Mr Thorpe."

It was a lie. She knew kindness and consideration, but not the burning force that was said to be all-consuming.

Thorpe snorted. "To use the word passion suggests you don't understand at all. A man feels nothing when he pays for services rendered. Satisfaction is but a fleeting moment."

"Forgive the error. Lust would have been a more appropriate term." The blood rushed to her cheeks. Heavens, this would not do. "Even so, as your colleague it is not for me to pry into your personal affairs."

Glass in hand, Daphne crossed the room and offered him the drink. He gripped the vessel awkwardly around the rim to avoid touching her fingers. Never in all their previous meetings had she noticed the marks on his hand. One raised white line ran from thumb to wrist. A patch of pink almost silvery skin covered one knuckle. They were the hands of a man who'd fought for his position. Was his body littered with similar scars? Was his hollow heart battered and bruised, too?

Thorpe cleared his throat. "As your colleague, I have nothing to hide. If I'm to help give perspective on your case, it is important we understand one another."

It took all the willpower she possessed not to laugh. The man was a mystery. Opaque. Completely unreadable. Scholars skilled in cracking codes would struggle to decipher his intention.

Daphne gestured to the chair once again. "Then let us sit and get to the matter at hand."

Only once they'd taken their seats did the size of the room feel inadequate. With barely a few inches between their knees, Daphne focused on his face and the silly beard that hid the sculptured jaw she found far more appealing.

Thorpe swallowed a mouthful of brandy. "Are you moving house?"

Daphne followed his gaze around the room. "Why do you say that?"

"You love to read I recall, yet the shelves are bare. You adore the countryside and yet dusty paintings of fruit hang on the walls. Nothing in this room fits with what I know of your character. Everything is dated, dull and uninspiring."

Like a naive debutante responding to her first compliment, Daphne's heart fluttered. Did he think her intelligent and interesting then? "How astute of you. I'm sure if you delve deeper you will find the answer you seek."

Thorpe inclined his head at the challenge. "When considered in context to what I know of our profession, I'd say you never remain in the same place for long."

"This is my current abode, not my home. As I'm sure you're aware, I must be ready to leave at short notice. Personal possessions can be a hindrance. Everything I hold dear fits into a reticule." Daphne assessed his stern expression. Only a satisfied sigh revealed the true nature of his thoughts. "Am I to assume you approve of my logical approach to work?"

"Regardless of your approach, I have never approved of your work," Thorpe replied bluntly, his eyes as cold and lifeless as the ash in the grate. "But when one understands the dangers, as you obviously do, one can avoid any mishaps."

It was Daphne's turn to sigh. Despite taking numerous precautions over the years, her quarry always found her. The stranger never approached her directly, never sent threatening letters or hid in dark doorways waiting to pounce. Even so, she knew the moment he'd entered her house. The faceless creature touched nothing, took nothing. Like a ghost, he breezed in and out without a trace though his ominous energy lingered.

"What happened to Madame Fontaine's window?" Thorpe's voice drew her attention.

"Someone threw a stone and smashed the glass."

Thorpe shuffled in the chair. "Someone?"

"We were in our beds and woke to the sound of it shattering." Whilst in a dreamlike state, Daphne had thought it was thunder.

"What time was this?"

"Around six o'clock. The costermongers were passing through with their barrows, and the milkmaid was delivering to a house in the street. A penny each bought a description of the culprit. The man was tall, lithe, staggered along the pavement mumbling to himself."

"And his clothes?"

"Clean. Neat. Those of a gentleman."

"And what conclusion did you draw?" Thorpe swallowed a mouthful of brandy, his beady gaze watching her intently over the rim of the glass. Possessing the power to unnerve with a single look, the man should have donned a wig and taken the bench. "Do you believe it a drunken prank?"

"I rather hope so. But you would be surprised what secrets ladies tell their modiste. As you know, information from Madame Fontaine assisted me in our last case. But disclosing personal information can be dangerous."

"That does not answer the question."

Daphne shrugged. "The truth is I have no idea. It could have been a drunken prank. It could have been someone with a grudge. Madame Fontaine is making a gown for an important client and has until tomorrow to finish it. Consequently, I have not had an opportunity to question her fully on the matter."

"But you do not think it is the same person who broke into Madame Fontaine's shop earlier this week?"

Thorpe was speaking of the theft, not of the mysterious shadow-of-a-man who followed Daphne from place to place.

"Logic would suggest they are different men," she said. The thought of three unidentified gentlemen with revenge in their hearts proved unsettling. "The thief entered the shop at night under a blanket of darkness. He stole two of Madame Fontaine's gowns, slippers and gloves to match. The gentleman who smashed the window did so in front of witnesses. Such erratic behaviour suggests anger, resentment, an irrational person."

13

Thorpe straightened. His broad, impressive shoulders filled her line of vision. A lady would have nothing to fear in his company. Wrapped in his arms, one would fall into a deep and peaceful slumber.

"Tell me about your last case." Thorpe's business-like tone shook Daphne from her fanciful musings. "The one prior to the work we did for Lord Harwood and Mrs Dempsey."

"What, you think a previous client is responsible for the incidents that have occurred here this week?" Daphne had considered the possibility. In their line of work, one expected a level of animosity.

"Perhaps."

"While I am happy to disclose information, for obvious reasons I shall be vague." Clients insisted on anonymity. If she broke a trust or confidence, she'd never work again. "My client hired me to gather written proof of her husband's infidelity, proof he kept a mistress in town. The lady—"

"I want names and places," Thorpe interjected.

Others did his bidding without question. Out of loyalty. Out of fear. She was not so easily intimidated.

"You know I cannot divulge the name of my client." Daphne stared into his dark eyes, determined to remain resolute. In the warm glow of candlelight, the faint amber flecks accentuated his wild, feral appeal.

Thorpe stood abruptly. The sudden movement caused Daphne's heart to shoot up to her throat. "Then there is little point me being here." He stomped over to the side table and placed his glass on the tray. "I'm not in the habit of investigating ghosts."

Ghosts!

Did Mr Thorpe possess the ability to read her mind?

"Why … why do you say that?" Daphne rose slowly from the chair. "Do you know something? Is that the real reason you watch the house?"

14

The deep frown marring his brow answered her questions. Confusion and then suspicion flashed in his eyes. "There is something you're not telling me." With a sense of urgency he scanned her from head to toe. His assessing gaze moved past her shoulder and swept the room once again. "Despite your efforts to hide it, you're frightened."

Daphne sucked in a breath. "As you've said many times before, though I work in a man's world I am still a woman." His gaze dropped briefly to her breasts swaddled in the thick pelisse, and for a moment she struggled to breathe. "What is the point of pretending I have your strength and hardened heart? Yes, I'm frightened, Mr Thorpe. Is that what you want to hear?"

Thorpe stepped closer, his menacing aura replaced by something else though she knew not what. "Then trust me. Let me help you. Together we will discover who stole Madame Fontaine's clothes, who smashed her window."

Would he find the man who haunted her, too?

Though loath to admit it, she needed him. Recent events had left her mind muddled.

"But you must be honest with me," Thorpe continued. "If I'm to help find the thief, I need to build a full picture of your life. I need names, details of previous cases."

Daphne shook her head. "Would you divulge personal information if I asked about your work?"

"Colleagues may share notes. Equally, if you hire my services, I guarantee utmost discretion."

"Hire your services?" Daphne smiled. "And remind me of your fee, Mr Thorpe."

"What I want money cannot buy, Mrs Chambers. All I ask is that you trust me with the truth."

The cryptic comment intrigued her. Thorpe didn't strike her as a man who craved material possessions. So what was he searching for? How did he define happiness when he appeared detached from all emotion?

A vision of him sitting alone in a dark room, his brooding gaze focused on the dying embers in the hearth, flashed into her mind. The life of an enquiry agent was often lonely, one fraught with mistrust and suspicion. No one would blame him for having a cynical view of life. But that was not the reason he wore an impenetrable suit of armour.

"If the truth is the price I'm to pay for your expert opinion, then so be it." Daphne resisted the urge to place her palm on his chest. Would she feel his heart beating beneath the shield of steel? Or was it buried so deep not even he knew it was there? "But you must allow me to invite you to dinner by way of thanks. I am considered quite a good cook, and from the breadth of your chest and shoulders I imagine you have a healthy appetite."

For a fleeting moment his eyes brightened, but he blinked and it was gone. "I have yet to meet a servant who's happy to share her chores with her mistress."

"And you certainly won't meet one here. I have no use for a maid or housekeeper."

"Are you telling me you live here alone?" The hard edge to his tone spoke of disapproval.

"Not entirely alone. Betsy occupies the rooms downstairs."

Thorpe stared at her, his expression unreadable. "A lady should not be without an attendant."

"In the same way it is objectionable for a lady to work?"

"Indeed." Thorpe muttered something, the words incoherent. "Thomas would never have permitted you to wander the streets at night without a chaperone."

The mere mention of her husband brought a host of memories flooding back. Was the ghost haunting her the same man who'd killed Thomas and discarded his body in the Thames?

"Thomas is dead, Mr Thorpe. As his oldest friend, I would expect you to share his concerns, but there is little point dwelling on the way things should be. I am a widow without means and must make my own choices."

"The man I know would not have left you in such a financial predicament."

Daphne raised her chin. "Some things are unavoidable. But you're right, he would be livid to learn I work for a living." Now was not the time to reminisce. "And regarding the matter of servants, is it not a rule of business never to form emotional attachments?" Caring for other people was considered a weakness. "A servant or paid companion would be an easy target for a man with a mind for revenge."

Thorpe's cheek twitched. "Unless one's companion is Bostock."

"Regardless of what others perceive, Mr Bostock is your friend and associate, not your servant." Even so, she imagined Bostock's hulking frame and meaty fists proved useful when dealing with scoundrels. "And yes, I would sleep easier in my bed knowing so capable a man was but a few feet away."

"I can arrange for Bostock to accompany you on your outings, to keep guard at your door, though I must advise against taking another case until we have confirmed that the incidents regarding Madame Fontaine bear no real threat."

"Surely Mr Bostock has more important things to do." Taking a new case was the last thing on her mind. Renting new rooms was her priority—and ensuring no one wished Betsy any harm.

Thorpe took a step closer. "Nothing is as important as your safety."

The hint of sincerity in his tone stole her breath. Did he care? Or did he feel duty bound to protect his friend's widow?

"And so I shall return mid-morning," he continued. "In the meantime, you should prepare Madame Fontaine for questioning."

"Prepare her?" Daphne snorted. "Is it to be an inquisition? Should I ready a potion that loosens the tongue?"

"As you know, I am not a man to mince words. Most people find my approach intimidating. Like most people, your modiste will no doubt consider me rude."

Daphne resisted the urge to chuckle. Never had she met a woman as direct as Betsy. The personae of elegant modiste was so opposed to her true character. Not that Thorpe would care. The man was adept at handling any situation. Even so, Daphne welcomed the opportunity to test his resolve, to see surprise or any other emotion spark to life in his eyes.

"Very well, I shall warn Betsy of your stern disposition."

Thorpe brushed a hand through his dark hair and covered the few steps to the door. "Stay inside. There is no need to see me out." He glanced at her boots. "A lady should not stand at the door in her nightdress, even if a pelisse covers her modesty."

"And a gentleman would have left the moment he noted the state of her undress."

"I am not known for my gentlemanly qualities."

"And as a working woman, I am not considered a lady."

Thorpe raised a brow. "Don't press me on the topic. I doubt you want to hear my opinion."

"Then I shall bid you goodnight."

Thorpe opened the door and stepped out into the hallway. "I have an early appointment but should be finished by eleven. I trust Madame Fontaine can spare the time."

"Eleven is perfect."

He lingered in the dim corridor. "Should there be any new developments, send word to the Museum Tavern on Great Russell Street. Tell the landlord that your father worked at The Dog and Duck. He'll ask for a description. The answer is Black-beard. Tell him you have a design for a new dress and I shall know where to come."

Daphne stared at him, impressed by the system he used to

protect his identity. Taking precautions was an inevitable part of their business.

"Thank you, although I doubt we'll need to pester you further."

Thorpe inclined his head. "Goodnight, Mrs Chambers."

"Goodnight, Mr Thorpe."

Daphne watched him descend the stairs. He stopped halfway down and looked at her through the gap in the balusters. "Perhaps you too should take the time to prepare yourself for an interrogation. Once I've spoken to Madame Fontaine, you will tell me the real reason you struggle to sleep at night."

CHAPTER 3

THE HEAVY SCENT OF PERFUME IN THE AIR ALMOST CHOKED HIM.
Daniel put his clenched fist to his mouth and coughed. Madame
Fontaine's parlour reminded him of Mrs Cooper's brothel, and of
the stuffy rooms in the molly-house where he'd once questioned
gentlemen wearing powdered wigs and an excessive amount
of rouge.

"Don't sit there," Madame Fontaine snapped, shooing him
away from the chair. The woman pulled the pins from the
padded arm and stuck them into the cushion in her hand. "Sit on
the sofa."

Daniel glanced around the room. Luxurious fabrics, reams of
ribbon, and an assortment of silk slippers cluttered every available space. The row of wig stands on the sideboard had painted
faces and sat watching the proceedings like disapproving jurors
on a bench.

Mrs Chambers stepped forward and assisted the modiste in
clearing the seats.

Daniel couldn't help but sigh while he waited.

"Trust me, Mr Thorpe," the modiste said, reacting to the
sound of his impatience, "if I ruin these fabrics there'll be little

point investigating the theft and broken window. Lady Arnshaw will have me strung up outside Newgate if her gown isn't ready on time."

"Surely you have room to store your work elsewhere."

Madame Fontaine straightened though still only measured an inch over five foot. While her height and slight frame gave an innocent, childlike impression, the woman had the sharp tongue of a seasoned market seller.

"Do you know how much material it takes to make one gown?" Madame Fontaine pushed a strand of golden hair behind her ear like a man seeking satisfaction would cock a pistol. "Only thing is ladies don't want to see one dress. No. They want a choice of designs, of colours and—"

"Yes, yes." Daniel waved his hand to silence the woman. "I've not come here to discuss dressmaking." Were it not for his concerns regarding Mrs Chambers' safety, he'd not have bothered with the modiste at all.

Mrs Chambers appeared at his side and touched his arm. "Let us sit on the sofa, take tea and hear Betsy's theory about the thief."

The inquisitive part of his character longed to examine the modiste's logic, to pick fault, find flaws. Yet the warm hand resting on his sleeve served as a distraction. The gesture was supposed to calm him. So why did the feel of Mrs Chambers' fingers ignite a fire in his belly that robbed him of all sense and reason?

Daniel fought the urge to stalk from the room, climb into his carriage and race through the streets at breakneck speed, to distance himself from temptation. Only when she dropped her hand and took a seat was he able to think clearly again.

"I shall stand." He clasped his hands behind his back as men often did when they needed to think.

"Nonsense." Mrs Chambers patted the worn green cushion next to her. "There's plenty of room. If you start pacing, I'll struggle to concentrate." Her amused gaze scanned his shoulders. "Besides, you're blocking the light and Betsy can't afford to burn candles during the daytime."

"These late nights spent sewing cost me a fortune," the modiste agreed.

With a huff loud enough to raise the roof, Daniel dropped into the seat next to Mrs Chambers. The sooner he dealt with the theft, the sooner he could get to the real matter at hand. While he respected Mrs Chambers' skill as an enquiry agent, she lacked the ability to hide her emotions. A sleepless night was not the cause of her pale complexion or the haunted look in her eyes. The woman was too proud, too stubborn to come to him and ask for his help. In that respect, he was grateful to the thief, and to the man responsible for smashing the window. They had paved the way for him to delve a little deeper into the lady's affairs.

"Someone must have told you that beards are not considered the height of fashion." Madame Fontaine's voice dragged him from his reverie.

Daniel shrugged. "Fashion is for fops and dandies. Men make up their own minds."

"When you decide to lose the beard, I have a use for the hair." Madame Fontaine nodded at his chin. "Mr Curser on Mill Street makes accessories for men who struggle to grow thick side-whiskers."

"I'd rather burn in hell than know some man is walking around town with my offcuts stuck to his face. And as time is precious, I suggest you stop talking nonsense and focus on our business."

"Ooh." The modiste grinned. "Someone woke with a sore head this morning."

"Not at all. I take my work seriously. What a shame you lack the capacity to do the same. I suspect if you'd kept your tongue you wouldn't be in this predicament."

Madame Fontaine's face flamed red. "Now you listen here—"

"Do you want my help or not?" Daniel was forced to be blunt else they'd be bandying words till nightfall.

Mrs Chambers touched his sleeve again. "Of course we want your help. Don't we Betsy?"

The modiste and Mrs Chambers exchanged wide-eyed glances.

"There is nothing to stop the thief returning," Daniel added. "Silk gowns fetch a pretty price if one knows where to sell them. Not all actresses and courtesans have wealthy benefactors. While I have no idea how much silk it takes to make a dress, I know you cannot afford another loss."

The modiste exhaled deeply. "Nor can I afford for any old strumpet to be seen wearing my exclusive designs."

"Indeed." Daniel inclined his head. "Now perhaps we should begin the investigation with the gentleman who smashed the window."

"As it's the most recent event, your memory will be clearer," Mrs Chambers said by way of clarification.

The modiste frowned and shook her head. "But there's nothing to tell. I'd been in bed but a few hours when I woke to an almighty noise and thought the heavens were falling."

Those disturbed from sleep often had a distorted view of the facts.

"At any time during the day did you have a disagreement with anyone?" Daniel monitored the woman's expression with interest. "Had a client complained about your work, argued over the price?"

Madame Fontaine looked aghast. "Don't be ridiculous. I go to great lengths to ensure all my clients' needs are met. And no, it was a pretty uneventful day."

"Who boarded the window?" Daniel asked.

"Mr Brown. He owns the pawnbrokers across the street. Mr

23

Brown said that a quick reaction is the best way to deter thieves. Told me to wait for a while before displaying anything of value in the window."

"Mr Brown appears to be a fountain of knowledge. Is he married?"

"No."

"Do you get the impression he admires you?"

"No."

"Do you have a lover?"

Madame Fontaine looked down her nose. "Do you?"

For some reason unbeknown, Daniel glanced at Mrs Chambers. The lady's gaze fell to his lips, but she shook her head and said, "Mr Thorpe is attempting to ascertain if jealousy might be a motive. To throw a stone through someone's window suggests the culprit harbours anger towards the recipient. Such crimes can stem from a jealous rage. A sudden, passionate reaction to something said or witnessed."

"Then the answer is no, Daphne. I do not have a lover, and Mr Brown is old enough to be my grandfather."

Hearing Mrs Chambers' given name spoken aloud sent the blood coursing through Daniel's veins. It had burst from his lips twice during their acquaintance, both times out of fear and frustration for her safety.

"And I don't think it was a sudden reaction either," the modiste added.

Daniel sat forward. Now they were getting somewhere. "What makes you say that?"

"Because the blighter had taken the time to wrap an engraving around the stone. I found it lying amongst the shards of glass. Now you can't tell me a man walks around with those sorts of things in his pocket."

"An engraving?" Daniel mused. "Tell me you still have it."

"Of course. I'm not a dimwit." Madame Fontaine rose from the chair and strode over to the sideboard. Distracted by a pair of stained slippers on top, she muttered a curse before pulling open the drawer and removing the paper. "Did you think me stupid enough to use it as kindling for the fire?" she said, thrusting it at him.

Daniel took the engraving and studied the picture. Upon first inspection, it appeared to be an image of a man and woman taking tea at a small table in a bedchamber. While trying his utmost to focus, Mrs Chambers edged closer and peered over his shoulder.

"Besides the admiral's hat balanced on her head, the lady is wearing gentlemen's shoes." Her arm brushed against his as she pointed to the woman. The muscles in his lower abdomen hardened instantly at her light touch.

Bloody hell!

The years apart had done nothing to ease his craving.

"With her feet wide apart and hands braced on her hips, the lady's stance is overtly masculine," Mrs Chambers added.

Daniel stared at the engraving. Distracting his thoughts was the only way to temper his body's reaction to her. "Upon closer inspection, you can see that the gentleman is wearing rouge and is holding a fan in his lap." A hint of lavender filled his nostrils as Mrs Chambers bent her head to consider his assessment. Suppressing the need to exhale loudly, he glanced at Madame Fontaine. "Has a man approached you and asked to buy a gown? He may have given the excuse that it is to be a gift for a wife or sister, even produced measurements?"

Mrs Chambers looked up at him. "But you think the gentleman wanted to purchase a dress for himself?"

"The engraving tackles the delicate subject of gender roles. It is not a coincidence."

"Yes," Madame Fontaine frowned. "A gentleman did ask me to make a gown. He got into a right old tizzy when I told him I had no appointments for three weeks. After a few muttered curses, he insisted on buying the dress in the window."

"And again you refused," Daniel clarified.

"No respected modiste would sell a dress without making sure it's a perfect fit. A saggy bodice can ruin a reputation."

"Did you not consider the fact that your disagreement with the gentleman resulted in his need to make a point?"

Madame Fontaine shook her head. "It's been nigh on two weeks since he came into the shop and I've not heard a peep from him since."

"Does it not stand to reason that the thief and the man who smashed the window could be one and the same?" Mrs Chambers offered. "Theft being the primary motive in both cases."

"On the surface, one might assume so." Daniel made the mistake of looking at Mrs Chambers when he spoke. Her emerald eyes dazzled like precious gems whenever she expressed confidence in her assumptions. "But as you've said, the thief was careful, calculating. Reckless and unpredictable is the best way to describe the man who threw the stone at the window." In which case, he carried the engraving around with him as one would a portrait of a family member. "And one must ask, why did he not steal the dress?"

"Perhaps he did not have time or feared he might injure himself on the broken shards."

"Or perhaps his conscience got the better of him," Daniel said.

Mrs Chambers' mouth formed a pout while she considered his reply. Her lips natural hue was rosebud pink. Many women used balm to achieve a similar effect, but most lacked the fullness necessary to tempt a man to taste them.

"Someone struggling with their identity may be prone to bouts of melancholy," Mrs Chambers replied, "equally capable of displaying a volatile temperament. Guilt and shame are often common characteristics, too."

"Precisely." Had Daniel been a man of great emotion, his tone would have conveyed a hint of admiration for her insight.

26

"Which is why I'm confident I can find the person responsible before the day is out."

"Well, when you do," Madame Fontaine blurted, "tell them if they pay for the damage I'll say no more about it."

Daniel nodded. "Now let us address the matter of theft. As it's been days since the thief found a way into the shop, I assume Mrs Chambers has a theory."

"A theory? I ... I have been a little preoccupied of late." Mrs Chambers looked at her hands resting in her lap. The air of confidence that oozed from every fibre of her being had vanished. "The matter should have been a priority but ..."

Her lack of attention proved worrying. "Then tell me all you know."

When she met his gaze, a look of vulnerability passed over her features. The hairs on his nape stood to attention. Damn it. Something was wrong.

"The thief entered via the basement door," she said. "As I've already told you, he stole two dresses, gloves and slippers."

Madame Fontaine tutted. "He was so quiet we never heard a thing."

Daniel was puzzled by the thief's chosen booty. Why steal accoutrements that held little value when he could have carried another silk dress?

"Were the accessories matching?"

Madame Fontaine nodded. "Once a garment is ready for collection, I box the accessories and keep them together."

"Did the thief take the boxes?" One man would struggle to carry the packages on his own.

"Yes."

"Then the appropriate term is thieves."

"It occurred to me that there might be two men," Mrs Chambers said, and Daniel was relieved to find that logical thought had not completely abandoned her.

"Who were the dresses made for?"

Madame Fontaine shuffled to the edge of her seat. "One was a mourning gown for Mrs Armstrong-Clarke. The other a ball gown for Miss Cartwright. From the random choice, it's obvious the thieves took the first garments they came across."

"Is it?" Daniel suspected otherwise. When it came to the motive for committing a crime, obvious assumptions were often wrong. "Did you have any doubts regarding your clients' ability to pay?"

"No." Madame Fontaine averted her gaze, only briefly, but it was enough to rouse Daniel's suspicion.

"Has either lady ordered dresses from you before?" he said, determined to receive an answer.

"Mrs Armstrong-Clarke has been a loyal customer for two years or more."

"And what about Miss Cartwright?"

Madame Fontaine batted her lashes far too rapidly. "It's the first time I've made a dress for her."

"As the woman is unmarried, are her parents paying the bill?" Daniel would drag the truth from the modiste if he had to sit there until Michaelmas.

A brief silence ensued.

Madame Fontaine opened her mouth but snapped it shut.

"What's wrong, Betsy?" Mrs Chambers said, as it was apparent the woman was reluctant to reply. "Can you not answer Mr Thorpe's question?"

A faint blush touched the modiste's cheeks. "Miss Cartwright's order was cancelled."

"Cancelled? Why did you not mention it before when I asked you about the theft?" Mrs Chambers' eyes widened. "You said there was nothing unusual about the transactions."

Madame Fontaine raised her chin, but her trembling lip belied her confident facade. "That's because I knew what you'd say if I told you what had happened."

"What did happen? Could the Cartwrights not afford to pay

the bill?" Daphne Chambers sounded most perturbed. Daniel suspected her anxious tone stemmed from embarrassment. Her failure to uncover a vital clue for the motive of the theft spoke of incompetence.

"The lady has no parents," Madame Fontaine replied. "I doubt Cartwright is her real name. No, her patron was to pay for the new gown."

In this case, patron was just a polite term for lover.

"I assume this patron agreed to cover all the lady's expenses," Daniel said, not bothering to curb his cynical tone.

"Isn't that what patrons do, Mr Thorpe?" the modiste snapped back.

Mrs Chambers frowned. "I still don't understand why you didn't mention the cancelled order. It changes everything. It gives Miss Cartwright a motive. Why should it matter so much to me if the lady's patron refused to pay for her dress?"

Daniel stroked his beard while examining the facts. There were only two reasons why a man refused to cover his mistress's expenses. Either the gentleman had exhausted his funds, or his wife discovered his secret and demanded he put an end to it.

But why did the modiste fear mentioning the fact to Mrs Chambers?

"I hear a modiste is often party to all the latest gossip," Daniel said, deciding any man who wanted to please his mistress would simply take the dress and add Madame Fontaine to his list of creditors. To his mind that left one possible avenue of investigation. "The problem with gossip is that one never knows who is listening."

As expected, Madame Fontaine's cheeks glowed berry red, and she squirmed in her chair.

"Oh, tell me you didn't, Betsy." Mrs Chambers gave a frustrated sigh. "Tell me you kept your tongue and were mindful of your comments. It takes but a word in the wrong ear to ruin your reputation."

"How was I to know Miss James was the goddaughter of Lady Tranmere? The girl noticed the lilac gown and demanded one similar. I told her the bodice was cut far too low for a debutante." Madame Fontaine paused for breath. "But the girl's sister panders to her every whim. Only a courtesan wears a gown that shows so much cleavage, but they insisted on lecturing me on the latest fashions from Paris. Tranmere would chase me out of town if he discovered another woman wore the same gown as his mistress, I said."

Mrs Chambers sucked in a breath. "Good Lord, Betsy!"

"So, Lady Tranmere discovered the truth about her beloved husband and forced Lord Tranmere to cancel Miss Cartwright's order," Daniel clarified.

"Yes." Madame Fontaine's shoulders sagged. "Miss Cartwright came to see me and asked to purchase the lilac gown, but the thief stole the dress the night before she was due to collect it."

Daniel sat back and folded his arms across his chest. "Then the theft and the smashed window are two separate incidents. Both culprits have motive, but I'm confident that neither of you need fear for your safety."

Daphne Chambers should have taken comfort from his words, but her weak smile and inability to meet his gaze confirmed his suspicion. Something sinister occupied her thoughts. Was it a secret she was willing to share? Was it something from the past or present?

Clearing his throat, Daniel stood. "Well, I'm sure you're eager to know the names of those responsible, and so I bid you both good day." He inclined his head and strode towards the door.

"Wait." Mrs Chambers jumped up from the sofa and rushed to his side. "If you're to investigate both matters, then I am coming with you. Two heads are better than one when it comes to solving puzzles."

Damn right she was coming with him; had he insisted upon it, she would have fought him. Time spent alone in his conveyance would give him an opportunity to uncover her secret.

"My first call will be at a molly-house in Covent Garden. You may wait in the carriage whilst I go inside. You know my views regarding what is considered inappropriate for a lady."

She pressed her lips together tightly in response, and the surrounding air turned chilly. With a deep sigh and some reluctance, she said, "Very well."

Daniel was not a fool. There was more chance of a giant eagle swooping down to carry him off than there was of Daphne Chambers following orders. Still, it gave him a means to bargain.

"Then I suggest you fetch your pelisse," Daniel said. "Wait for me in my carriage. I wish to call in and thank Mr Brown for his help in boarding the window." And to ask a few questions relating to the identity of the vandal responsible for the damage.

The sudden smile illuminating Mrs Chambers' features almost melted his steely resolve. The woman had the power to get under his skin. She was the only person alive who roused any emotion in his chest. But she had been quick to refuse his offer of marriage three years ago, saw him as nothing more than an acquaintance, a colleague.

Mentally throwing on his metal breastplate, Daniel straightened. The case of the stolen gowns and smashed window was a simple one. Working closely with Daphne Chambers would prove to be a little more complicated.

CHAPTER 4

DURING THE FIVE YEARS DAPHNE HAD KNOWN DANIEL THORPE, she'd had the pleasure of travelling alone with him in a carriage twice.

The first time occurred a few weeks after her husband's death. Mr Thorpe thought a change of scenery might lift her spirits. But then he'd offered marriage—purely out of a sense of duty—and Daphne had politely declined.

The second instance took place two weeks ago. After discovering Daphne at the docks dressed as a prostitute while investigating Emily Compton's disappearance, Thorpe had escorted her home.

On both occasions, the tension in the vehicle had clawed at her shoulders. The uncomfortable atmosphere—enhanced by Thorpe's glare of disapproval—would have made most females cower in the corner. But Daphne refused to let him see that his mood affected her and excelled at hiding emotion.

Yet now, as she sat opposite him in the dark confines of his carriage, he seemed different. Yes, his tone was blunt, his broad shoulders cast an ominous shadow, but those black eyes had softened to a rich, chocolate brown.

"You must think me extremely lapse," Daphne said over the noise of the rain lashing at the window. She was grateful for the miserable weather as it gave her an opportunity to look at something other than Thorpe's intense gaze. "Instinct should have told me that Betsy had omitted certain parts of the story."

Mr Thorpe stroked his chin, pulling the facial hair into a point. Heavens, she wished he would do something about his ridiculous beard. There were far better ways to disguise one's appearance.

"Under normal circumstances, I would have questioned your lack of insight," Thorpe agreed. "But we both know that the problem plaguing your thoughts is affecting your ability to work."

"And what problem would that be?" Daphne swallowed down a rush of panic. For a man with his level of intuition, a raised brow or muscle twitch was as good as a confession.

"The problem that made you jump when I mentioned the word *ghost*. The problem that forces you to move house when it's obvious you enjoy the modiste's company." He paused. "So, are you going to tell me what's troubling you?"

Blast!

"I doubt you want to be party to my thoughts." Daphne gave a weak chuckle. "A man with your rational mind would think me just another delusional woman spooked by her own shadow."

Without warning Thorpe sat forward, their knees almost touching. "I might disapprove of your need to work, but I consider you more intelligent than most men of my acquaintance. I would never attempt to discredit your opinion."

"Oh." A warm glow crept up her throat to toast her cheeks. "Well, your good opinion is rarely bestowed, and so I shall take it as a compliment."

"Then you have understood my meaning perfectly."

Silence ensued.

Daphne was used to dealing with his criticism, but this …
this was uncharted territory.

"Was it not your perceptive skills that helped solve the
Harwood case?" he added.

An image of him stalking up behind her at the docks flashed
into her mind. When his large hand had covered her mouth to
prevent her from screaming, she'd almost expired on the spot.
Yet it was his tortured expression that tore at her heart, not his
rants and curses.

"So why make me feel foolish for following that line of
enquiry?"

"Day or night, the docks are no place for a lady." He pushed
his hand through his hair as a weary sigh left his lips. "Anything
could have happened to you."

"I am quite capable of warding off a drunken sailor."

"And what if there'd been three of them? Despite your skill
with a blade, you wouldn't stand a chance." Thorpe mumbled
something to himself. "No matter how hard I try, I cannot understand why you would put yourself in such a predicament."

Daphne knew the risks involved when she went out alone.
But the circumstances surrounding Thomas' death had left
many unanswered questions. Chasing the truth had become a
passion, grown into an obsession. Helping other people solve
their problems gave her a sense of purpose. She was as
addicted to solving mysteries as some women were to
laudanum.

"When one finds oneself on an unfamiliar road one has but
two options," Daphne said. "With the life I knew lost, I chose to
follow a different path, curious where it might lead. Yes, the
journey has been treacherous at times, but the sense of achieve-
ment is rewarding."

Thorpe dragged his hand down his face. "There are other
ways to feel fulfilled. I hear needlework can be quite a stimu-
lating hobby." There was a faint hint of amusement in his tone.

"Can you honestly see me sitting at a frame for hours mulling over which is the right colour thread?"

"No, though I'm sure you would find use for a needle amongst your arsenal of weapons."

Daphne laughed. It occurred to her that Mr Thorpe could be quite humorous. "While a loaded pistol is a perfect deterrent, my tongue would be my weapon of choice." Talking was the best way to avoid conflict.

"Indeed." His penetrating gaze travelled over her chest and face, lingered on her lips. "As with everything else you put your mind to, I imagine you possess a high degree of skill in that regard."

Like a naive debutante hearing the polished words of a seducer, Daphne's heart fluttered. Had she mistaken the warm notes in his tone? Had she imagined his effort to tease?

"Then why not take advantage of the opportunity and judge for yourself?" she replied, suppressing a grin when he sucked in a sharp breath. "Let me accompany you to the molly-house. I can talk my way out of the most awkward conversations."

Thorpe raised a brow. "As a consummate professional, you know I cannot do that."

"Why ever not? I shall be perfectly safe with you at my side."

"We have established that you currently lack the ability to concentrate. The men require a firm hand if we're to learn anything useful." Mr Thorpe paused. "Of course, perhaps if you told me what plagues your thoughts, I might consider you less of a liability."

She would have to tell him about her mysterious stalker eventually. Once his suspicions were roused he was like a bloodhound hunting out the scent until he'd located his target.

"You'll think me foolish when I tell you," she said, wondering where on earth she would start.

"Do not presume to kn—"

The carriage jolted to a halt. Daphne gripped the seat for fear of tumbling into Mr Thorpe's lap. But he reached out and put his hand on her knee to prevent her from falling forward. The intimacy of the action forced them both to gulp down a breath. They stared into each other's eyes as the coachman's shouts and protests could be clearly heard as he chastised someone for running out into the street.

Once the carriage was on its way and they had settled back into their seats, Thorpe cleared his throat. "Despite the distraction, I'm still waiting for your answer."

Daphne decided the best way to reveal her secret was to start with the most implausible deduction. "After our experiences during the Harwood case, I'm beginning to wonder if … if Thomas is still alive."

Mr Thorpe frowned. "You think Thomas is alive?" He shook his head too many times to count. "Trust me. I identified the body. Thomas was the man they pulled from the Thames on that godforsaken night."

Hearing Thorpe's assurance should have been enough to put the ludicrous idea to rest, yet instinct said something was amiss. "I said you'd think me deluded."

"Deluded, no. Confused, perhaps. The mind conjures all sorts of strange things when one is frightened."

He was right, of course. She often imagined waking in the dead of night to find Thomas looming large over the bed, his face puffy and an odd shade of green, his skin possessing a silvery incandescent sheen from time spent in the water.

"No doubt you have never felt the strangling effects of fear." She'd been so scared she'd struggled to breathe.

"That depends on your definition of the word. Do I fear dying? No. I would storm into a room of a hundred armed men if I had a point to prove." Thorpe glanced at the carriage floor before meeting her gaze again. "Do I fear the pain that comes from losing someone I care about? Yes."

It was hard to imagine him caring about anyone. "Then despite popular opinion, you are human," she said to lighten the sudden air of melancholy that settled over him.

"Oh, I'm human." Thorpe thrust out his arm. "Touch me and see."

Daphne stared at the sleeve of his coat. Good Lord. All she had to do was pat his arm and offer a witty retort. Yet the thought of touching him in the intimate space sent her heart shooting up to her throat.

Mr Thorpe dropped his arm, and she cursed herself for the missed opportunity to further their connection.

"From your irrational comment about Thomas," Mr Thorpe began, "along with your desire to move house and the flash of terror in your eyes when I mentioned the word *ghost*, one would assume Madame Fontaine's shop is haunted." He narrowed his gaze. "Yet it is something more troubling than that."

As always, the man could read her mind, see into her soul.

"If only it were as simple as me waking to find a spectre at the foot of the bed." A weak chuckle left her lips. "One has nothing to fear from the dead."

Thorpe remained silent—a ploy he often used to force her to continue speaking.

"Do you remember what I told you when they heaved Thomas' bloated body from the river?" She shivered as the memory of that fateful night flashed through her mind.

"You said Thomas was not so careless as to drink himself into a stupor or stagger alone from a tavern in such a seedy part of town."

Nor was he a man foolish enough to wander aimlessly through thick fog and tumble into the Thames.

"Yet you thought them nothing more than the words of a grieving widow."

Thorpe shrugged. "In part, though I tried to speak to the witnesses but failed to trace them."

"You did?" Daphne sucked in a breath. So she *had* planted a seed of doubt. "Then their disappearance is odd, don't you agree?"

"The men who live and work around the docks are often away at sea. Equally, those who frequent The Mariners Tavern are keen to avoid all dealings with the law and spend their lives dodging the hangman's noose. The fact that I could not locate the men concerned does not seem odd to me."

His logical reply failed to appease her. She'd learnt that one should never ignore the hollow feeling in their gut.

"And I suppose it's normal for a gentleman of good breeding to drink with sailors in a ramshackle tavern?" she said.

"Surely, with the experience you've gained during your work these last three years, you understand a man's need for privacy." His condescending tone prickled the hairs on her nape. "A tavern in that part of town offers a degree of anonymity. You'll find no nosey matrons scrambling about for juicy morsels of gossip. A man of good breeding often seeks entertainment in quieter pastures."

She was not a fool and knew men went to taverns to quench more than their thirst. "Is that a polite way of telling me that Thomas sought more than a mug of ale and a meat pie?"

"I have no notion why Thomas was there."

"Most men look for excitement outside the marriage bed." She didn't want Thorpe to think her naive.

Thorpe stared down his nose, his gaze hard, dangerously dark. "Not all men. Some prefer to dedicate their life to one woman. Some understand the true value of a woman's love."

The surrounding air was suddenly charged with a magnetic energy that awakened her attraction to him. What would it feel like to be loved by Daniel Thorpe? She suspected he hid an intense passion beneath his austere facade. The thought caused her heart to skip a beat, brought beads of perspiration to her brow.

"Then my faith in men is restored," she said, knowing that Thorpe would protect his lady love until he drew his last breath. "Perhaps love does exist. Perhaps there's hope for us all."

Mr Thorpe shuffled uncomfortably in his seat. "We seem to have strayed from the topic. You were telling me why a ghost is the least of your fears."

"Oh, yes. Then I shall come straight to the point." For three years she had kept her fears a secret. In her mind, she repeated the sentence that was about to change everything. "Someone is following me, Mr Thorpe. When I'm walking along the street, trying on gloves at Masons, eating an ice at Gunters, I am aware of him watching me. It doesn't matter how many times I move to new lodgings, he always finds me."

Thorpe sat bolt upright. "Why the blazes didn't you say so before? Do you know him? Do you know why the hell he's following you around town?"

Daphne squirmed. "No. I have no idea who he is." This was going to be the hardest part. He would think her fit for Bedlam. "I have no idea who he is because I have never seen him."

Thorpe jerked his head back. Two deep furrows appeared between his brows.

"Please do not offer words of wisdom or question my judgement," she said before he could open his mouth. "The man enters my house, takes nothing, leaves no trace but for his unique scent in the air. I've spent years scouring the recesses of my mind in search of another explanation. Years trying to understand if it has anything to do with Thomas."

"Years? How long have you had these suspicions?"

"Three years."

"Since Thomas' death?" Thorpe appeared shocked.

"A few weeks after, yes." Due to the dulling effects of grief, it was impossible for her to recall when she'd felt that first prickle of awareness.

Thorpe bowed his head.

With a heavy tension in the air pressing down on her shoulders, Daphne watched the rivulets of rain trickle down the windowpane. Mr Thorpe was often silent when he was thinking. He was often silent when attempting to control his temper.

When he looked up, the despair in his eyes stabbed at her heart. "You should have come to me sooner. I would have found this rogue and put an end to the matter."

He believed her!

They had never shared the sort of trusting friendship that allowed a person to declare their innermost feelings. "Forgive me for being blunt but, prior to Lord Harwood's case, your constant need to remind me of my failings only served to place distance between us."

He gritted his teeth and shook his head. "For heaven's sake, Daphne, I was worried. What did you expect me to do, say nothing about your work? Did you imagine I could simply stand back and watch knowing your life was in jeopardy every time you walked out of the door?"

"There is little point discussing our past mistakes," she said. "Perhaps I should not have been so stubborn. Perhaps you should have tried a different approach to deter me from my course."

Thorpe threw himself back in the seat and gave an exasperated sigh. "I tried a different approach if you remember."

He was talking about the marriage proposal. Now was not the time to debate the difference between duty and love.

"Then let us agree to be honest in future. I shall tell you when you're charging about like a bull in a pig pen, and you can tell me when your glare of disapproval stems from fear for my safety." Daphne chuckled to herself as she imagined Thorpe's pained expression upon declaring his true feelings.

"Agreed." He folded his arms across his chest. "Then let us start as we mean to go on. As a friend and colleague worried for your safety, I insist—" He stopped abruptly and tutted. "I suggest you allow Bostock to act as your chaperone until I can investigate the matter further."

A few weeks ago, she would have given him a lecture on a woman's ability to be independent, but she couldn't shake the strange sense of foreboding.

While still contemplating her response, the carriage jerked to a halt near the entrance to the market in Covent Garden.

"Let me accompany you to the molly-house, and we can discuss the matter of Mr Bostock on our return journey."

The corners of Thorpe's mouth twitched. "Your attempt at manipulation is unnecessary. After what you've told me, I don't intend to let you out of my sight."

CHAPTER 5

Covent Garden bustled with people eager to buy from the vast array of market traders hawking their wares. Amid the loud cries of sellers desperate to attract attention now the rain had stopped, a man could hardly focus on a thought. Over-laden carts blocked the street. Strewn baskets of rotten vegetables failed to draw paying customers though the rats made the most of the bounty of opportunity.

Daniel gripped the tips of Daphne Chambers' fingers as he assisted her from the carriage. "The house we want is a few minutes' walk, but with this rabble blocking the road Murphy has no hope of dropping us any closer."

As soon as he released her, Mrs Chambers slapped a gloved hand over her nose. "Heavens above," she mumbled.

"The residents have petitioned for something to be done about the putrid stench. It's worse when it rains and the market's busy."

Mrs Chambers lowered her hand. "Once the initial shock has subsided, and my stomach decides not to cast up its contents, then I know it's safe to breathe."

Daniel offered his arm and, after staring at it for longer than necessary, she placed her hand in the crook.

They'd taken no more than ten steps when a man with a beaten top hat and threadbare coat approached them. From his shifty gaze, it was obvious whatever he was selling had been acquired by ill-gotten means.

"Can I interest you genteel folk in a fine bottle of rum?" the fellow said in a broad Irish accent as he whipped open his coat to reveal a dusty brown bottle. "Five gills will cost but three shillings."

"Three shillings?" Mrs Chambers said in astonishment. "I could buy two bottles for that price."

The fellow winked. "Bless the Lord. The lady is canny when it comes to business. Two shillings and sixpence and it's yours."

"Do I look like a man who enjoys drinking watered-down pizzle?" Daniel countered.

"Pizzle? This fair stuff's so strong it'll burn your throat. It was given to me by an old sea-faring captain who's just returned from the Indies." The fellow offered a toothless grin. "Will ya not help a poor man fill his belly?"

"I'll help any man with manners." Daniel straightened to his full height. "Had you resisted the urge to accost a lady in the street, then I might have offered assistance."

"Then a fool I am, sir. A man's mind is muddled when his stomach's growling," the fellow replied, but Daniel ignored him and led Mrs Chambers away.

"It wouldn't have hurt to give him a penny," she said, glancing back at the beggar as he moved to try his luck with another punter.

It was such statements that reinforced her unsuitability to work on the streets. "And do you honestly think he'd use the money to buy food?"

"We could have bought him a meat pie."

"And watch him turn his nose up at our generosity. There are better ways to help the poor than supporting their need to sell stolen spirits."

Mrs Chambers sighed. "As always, I suspect you're right."

After dodging two boys clutching a stolen loaf while a baker chased their heels, Daniel turned the corner and escorted his companion to the house on Maiden Lane.

"As I've never been to such an establishment before," Daphne Chambers began as she searched the facade with some curiosity, "I doubt it is as easy as you knocking the door and fluttering your long lashes."

"Is that your way of saying you think my eyes possess a feminine quality?" Daniel mocked.

A sweet smile lit up her face as she stared into his eyes. It was a vision he'd pictured on many a cold, lonely night.

"I know many ladies who would give everything they own to have eyes as attractive as yours." She paused, then added, "Unless you're in a bad mood, which I understand is fairly frequently, then they lose their lustre."

Compliments usually failed to penetrate his steely composure. He was not a man who needed praise to feel worthy. Far too many people spouted drivel in order to win favour. But Daphne Chambers was not one of them. When she gave praise, she meant it.

"Then I shall try my best to convey a positive disposition when in your company."

"Perhaps if you lost the beard, I might be granted the opportunity of seeing you smile," she replied with a hint of amusement.

Daniel stroked his facial hair. "Does it not make me look more distinguished?"

"If distinguished means looking ten years older, and like a man who's slept in a bush for the past year, then yes." Avoiding his gaze, she glanced at the downstairs window. "With the price of candles, you'd think the occupants would avoid closing the drapes during the day."

"What the eye doesn't see the lips can't tell," he said. "Privacy is a priority when dabbling in unlawful pursuits."

"Yet you presume the occupants will allow you entry."

Daniel stepped up to the door, raised the brass knocker and let it fall. "Mr Cutter knows he can rely upon my discretion."

"Mr Cutter?"

"The custodian. One of his patrons blackmailed him, and he hired me to fix the problem." Cutter was more like a mother to the gentlemen who sought the freedom to dress and act how they pleased. "Periodically, he pays me to wander the house and search the rooms as a deterrent to those who might have similar ideas. I usually send Bostock."

Before another word was spoken, Cutter opened the spy hatch, which to anyone passing looked like any other wooden panel, and with a narrow gaze scrutinised them from head to toe. It took but a few seconds for his suspicious expression to brighten into an inviting smile.

"Mr Thorpe! What an honour it is to have you call upon us." Cutter's chubby cheeks glowed and his tone brimmed with admiration. Daniel found it somewhat unnerving though he would never admit so to Mrs Chambers. "Let me open the door for you at once, sir."

The rattling of keys accompanied the clunk of a lock or two. Cutter hid behind the door, his flamboyant hand gesture beckoning them into the hall. As soon as they crossed the threshold, he slammed the door shut with the urgency of a man seeking sanctuary from a pack of bloodthirsty wolves.

"Goodness me." Cutter patted his brow with the lace-trimmed handkerchief and sucked in a deep breath. "Blasted street urchins will be the death of me. Lord knows how they sneak in here. We found one hiding under the bed in Catherine

Parr's room. The blighter was stealing from the guests when they were otherwise engaged."

"Catherine Parr?" Mrs Chambers said.

"All the bedchambers are named after the wives of Henry VIII," Daniel informed.

Daphne Chambers raised an amused brow. "Then I assume there are not many who want to stay in Jane Seymour's room. The poor lady is said to have died in her bed."

Cutter turned his attention to Mrs Chambers, his wide eyes settling on the generous bosom ensconced in green silk. A sight Daniel found equally hard to ignore. "Ah, my initial assessment was correct. I need hear but one word to confirm a person's gender."

Mrs Chambers frowned.

"Many ladies knock Mr Cutter's door," Daniel said, "though their clothing does not always convey their sex."

Mrs Chambers gasped as recognition dawned. "You thought I was a man?"

"One can never be sure." The custodian fiddled nervously with the ruffles on his shirt. "Patrons spend months perfecting the grace of the feminine form. Even so, a lady's soft melodic tones are harder to master."

"Well, I do not know whether to be flattered or offended." Mrs Chambers ran her fingers over her lips and patted the ebony hair below the rim of her bonnet.

"Oh, you must be flattered, my dear." Cutter took to waving his handkerchief around again. "It takes layers of powder to create such a clear complexion. Now, follow me through to the drawing room where we may speak in private."

As Daniel gestured for Mrs Chambers to follow Mr Cutter along the gloomy hallway, he bowed his head and whispered, "Don't look so glum. There is nothing masculine about you. Every part of you oozes feminine appeal."

She looked up at him, a little startled. "Are your kind words merely a means to appease my injured pride?"

Daniel cursed inwardly for giving a voice to his thoughts. "No, purely to convey what is apparent to most virile men."

"And you count yourself a member of this group?"

"Have I not just said so?"

Mr Cutter escorted them into a dimly lit room at the rear of the house. The thick burgundy drapes were drawn. The only light came from the candles burning in the wall sconces, and it brought to mind thoughts of a previous case where Daniel had been hired to prove it wasn't a ghost rattling the door knob at night.

"Pray take a seat." With a few flicks of his handkerchief, Cutter dusted the cushions on the carved mahogany sofa. "I shall ring for refreshments."

"Do not go to any trouble on our account." Daniel raised his hand hoping the man would stop flapping. "We have an urgent appointment elsewhere, and so I shall come straight to the point."

Cutter stopped abruptly and gave them his full attention.

"There was an incident at a modiste shop," Daniel continued. "I have a strong suspicion that the person responsible spends time here." Mr Cutter's molly-house was the only establishment to cater to those gentlemen in society who considered themselves progressive. "We mean the man concerned no harm, but simply seek to confirm he is the culprit."

Cutter put a hand on his portly stomach. "Am I allowed to ask as to the nature of this incident?"

"The fellow smashed the front window," Mrs Chambers said, "and then staggered away from the scene mumbling incoherently. Witnesses describe him as tall and lithe, wearing the clothes of a gentleman."

"My dear, you have just described half the gentlemen in Mayfair." Cutter shook his head. "What led you to my door?"

Daniel cleared his throat. "I believe the same man who asked the modiste to make a gown with nothing more than measurements, is the same man who smashed the window." Even logical thought required a certain creativity. "Humour me, Mr Cutter. The gentleman will be of good breeding, intelligent, yet emotionally unbalanced."

Mrs Chambers took a step forward. "Maybe the internal struggle between the heart and mind affects his ability to reason."

At some point in their lives, most people experienced the imbalance between what they wanted to do and what they should do. Sometimes, cutting the heart off to all emotion was the only way to achieve a peaceful existence.

"The majority of men who spend time here display excessive bouts of sentimentality," Cutter said as he rubbed his chin. "Though they tend to swoon rather than smash windows."

"Can you think of anyone whose internal conflict is apparent to all?" Daniel said.

With meditative strokes of his neat white beard, Cutter contemplated the question. "There's Mr Harrison, or Rosalyn Harrison to us. She is forever complaining about her inability to pass for a woman. I found her gargling a strange liquid bought from the apothecary that is said to soften the voice."

"So, Mr Harrison dresses as a woman when here?"

"Yes," Cutter nodded. "When in a good mood, Rosalyn is quite popular."

Daniel cast Mrs Chambers a sidelong glance. As a working woman she challenged accepted modes of conduct, yet with her tilted head and slack expression, it was obvious she found the thought of Mollys bemusing.

"And Mr Harrison is often volatile, easily angered?"

"Not always, no. I'd say his moods tend to border on self-pity. It's his limp." Cutter spoke softly. "One struggles with the feminine graces when hampered by such an obvious affliction."

"His limp," Daniel repeated. The pawnbroker mentioned seeing a gentleman with a similar impediment hovering outside the modiste shop. Perhaps the man seen staggering away from the scene was not drunk at all. "Can you tell me where I might find Mr Harrison?"

"Why, he is upstairs practising for the play." Cutter leant forward. "You are welcome to speak to him, but the lady must remain here."

As though a bitter wind had swept in from the north, the air in the room turned frosty.

"I am Mr Thorpe's partner in this case, not a wanton widow eager for entertainment." Daphne Chambers squared her shoulders and raised her chin. "As such, I shall accompany him when he makes his enquiries."

Cutter held up his hands. "Please, my dear, I mean no offence. But it is not wise to parade about the upstairs rooms when we are open for business." Cutter squirmed when the last few words tumbled awkwardly from his lips. "Certain assumptions will be made."

"Mr Cutter, besides the fact I am more than capable of dealing with most situations, have you failed to notice the impressive breadth of Mr Thorpe's chest? Does he look like a man who would see a lady harassed or harmed? No. I would enter a pit full of vipers if he were my companion, and so I hardly think gentlemen in gowns will prove to be a problem."

A hard lump formed in Daniel's throat. Her faith in his ability was not unfounded. He had saved her life once. The memory of chasing away the mugger, of seeing her body tremble as she crumpled to a heap in the dark alley, roused a pain like no other. He'd taken her home, sat with her while she slept, until her neighbour came to relieve him. That night, he took solace in a bottle of brandy. And he prayed for a way to bring his friend back from the grave so someone could protect the reckless widow.

"Mr Thorpe." Cutter coughed to get Daniel's attention. "I said I trust you do not object to the lady's request."

"Mrs Chambers is a highly skilled enquiry agent," Daniel said. Well, that's what he'd told himself when he stopped following her at night, when she refused to listen to reason or obey his command. "And she's right. Anyone wishing to hurt her will have to deal with me."

Mrs Chambers looked up at him and smiled.

Cutter shook his head numerous times. "This is a place of sanctuary for those who seek to escape from the prejudices of the world. The ladies are not comfortable with men brawling."

"Trust me." Daniel cast the custodian an arrogant look. "One word is all it takes for me to bring calm to a situation." He was aware of Mrs Chambers' gaze drifting over his face, searching, probing. "You'll not hear a raised voice or cross word. I promise you that."

"Then you may proceed upstairs." Cutter flicked his chubby fingers at the door. "You will find Rosalyn Harrison with the other ladies in the private parlour. It's the first door on the left in what used to be the Seymour bedchamber. The name is on the plate. Oh, and if anyone questions you, Thorpe, just say I asked you to call, but you're yet to discover why."

Daniel nodded and escorted Mrs Chambers to the upstairs floor. They followed the dull tinkling of an out-of-tune pianoforte and the high-pitched screech that occasionally broke into a baritone.

The door to the Seymour room was ajar, and so they slipped inside so as not to cause too much of a distraction.

"Bravo, Miss Melinda. Bravo!" a man cheered from the small row of seats positioned in front of the pianoforte. His greasy hair was parted in the centre, and his hand shook as he held up his monocle to examine the ladies. "You have the voice of a nightingale, so sweet and full of gaiety."

"Oh, my lord," the lady replied, though her hook nose, and

the dark shadow gracing her square jaw, confirmed the silk gown and white wig were merely a means to create a facade. "Were it not for Miss Brown's excellent playing I fear I would sound rather mediocre."

"Nonsense," another gentleman cried from his seat at the card table at the back of the room. "You are an accomplished young lady, Miss Melinda."

The lady put her hand to her lips and tittered as she batted her lashes and looked to the floor.

"And we have two more come to hear your delightful playing, Miss Brown," came another masculine voice from somewhere in the audience.

All heads turned in their direction though it was Mrs Chambers who captured their attention. Greedy gazes travelled over her curvaceous form. The lady known as Miss Melinda cast a jealous scowl while Miss Brown stared in awe.

"Please," Mrs Chambers began, "continue with the delightful show."

Her voice possessed the soft, soothing quality that stirred the senses. It was a sound that appealed to most men. A sound the other *ladies* in the room struggled to master.

"Yes, please continue," Daniel reaffirmed leading Mrs Chambers to the empty sofa before a patron made an illicit proposition and fists flew.

There was an awkward moment of silence. Miss Brown tinkled her keys to distract the gentlemen in the seats from the stunning beauty who had just entered the room. Of course, it wasn't the feminine form they sought. The lady at his side lacked the tools necessary to satisfy these particular men.

"Why are they staring at me like starving dogs eyeing a juicy slab of beef?" Mrs Chambers said as Miss Melinda's barely adequate rendition of *The Mermaid's Song* drifted through the room.

"The women who frequent this establishment are not women

at all," he replied, unable to hide the hint of amusement in his tone. "No doubt the men are mesmerised by your perfect disguise. The ladies only wish they were half as attractive." He met Mrs Chamber's gaze, and she swallowed deeply.

"Heavens, Mr Thorpe. I've barely heard a word from you in the last few years and yet you have paid me three compliments in the last hour alone. Perhaps you're keen to unsettle me."

Damn.

As a man detached from emotion, he often spoke his mind. What need had he to hide the truth? People's opinions mattered little. So why did he fear telling Daphne Chambers his innermost thoughts? Probably because the more time he spent in her company, the more likely he was to drop to his knees, clutch her hands and beg to know why the hell she refused his suit three years ago.

"It was merely an observation," he countered. "I state the facts as I see them."

"A general observation or a personal one?" When he frowned, she added, "Is it your personal opinion of my countenance or how you deem others see me?"

Bloody hell.

Why could she not nod and giggle like the simpering miss murdering Haydn's masterpiece on the pianoforte?

While Daniel endeavoured to form a reply, his attention was drawn to the insipid lady shuffling past, her gaze rooted to the floor.

"Come." Daniel stood abruptly and offered his hand to Mrs Chambers. "Our business demands we leave."

"What, so soon? But I've only just sat down."

He pulled her to her feet. "Mr Harrison is leaving the room."

Mrs Chambers turned and stared at the figure attempting to squeeze unnoticed through the narrow gap in the door. "But how do you know that's—"

"Never mind. I'll explain later." They hurried out into the

hall. Only the missed note on the pianoforte and a sudden screech from Miss Melinda indicated anyone had noted their departure. "Mr Harrison," Daniel called out to the figure hurrying across the landing.

The person ground to a halt but did not turn around.

"We wish you no harm," Mrs Chambers said.

Daniel stepped closer. "Surely you know why we're here."

With the information gathered from the pawnbroker, and from the gentleman's impediment, it was obvious they'd found the right fellow.

Mr Harrison turned slowly. "What … what do you want with me?"

"Two things," Daniel said bluntly. There was no time to pass pleasantries. They had one more visit to make to complete their business, and it was difficult to focus when all he cared about was discovering the identity of Daphne Chambers' mysterious intruder. "We require a confession and an explanation."

"A confession?" Mr Harrison's hollow cheeks accentuated his timid countenance. He was one of life's victims. No doubt problems followed him wherever he went. "But it is obvious to everyone that I'm a man. And don't ask me to explain that which I fail—"

"Do not play games, Mr Harrison. Admit to being the person who caused the damage at Madame Fontaine's shop and agree to pay for the repairs. That is all we require. Twenty pounds should suffice."

"Twenty pounds!" the gentleman cried, all trace of feminine intonation abandoned. "For a broken window."

Mrs Chambers sucked in a breath. "I believe you have just confessed, sir, as Mr Thorpe made no mention of the window. Though I agree, twenty pounds is far too steep for a pane of glass."

Mr Harrison clasped his hands together in prayer. "It was a stupid lapse of judgment. Perhaps Madame Fontaine will allow me to work to repay the debt for I do not have a spare shilling to my name."

Daniel reached into the inside pocket of his coat, removed the folded banknote, grabbed Mr Harrison's hand and thrust it into this palm. "That should cover all expenses. You're to call in at the modiste's and pay for the repair to the window as a matter of urgency. Ten pounds should suffice."

Mr Harrison unfolded the note and gasped. "Heavens above. But what shall I do with the change?"

"Spend it. Madame Fontaine's dresses are too expensive for your moderate income, so I suggest you call on Mrs Wilson on South Moulton Street, number fifty-nine if my memory serves me. She is a skilled dressmaker, but her prices are fair."

Mr Harrison's eyes brightened. "You're giving me the money to buy a new dress? You do not wish to call a constable and report the incident?"

"There is no need to involve anyone else." Daniel could show compassion when necessary. What was the point of punishing a man who spent his days punishing himself? "May I suggest you find a way to control your sudden outbursts? Accept your fate and make the best of it. As we have all had to do."

"Oh, thank you, sir." Mr Harrison bowed and then curtsied. "I'm a man of modest means, but should you need any assistance in the future you only need ask."

Now Daniel's interest was piqued. "And what is your profession, Mr Harrison?"

"I work as a clerk for—" He stopped abruptly. "I draw up contracts and legal papers."

"Excellent." Daniel inclined his head. "I shall bear that in mind should I be in need of such services. Now, if you will excuse us, we have important business elsewhere."

Daniel placed a hand on the small of Mrs Chambers' back and guided her towards the stairs. Her penetrating gaze never left his face, and he had to grab her arm when they reached the top step for fear of her falling.

"Despite my years investigating the strange and unusual, I'm shocked to find that some things still surprise me," she eventually said.

Most ladies had no idea what went on inside a molly-house. Most ladies were unaware of their existence. "So you've never seen men parading as women before?"

"I've heard about them but never seen them in the flesh," she said with a little chuckle. "But that is not what I found most surprising. It is something else entirely."

"And what is this astonishing discovery?" he said with some amusement.

"It is not a discovery, merely what I always suspected—that beneath your austere facade, you have a kind and forgiving heart."

CHAPTER 6

"WILL YOU NOT ADMIT TO HAVING A GENEROUS NATURE?" Daphne stepped out onto Maiden Lane and turned to face Mr Thorpe. "Kindness is an admirable quality, not something to be ashamed of."

"Some people think it's a weakness."

She stared into dark brown eyes that too often looked cold and empty. "But you don't believe that."

"Punishing Mr Harrison serves no purpose," he replied, avoiding a more direct answer. "You saw the man. He could barely hold my gaze. It is evident this was his first offence. As long as he reimburses Madame Fontaine for the window, I see no need to pursue the matter."

"Why did you not simply give Betsy the money yourself?" Daphne knew the answer, but the opportunity to probe Thorpe's mind proved too tempting.

"Because if I ever need to call on Mr Harrison, I must be certain of his character."

Surely Thorpe was aware of the discrepancy in his tale. He'd given Mr Harrison the money before learning of his profession.

"You mean you require validation," she clarified. "You want to know that your faith in him is not unfounded."

"Something like that."

Large drops of rain landed on Daphne's face. One glance at the black clouds moving overhead confirmed the heavens were about to unleash a torrent on the mere mortals below.

Thorpe glanced up at the sky. "Come, if we're quick we might miss the worst of the weather." He cupped Daphne's elbow and prompted her to walk back to the bustling Covent Garden market.

"So if Mr Harrison fails to pay for the window and spends the money on gin, what then?" Daphne's words were lost in the din as they navigated the boisterous crowd rushing to finish their chores.

As expected, a succession of loud rumbles above brought a deluge of rain. Panic ensued. Sellers shouted, desperate to hawk their wares and be heard above the sound of the storm.

Two men barged between them, forcing them apart. A trader's cries of a sale for the first twenty customers caused a sudden frenzy. Wet or not, everyone wanted a bargain. Everyone wanted to finish their errands and find a dry place to shelter from the downpour.

"God damn," Thorpe cursed. "Watch where you're going, man."

A sea of people swept past them, jostling for a position at the front of the queue as they surged towards the market stall. Hunger made men desperate, but it was the women who abandoned their morals to nudge and elbow others out of the way.

"Thorpe!" Daphne stood on tiptoes, blinked away the rain from her lashes and scanned the crowd looking for a black hat towering above all others. She saw him on the opposite bank of this flood of eager customers.

"Keep moving forward," he shouted pointing to his carriage parked beyond the market square.

She tucked her arms into her chest—all the bumps and bangs were sure to leave ugly blue bruises—and did as he asked. Having much longer strides, and a frame large enough to make the Devil think twice before taking a swipe, Mr Thorpe reached his carriage before her.

Forced to push and shove, Daphne broke through the crowd. She heaved in a breath, more out of relief than a need for air, and moved towards Thorpe's vehicle.

Thorpe took two steps towards her but his sharp gaze shot to a point on her left. He shouted something, but the cries of the crowd rang loudly in her ears.

Bless him, he did worry so. With a torturous expression, Thorpe waved for her to hurry but then took to his feet and ran towards her.

The squelching sound of horse's hooves as it moved from trot to canter on the muddy thoroughfare was the only thing she heard before glancing up and seeing a cart charging towards her. The driver's broad-brimmed hat obscured his face, probably as a means of protection from the rain, yet he seemed determined in his course.

Could the man not see her?

Did he not realise she was there?

"Look out!" Thorpe cried, but the driver kept his head bowed. "Bloody hell, are you deaf?"

Out of fear of being trampled by the horse, Daphne picked up her skirt and ran. When the driver was but an inch from her shoulder, he glanced up. But it wasn't shock or fear she saw in his cold eyes—it was determination. The discreet swerve into her was deliberate and sent her flying forward.

Time slowed.

Anticipating the crack of broken bones when she hit the ground, Daphne squeezed her eyes shut as though that would somehow lessen the pain, and waited for the unavoidable impact.

But instead of landing with a thud, strong arms enveloped

her and cushioned the fall. Held tight against Thorpe's hard chest they rolled in the mud—twice, three times, before coming to a stop. They lay motionless for a moment, Thorpe's huge frame pressing down on her, acting as a shield. Daphne heard his ragged breathing. She gasped to catch her breath and caught the aromatic scent of nutmeg and exotic wood. A faint whiff of lavender added a hint of sophistication. Mr Thorpe smelt divine —so good, it took every effort not to press her lips to his neck and inhale.

When he stood, Daphne felt the loss of his warm body instantly. Blinking to clear her vision and to banish all amorous thoughts of Mr Thorpe, she grabbed his outstretched hand and came to her feet.

"My pelisse is ruined." She glanced down at the dirty, brown splodges and flicked away remnants of rotten vegetables. "I'll never get the stains out."

"Forget about your coat. I'll buy you a new one." Thorpe's voice was hard, stern. "There's no sign of the cart, but I never forget a face. I'll find him even if I have to camp here for a week." He took her hand and pulled her towards the carriage, his head whipping left and right as he scanned the area. "Get in," he snapped with some frustration as he held the carriage door open. "Get us the hell out of here, Murphy."

"Where to, sir?"

"To the house on Church Street," Thorpe said as he followed Daphne inside and slammed the door.

The vehicle jerked, jolted and trundled on a few paces. A silent minute passed while Murphy negotiated the crowd and until they were rattling along the road at a steady pace. Thorpe shrugged out of his greatcoat and used a handkerchief to wipe rainwater and splashes of mud off his face.

"Remind me to avoid Covent Garden in the afternoon," Daphne said, removing her filthy coat, rolling it into a neat package and placing it on the seat. The hint of amusement in her tone was intended to settle her companion. In truth, she had to sit on her hands to stop them shaking, had to smile to stop her lip from trembling. The image of a giant horse bearing down refused to leave her. Those cold black eyes would revisit her in her sleep.

Thorpe removed his hat and threw it onto the seat next to him. "How the hell are you able to remain so calm when that bloody idiot almost killed you?"

Daphne swallowed. The sound of her erratic heartbeat echoed in her ears. "I doubt the fellow could see where he was going in the rain."

Thorpe shot forward. Anger emanated from every fibre of his being. "You may be capable of fooling other people, but you cannot fool me. You know damn well he swerved into you intending to cause you harm. The question remains why."

"Perhaps his hands slipped on the wet reins." Her tone lacked the conviction necessary to persuade him.

"Or perhaps you've not told me everything about this invisible intruder that has stalked you for nigh on three years."

With a frustrated huff, Thorpe threw himself back in the seat, the carriage rocking violently on its axis. The depth of contempt in his voice was enough to send most men scurrying for cover, but she'd seen enough of fear to know anger was merely a mask.

A tense silence filled the air.

What was she to say—that she suspected Thomas spied for the Crown? Lengthy trips to France stemmed from more than a need to avoid intimacy. Daphne was convinced his appointment at the tavern on that fateful night held the key to the mystery. If only one of the blasted sailors had talked, but loyalty was as ingrained as the sea-salt on their skin.

"My stalker has never threatened physical violence." No, he preferred to abuse her mind, invade her thoughts.

"So what are you telling me?" He threw his hands in the air.

"That the person who stole Lady Hartley's hat pin hired a man to murder you in Covent Garden?"

"Of course not. The accusations against the staff proved to be unfounded. Lady Hartley suffers from—" Daphne stopped abruptly and drew her head back. "How do you know the lady hired me to find the thief at Hampton Hall?"

Thorpe grunted and glared out of the window.

"Mr Thorpe," she said to get his attention. "That case was three months ago, long before we were both hired by Lord Harwood and consequently renewed our acquaintance."

"Lord Harwood hired *me*," he corrected. "You were hired by Mrs Dempsey."

"Does it matter? Together we solved the case." She offered the sweetest smile she could muster. "Have you been spying on me, sir?"

After a brief look of surprise at her direct approach, he offered an arrogant smirk. "I feel it my duty to keep abreast of your business activities."

"Your duty?" Oh, how that word irritated her. It brought to mind the letter he'd written after making his marriage offer. The word duty had left her cold then, too. "To whom? To your childhood friend who, through his stupidity, can no longer protect his wife? Or does your prying stem from a need to keep ahead of the competition?"

"You're no competition when it comes to gaining clients." He folded his arms across his chest. "When it comes to those needing protection, it stands to reason I'd be the obvious choice."

"I see. You mean a simple case of a stolen hat pin is nothing compared to storming a smugglers' hideout brandishing a pistol?"

Thorpe's eyes widened. "How the hell do you know about that?"

"It is my duty, sir, to keep abreast of your whereabouts

61

should you ever need assistance." It was pure guesswork on her part. Daphne had read about the case in *The Times*. No names were mentioned, but few men were willing to take on a gang single-handedly. No one else fitted the description of a dark, brooding fellow wearing a billowing greatcoat. Of course, Mr Bostock would have accompanied him. "Had you not taken Bostock, you could have called on me for help."

A range of emotions flitted across his face: confusion and suspicion being the most obvious. "It seems I'm not the only one with an interest in the competition. But with all due respect, a woman is no match for a man in those situations and certainly no match for Bostock."

The obstinate oaf had no measure of her skill. "I can assure you, my ability with a blade and pistol surpasses that of most men of my acquaintance."

"What men?"

"Excuse me?"

"Who are these men you're acquainted with?"

"Why?"

"Because I want to know."

"Then I suggest you check your notebook. That is where you keep a record of your spying activities, is it not?"

He raised a brow and snorted. "Though I have serious doubts over your physical strength in battle, your mind is sharper than a knight's sword."

The compliment made her smile. "And while I have no doubt you're the strongest man I know, I find your logic lacking. Anyone who wields a weapon is a threat, regardless of gender."

"That is where your lack of experience fails you. The desperate need to escape the hangman's noose creates unpredictability. I've seen a man take a ball in the back so his comrades may escape." He leant forward, his elbow resting on his knee. "Confronted by a woman, they would take their pleasure before leaving her for dead."

Thorpe spoke with such conviction Daphne wondered what horrors he had witnessed during his time as an enquiry agent.

"After what I've seen of gentlemen's habits at the molly-house, there is nothing to stop you from suffering a similar fate," she replied.

Thorpe's expression darkened. "Trust me, I'd rip their heads from their shoulders before they could rouse an immoral thought." His penetrating stare travelled slowly down the length of her body. "You, I fear, would be helpless."

Despite a burning need to prove him wrong, Daphne recognised the truth in his words. While a pistol worked as a deterrent, there were men savage enough, conniving enough, to manipulate events to their advantage. Still, she couldn't help but tease the sour-faced gentleman sitting opposite.

"I do have some skill with my fists." Monsieur Tullier insisted she tell no one of his private tuition in the art of pugilism, fearing he might be bombarded with feisty women too headstrong to do as they were told. "Probably not as powerful as the punches you throw." An image of a hammer smashing down on an anvil sprang to mind. "But I'm confident I could break a man's nose if necessary."

Thorpe's nostrils flared. The surrounding air sparked with a volatile energy. The temperature within the small space rose till Daphne thought the carriage might combust.

"Despite disapproving of your work, I've never taken you for a fool." Thorpe had the look of a man doing Lucifer's bidding. "So let us put an end to this matter once and for all. Let's see how capable you are with a man intent on getting his way."

Without warning, Mr Thorpe grabbed her wrist and pulled her to the opposite side of the carriage. There was no time to react as she tumbled into his lap.

"I am only holding one hand," he said in a slow, arrogant drawl. "Let us see if your iron fist can render me helpless."

Anger should have been the primary emotion coursing through her veins. She was eager to prove her worth, equally frustrated at his high-handed approach. But sitting across his muscular thighs, inhaling the potent scent that clung to his clothes, his hair, his skin, proved too much of a distraction.

How quickly logical thought abandoned her when presented with an opportunity to experience close human contact.

"One's weapon of choice must suit the circumstances," she whispered, the seductive lilt in her voice evident as her mind raced two steps ahead. "And I do have another weapon in my arsenal. One you have not considered."

The element of surprise was crucial in any form of attack. Pushing aside her doubts—for when in combat only the confident prevailed—Daphne pressed her mouth to his, leant into his hard body and kissed him.

The hair on his chin proved to be less irritating than expected. The lips hidden beneath were warm and surprisingly soft. Thorpe remained rigid, motionless, while she moved her firm mouth over his. The kiss was supposed to shock him. And so to that end, it served her purpose. But she wanted a reaction.

She demanded a reaction.

With that in mind, she altered the pressure, running featherlight kisses across his lips, nipping at the corners.

Still, he gave nothing.

Damn the man. Was it stubbornness that made him refuse to surrender? Was it his determination to prove a point?

Well, she had a point to prove, too.

For fear of looking foolish, Daphne tried the only other option available—she ran her tongue over the seam of his lips hoping to delve deeper inside.

Daniel Thorpe reacted instantly.

The passion that lay dormant burst to life with a sudden flurry of activity. A deep groan resonated from the back of his throat. His free hand slid around her back, gathered the material of her dress in his fist and crushed her to his chest.

Responding in the way she hoped, he let her inside his warm, wet mouth, let her taste him as she wanted to. The wild dance of their tongues was accompanied by the sound of their ragged breathing. The sudden urgency to sate a physical need Daphne had denied for so long pushed to the fore. Before her mind could catch up with her movements, she was straddling Thorpe's lap. Releasing Daphne's wrist, his other hand crept under her skirt to caress her thigh.

"God damn, Daphne," he whispered, trailing kisses down the column of her throat. "Are you determined to drive me insane? Is this to be my punishment for challenging you? Am I to sample something heavenly only to have it ripped from my grasp?"

Thorpe was a man of sound mind. He spoke with care and clarity. These unrestrained ramblings were so unlike him.

"When presented with a problem," Daphne began, though the liquid fire pooling between her legs made it almost impossible to focus, "a lady must find a way to gain the upper hand."

Thorpe pulled away abruptly, snatched his hand back from under her dress as though he'd touched a nest of spiders.

"Then my first instinct was correct," he said with a hint of malice that belied the look of longing swimming in his eyes. "This is a game to you. In your bid to teach me a lesson, you would drag me through the hot fires of hell."

Daphne slid off his lap and tumbled into the seat opposite. "My initial intention was to do just that," she said, batting the creases from her dress. Her cheeks burned, but she did her best to hold his gaze. "But it has been a long time since I've felt close to anyone. I think it's fair to say we both got a little carried away."

He glanced down at his boots. "Such a misunderstanding will only hinder our working relationship."

A misunderstanding? What did he mean?

So she'd kissed him. Like a wild wanton, she'd sat astride those muscular thighs straining against the confines of his breeches. One did not need an education in human emotions to know they had enjoyed the experience.

"There is no misunderstanding." A working woman did not need to skirt around the truth. "Once our lips met, and you finally responded, it was our mutual desire that took over." Had her words not dampened his ardour, heaven knows where their passionate encounter would have ended.

The carriage rumbled to a halt in Church Street, prompting a change in conversation.

Thorpe shuffled forward. "Give me a few minutes to find a clean coat, and I'll be back. Wait here."

He opened the door, jumped to the pavement and inhaled like a man starved of air.

Daphne peered out. "Where are we to go next?"

Thorpe turned, reached into the carriage and snatched his hat from the seat. "I am going to visit Lord Tranmere. And you, Mrs Chambers, are going home."

CHAPTER 7

"I AM A MATURE WOMAN NOT A CHILD IN NEED OF CODDLING." Daphne followed him into the house in Church Street, her constant complaining a means to rouse a reaction.

Daniel mounted the stairs two at a time to place some distance between them but she raced up behind him, the thud of her boots on the wooden stairs evidence of her frustration.

"Surely your client's wishes take precedence over your own," she persisted. "What if I don't want to go home?"

Daniel swung around and grabbed the bannister at the top of the stairs for fear of throttling the woman to her senses. "What part of your supposedly logical brain fails to appreciate the severity of what has just occurred?"

She climbed the last step and came to stand before him. "Forgive me, but I fail to see why a man of your experience places so much weight on the event. Frankly, you're over-reacting."

Daniel stared at her, baffled by her nonchalant manner. "Do you take pleasure in causing me distress?"

"Distress? Come now, is that not an exaggeration?" A coy smile touched her lips. "I'm not a woman of vast experience, but

I know it can be difficult for a gentleman when passions are roused to such a degree. It can cause an emotional imbalance that men struggle to deal with. After all, it was over so quickly. You're bound to feel a lingering need for satisfaction."

"Satisfaction? Rest assured, Mrs Chambers, when I catch the blasted driver of that cart, I'll string him up outside Newgate and leave him as food for the crows." Daniel's hands throbbed at the thought of wringing the rogue's neck.

She drew her head back sharply and blinked numerous times as if still trying to bat rain from her lashes. "Oh, you're talking about the incident in Covent Garden. That's why you want me to go home."

"What else would I be talking about?"

A pink blush touched her cheeks. "I thought you were referring to our … to the incident in the carriage. You appeared most unsettled by it."

Unsettled was far too tame a word. Lonely nights spent imagining that exact scenario had failed to prepare him. God, the woman had no idea how she affected him, how much he'd wanted to unbutton his breeches and thrust home, to hear her pretty pants and sighs as he pleasured her until she called out his name.

"Lust can lead to frustration and can occasionally be distressing, but our kiss has nothing to do with my need to take you home." The comment held a grain of truth. Daphne's safety was paramount. But he'd spent years learning to suppress his desire for her. Now, having tasted the forbidden fruit, he wasn't sure how long he could keep it at bay.

"Do you think that's the first time someone has tried to hurt me?" she snapped.

Anger flared at the thought of anyone laying a hand on her.

Daniel turned on his heels and stomped off to the bedchamber. The whirlwind of emotion in his chest was set to spiral into a raging storm capable of causing total devastation.

She traipsed after him still muttering, but he busied about finding a clean coat and changing his boots, though the image of her ashen face as the cart knocked her to the ground still plagued him. Without saying a word—silence was the only way to guarantee he'd not say something he might regret—he strode past her and waited at the front door.

"You know I'll not sit at home and wait for your updates." She sauntered past and climbed into the carriage. "Don't force me to investigate the matter alone," she said as he settled into the seat opposite. "I've spent far too much time on my own of late. Can we not work together? Can we not put our personal feelings aside and concentrate on the case?"

Her soft, melodic tone spoke to him in a way no other woman ever had. For the umpteenth time, he would have to bow to her whims and demands. The woman was a menace when left to her own devices. And despite being a man of strong conviction, he found he couldn't refuse Mrs Chambers anything.

Daniel removed his watch and checked the time before replacing it in his pocket. "At this hour, we should find Tranmere at White's. I'll call in and speak to him. Then we'll visit his mistress, Miss Cartwright. Once there, you can leave your stained pelisse in the carriage and accompany me inside. Miss Cartwright's opinion of what is deemed appropriate hardly matters."

The smile illuminating her face robbed him of breath.

"You're a member of White's?" she said with some surprise.

"Of course not. Do I look like a man with nothing better to do than cross my legs, puff on a cigar and read the newspaper?"

"Then how do you propose to gain entrance?"

There were no doors barred to him. "There's not a gentleman in the *ton* who doesn't owe me a favour. While you harass the modiste for information, I build a list of those in my debt. Ask me for anything, and I can get it for you."

She tapped her finger to her lips and hummed. "I suspect most ladies would ask for a ruby the size of an apple. Or a chestnut mare with white feet and a pleasant temperament. If I were a woman who believed in whimsical dreams, I'd ask for a home in the countryside, nestled deep in a valley amidst rolling hills."

Though he knew of her love for the country, she'd never mentioned it before. "Thomas said you grew up in Aylesford, that your families were neighbours. I hear it's a pretty village, although I've never been."

Thomas had spoken with enthusiasm about long walks by the river, of the quaint church, of time spent enjoying picnics in the meadow. For that reason, Daniel should have hated the country-side, yet he saw it as a symbol of all that was good with the world.

"Oh, it's so peaceful there." Her eyes glistened like never before as a satisfied sigh left her lips. "When I have the funds, I plan to move out of London," she said, and Daniel thought the day couldn't come quick enough. "I want to wake to nothing but the birds' beautiful song, to breathe clean air, to feel so safe I can leave the bedchamber window open at night."

"What of your work?" he said, relishing the prospect of a peaceful night without worry, too. "The case of the missing lamb hardly rouses intrigue."

She chuckled at that. "This might surprise you, but I hope my work as an enquiry agent will soon be at and end. Truth be told, I'm tired, tired of … well, solving crimes can be exhaust-ing, as well you know."

Relief coursed through his veins though he couldn't quite bring himself to punch the air and cheer. Moving to the country meant there'd be no excuse to keep abreast of Mrs Chambers' cases, no reason to show an interest in her life.

"Then why chastise me for my opinion when you seek a better life for yourself, anyway?"

The question seemed to rouse her ire. "Because I'm a woman

who detests the patriarchal dominance too often displayed in our society. Because I will lead the life I choose and no one shall tell me otherwise."

"What you see as dominance I consider to be a duty to protect."

Tiny furrows appeared on her brow. "Then you must know I have a problem with the word duty, too."

"Again, I must disagree. Your dedication to your work proves otherwise."

"You can't disagree with my opinion, Thorpe. I think I know my own mind, and I was not referring to my work."

"Then you should speak plainly to avoid confusion."

"Must you always challenge my position?"

"Must you always assume my intention is to belittle you?"

They both exhaled deeply.

The carriage jerked to a halt on St James' Street. "Wait here," he instructed even though she had no choice in the matter. Never had a woman been granted entry into White's. "I'll be but a moment."

"There's nothing to fear on that score. Dressed like this, I'm not fit to beg for scraps."

"Yet I get the impression that would not deter you." Offering a curt nod, he opened the door and jumped down to the pavement. "Mrs Chambers' safety is a priority," Daniel shouted to Murphy. "Should you have need to leave, I'll meet you in the yard of The Cock Inn."

"Right you are, sir."

"Stay alert," Daniel reiterated.

"I've the eyes of a hawk to be sure."

Horbury greeted Daniel at the door, his ragged breathing belying his calm facade. The fellow was employed to cater to the guests' ridiculous demands. Daniel made good use of the fact, paying him handsomely to run errands, gather and relay information. Consequently, the man was like an obedient dog, rushing to his master's heels whenever he appeared.

"Is mine the only carriage in town you recognise," Daniel said with some amusement as Horbury dabbed at the beads of perspiration on his brow.

"Most carriages display golden crests, have liveried footmen in tow and are pulled by chestnut or dapple grey matching pairs." The fellow nodded to the door leading out onto the street. "Your black stallions and unmarked conveyance could belong to Lucifer, and most people would believe it to be true."

Creating a menacing aura made men think twice before throwing a punch or drawing a weapon. "So, I'm Lucifer now. Have you forgotten who pays the rent on that little terrace house of yours?"

A look of mild panic flashed in Horbury's eyes. "Then you must forgive a man for his slack mouth."

Daniel gripped the lean man's shoulder, his firm fingers settling on nought but bone. "I'll let it pass, but I need an audience with Lord Tranmere."

"Lord Tranmere?" Horbury swallowed. "He's with Mr Trenton, his man of business."

"Tell him I wish to speak to him privately. It concerns Miss Cartwright. Should he be unable to spare a few minutes, tell him I shall have no option but to call on Lady Tranmere." Upon witnessing Horbury's trembling lip, Daniel reached into his coat pocket, removed three sovereigns and thrust them into the man's palm. "Time is of the essence."

Horbury scurried off toward the private dining room, leaving Daniel to wait in the hall. A minute passed before Tranmere burst through the door as though the seat of his breeches were on fire.

"What is the meaning of this?" Tranmere, a tall man with greying hair, nostrils wide enough to fill his lungs with a single sniff and a paunch that spoke of overindulgence, came to an abrupt halt before him. "If Georgina wants more money, tell her my hands are tied."

Witnessing the lord's agitation, Horbury made a hasty retreat.

"There was an incident at Madame Fontaine's shop," Daniel said, drawing the pompous lord away from the main entrance to a quiet corner.

"Madame Fontaine? Good. That bloody woman and her loose tongue ruined everything."

Tranmere was obviously referring to the fact Madame Fontaine had unwittingly informed Lady Tranmere that her husband kept a mistress. "I need to speak to Miss Cartwright. As Madame Fontaine has no record of her address, I want you to give it to me."

Tranmere's penetrating stare travelled over Daniel's face. "If you're looking for a mistress and plan on making Georgina an offer let me caution you. The woman is a leech intent on sucking every last drop from her victims. My advice is to find another doxy to keep your bed warm."

In a moment of fancy, Daniel imagined punching Tranmere on the nose, imagined his crisp white shirt stained red. Arrogant lords filled with self-importance gave women like Miss Cartwright licence to behave so shamelessly.

"Her address, my lord, and then I shall leave you to your business."

"Well, I'll not give it to you." Tranmere sounded like a spoilt child.

Daniel shrugged but kept his expression impassive. "You've recently invested in Mr Moorcroft's shipping company upon the advice of your man of business, I hear."

Tranmere's jaw dropped. "How the hell do you know? No one knows of it, other than Mr Trenton. Besides, what has that to do with Miss Cartwright?"

"You should know that Moorcroft specialises in illegal

opium smuggling from Calcutta to China. You should be aware that his nefarious dealings are well-documented. In the wrong hands, the evidence could be damning for all those involved."

Tranmere's limp hand flew to his mouth. "But Trenton assured me—"

"Then the question you should ask is can your man be trusted? My advice would be to find a more lucrative yet legal method to increase your coffers. But before you go, you will give me Miss Cartwright's address."

Tranmere still appeared somewhat dazed.

"Let me be clear," Daniel said. "The information I have imparted is worth a damn sight more than the address of a courtesan. Do not make me regret my decision. During my visit, I might persuade the lady to stop pestering you for money."

At that, Tranmere's shoulders sagged. "Georgina refuses to leave the house I rented for her in Broad Street."

"And the number?"

"Five. Number five."

Daniel inclined his head. "Then I shall leave you to your meeting. Should you need to hire an agent to investigate your man of business, Horbury has my details."

Once back in the carriage, Daphne wasted no time in demanding to know every word exchanged.

"Did Tranmere say anything else?" With wide expressive eyes, she sat forward. "How did he react when you mentioned the theft?"

"I made no mention of the stolen dresses. A man who keeps a mistress thinks with his ... with a part of his anatomy that isn't his brain." Tranmere would bed Miss Cartwright again if the opportunity presented itself. Daniel had noted the flash of jealousy in the fool's eyes when he'd asked for the courtesan's address. "While the woman is intent on making life difficult for Tranmere, I suspect he could still be won over by her charms."

"But did he tell you where you might find Miss Cartwright?"

Daniel nodded. "We'll make a quick call at her residence in Broad Street and then I'll take you home."

Only then could they get to the matter of the real case, the one that required a more thorough, in-depth investigation. Indeed, the burning question was who the hell wanted Daphne Chambers dead and why?

"A quick call?" she asked curiously. "So you're confident you'll gain a confession despite the lack of evidence?"

"A scorned lover is the prime suspect in any case. You know that."

CHAPTER 8

"Tell your mistress that Lord Tranmere sent us, and we must make the offer in person."

The maid's terrified gaze scanned the breadth of Mr Thorpe's chest. Her wide eyes flitted to his beard which she appeared to find equally alarming.

"We need but five minutes of her time," Daphne said to ease the servant's fears.

The girl nodded. "Wait 'ere a moment."

They stood on the doorstep while she scurried off to alert her mistress.

"Do you think Miss Cartwright will see us?" Daphne could not imagine Thorpe taking no for an answer. "If not, we must wait until she leaves the house and accost her then."

"Miss Cartwright will see us," Thorpe insisted. "The woman is desperate and will be curious to hear our offer."

The maid returned, opened the door wide and waved for them to enter. She escorted them to the drawing room where they found Miss Cartwright wearing nothing but a silk wrapper, her golden hair draped over one shoulder as she lay stretched out on the chaise.

"You are here at Tranmere's behest?" she asked weakly, her limp hand resting palm up on her forehead. "Forgive me, I am suffering from a strange malady and cannot sit up. It is a sickness of the heart no doubt."

Daphne suppressed a grin. When Miss Cartwright wasn't bedding married men, perhaps she took a turn on the stage.

"We're here with an offer," Mr Thorpe said bluntly.

Miss Cartwright squinted out of one eye, the corners of her mouth curling up when noting Mr Thorpe's thoroughly masculine form. "Please, if you will assist me, sir, I may be able to sit."

"For goodness' sake," Daphne muttered under her breath, keen to observe the line of Daniel Thorpe's gaze.

Did he find such overt displays of femininity attractive?

Despite his austere facade, did the frivolous lady before him speak to his most primal needs?

For some odd reason, Daphne's throat grew tight when Mr Thorpe stepped forward, took Miss Cartwright's hand and assisted her into a sitting position.

"What large hands you have, sir." Miss Cartwright looked upon Thorpe as one would a juicy piece of plum pie. "I'm sure your sister is grateful to have someone so strong to offer his protection."

Sister? The veiled insult did not slip past Daphne. What the woman meant to say was spinster. "That is why introductions are made before conversation commences," Daphne snapped. "It prevents either party from making foolish assumptions."

Miss Cartwright scanned the muddy hem of Daphne's plain dress with some amusement. "It could have been worse. With your inappropriate attire, I might have mistaken you for a maid."

Her inappropriate attire? This woman had gall. Forgoing a coat was not nearly as vulgar as greeting guests in a robe.

"I heard you find excessive clothes an encumbrance." Daphne could feel Mr Thorpe's gaze searching her face but ignored it. "For once it appears the gossips were right."

Miss Cartwright gave a light, airy chuckle as she trailed her fingers across the exposed skin at her collarbone. "From her stuffy manner, am I to assume she's your wife?"

"Mrs Chambers is my business partner," Thorpe informed in the tone of a schoolmaster quick to put an end to his pupils' childish banter.

"How quaint. I would ask you more about your business, sir, but I'm more interested in what you do when at your leisure."

Lord above. Surely Thorpe wasn't duped by her insincere flattery.

"Your interest must be great indeed," Daphne interjected, "since you appear to have forgotten all about your ailment of the heart."

Miss Cartwright moistened her lips as she studied Thorpe's impressive form. "If presented with a muscular stallion would one mourn the loss of a shabby pony?"

Thorpe cleared his throat. "As you currently have no claims on either, Miss Cartwright, I suggest we get to the matter at hand."

A smile formed on Daphne's lips and she squared her shoulders. A warm feeling filled her chest at Thorpe's complete lack of interest in the brazen beauty before them.

"If Tranmere wants me to take him back, he will have to make it worth my while. The humiliation alone is worth a substantial increase in allowance."

"Are you speaking of your humiliation or that of his wife?" Daphne said.

Miss Cartwright ignored the comment. "Well, how much is he offering?"

"The offer is not from Tranmere," Thorpe said. "It is I who wish to strike a bargain."

Like water breaching a dam, the blood rushed to Daphne's face. What in heaven's name was Thorpe going to offer?

"Oh, I am all ears, sir." The hussy moistened her lips. "A

lady rarely gets such a welcome proposition. I am inclined to say yes before hearing your terms."

"Then I shall not keep you in suspense any longer. You will explain why you saw fit to enter Madame Fontaine's shop and steal two gowns. Else I shall hand over the evidence to the constable."

Miss Cartwright blinked. Her hand flew up to her throat as her complexion turned a deathly shade of grey.

"I don't know what you mean," she said, her voice a strangled whisper.

"Don't you? You more than anyone should know that gentlemen like to boast of their conquests," Thorpe replied. "The poor blighter you persuaded to pick the lock has told everyone you're lovers. It seems true love makes a man do wild and reckless things, Miss Cartwright."

Daphne watched Daniel Thorpe intently. He had based his comments on nothing more than speculation, yet he had such an inherent confidence about his tone and manner he could persuade the Devil he was misguided.

Pride blossomed in her chest. Mr Thorpe was an expert investigator, and intelligence was a quality Daphne found highly attractive.

"Must I reveal your counterpart's name to hear your confession?" Thorpe continued. "Once his name leaves my lips, I fear my business partner may alert Lord Tranmere of your infidelity. Indeed, the magistrate will be interested to hear how you tricked a man into committing a crime."

Miss Cartwright jumped to her feet. "I did not trick Mr Reynolds. For heaven's sake, it was Tranmere's money that kept him out of debtors' prison. He had no choice but to help me. I should have known the fool had a loose tongue. One sip of brandy and he's staggering about the place like a drunken buffoon."

"In taking the dresses I assume your intention was to punish

Lord Tranmere," Thorpe said. "Stealing the mourning gown was simply a means to avert suspicion."

"I believe Miss Cartwright's intention was to punish both Lady Tranmere and her husband," Daphne added. Having spent five minutes with the woman it was obvious manipulation was her game.

Miss Cartwright snorted. "Imagine the scowl on Lady Tranmere's face when she sees me wearing the lilac gown. She knows full well her husband bought it for me. She will believe Tranmere and I are still lovers. He will want rid of me and will pay handsomely to secure my co-operation. And she will suffer humiliation in front of her precious friends."

"One's imagination can often run away with them," Thorpe said with a smirk. "Even the best plans go awry. So allow me to give you a realistic view of what will occur." He straightened to his full height and clasped his hands behind his back. "Your maid will bring the items you stole from Madame Fontaine and put them in my carriage. You have until tomorrow to be out of this house. I'm sure Tranmere will allow you to keep any gifts he purchased. But once he hears of your plan to drain him dry, I sense he will beg Lady Tranmere to forgive him."

"You're asking me to leave my home?" For the first time since they'd set foot in the drawing room, Miss Cartwright's arrogant countenance faltered.

"No, I'm telling you to leave." Thorpe reached into his pocket, withdrew a banknote and gave it to Miss Cartwright. "Tranmere will cover a month's stay at The Burlington. I suggest you accept else I've no doubt you'll face transportation, perhaps even the noose."

Miss Cartwright tightened the belt on her wrapper and with a disgruntled huff snatched the note from Mr Thorpe's hand. "What choice do I have?"

"None." Thorpe inclined his head. "We shall leave you to pack and will wait in the carriage for your maid to bring

Madame Fontaine's items. Rest assured, I shall have words with Mr Reynolds. Good day, Miss Cartwright. And may you find another gentleman foolish enough to fall for your womanly wiles."

With a tug of the bell pull strong enough to free it of its moorings, the courtesan summoned her servant.

Mr Thorpe touched Daphne lightly on the elbow and escorted her back to the carriage. One might have assumed it was anger at Miss Cartwright's disparaging remarks that caused Daphne's hands to shake and her breath to come quickly. But witnessing Thorpe's lack of interest in the courtesan, his cold and rather blunt tone when dealing with the ravishing creature, roused a strange sensation in her chest.

Thorpe was renowned for his abrupt manner and frosty tone, yet when with Daphne there was a warm, caring side he rarely showed anyone else.

As he assisted Daphne into the carriage, their gazes locked. Good Lord, her heart fluttered so erratically it was about to take flight. Their earlier kiss stemmed from a need to test a theory, to prove a point. Now, she imagined kissing him for an entirely different reason.

"I think Miss Cartwright fancied you as her new benefactor," Daphne said as they waited for the maid to bring the stolen garments out. A lump formed in her throat at the thought of Thorpe taking the strumpet in his arms and kissing her tenderly. "The woman was practically drooling."

"Some women find authority attractive, though I doubt I possess the refinement necessary to warm her bed."

"Nonsense," Daphne blurted. "You may not have a title, but you are every bit a gentleman."

He shuffled uncomfortably in the seat. "Are you suggesting I make Miss Cartwright an offer?"

Lord no! She would rather jump off a bridge into the Thames with an iron ball shackled to her ankle.

"That all depends. Do … do you want to warm her bed?"

"I wouldn't bed Miss Cartwright if she were the last woman in London." Thorpe's intense brown eyes studied her. "Intelligence and integrity excite me far more than fluttering lashes and a seductive pout."

For once, Daphne didn't know what to say. While she stared at him, her mind conjured a whimsical daydream, where the gentleman opposite did all sorts of amorous things whenever she offered an insightful argument or comment. The sudden need for Thorpe to see her as physically attractive pushed to the fore. She wanted to see those dark eyes filled with desire as he studied her naked form. She wanted to see his cool facade falter as he ran a hand over her bare skin.

Heavens above!

Daphne coughed and cleared her throat to banish her lustful fantasy.

Thankfully, the maid stumbled down the steps with the garments draped over her arm while she carried a tower of boxes. The coachman climbed down and offered his assistance.

Thorpe opened the door. "Put the parcels in here, Murphy. Arrange the boxes on the seat and lay the gowns flat on top. Mrs Chambers will sit next to me for the duration of our journey."

Despite the odd tickle in her belly at the thought of being squashed next to Thorpe's muscular frame, Daphne moved across to the opposite side of the carriage, sat down and assisted the servants in organising Madame Fontaine's stolen apparel.

"Do you know the gentleman Miss Cartwright mentioned?" Thorpe asked as the carriage trundled along on its way back to New Bond Street. "The one who broke into Madame Fontaine's shop?"

"Mr Reynolds? No, but Betsy might know of him."

"Pay it no mind. I shall find his address soon enough." Though said in a casual tone, there was a dangerous air about his countenance that prickled the hairs at her nape.

"What do you intend to do?"

One corner of his mouth twitched arrogantly. "Oh, I intend to visit him in his room at night and scare him half to death. To let him know it is never a good idea to frighten a lady in her home. When I'm done, he'll kiss my knuckles and thank me for not reporting his nefarious deeds to the magistrate."

The second comment was lost on her for it was his first statement that made her shiver. It was a poor choice of words on Mr Thorpe's part. Memories of nightmares flooded her vision, of imagined figures lurking at the end of her bed—of the ghostly intruder with the power to walk through locked doors.

In some respects, Mr Reynolds' crime paled in comparison. Daphne would rather her stalker stole something, emptied drawers, knocked over chairs and cupboards. To do nothing, to touch nothing, proved far more troubling.

"What is it?" Thorpe swivelled to face her, their legs brushing together in the process. As always, his instincts were in tune with her thoughts.

"Nothing." She shook her head too many times—a sure sign that her words and actions were not aligned.

Thorpe looked into her eyes, stared deep into her soul. "It's so hot in here one can hardly breathe, and so I imagine your sudden shiver stems from feelings of apprehension."

"Apprehension?"

"Now that we've solved two very simple cases, we are free to find your mysterious intruder."

If only it were that easy. Like the last wisps of cigar smoke disappearing from a room, the fellow left nothing behind but an odd lingering smell.

"Where will we start?"

"We'll start by taking you home so you may bathe after your ordeal in Covent Garden. I shall send word to Bostock as he will be your escort when you need to run errands in town."

"Is that because you will be otherwise engaged?" She had

taken up far too much of his time already. It was foolish to think he would act as chaperone as well.

"I will visit The Mariners Tavern. By all accounts, it is the last place Thomas was seen alive."

"So you do think my mysterious visitor is involved in Thomas' death?" Her eagerness for answers was evident in her voice.

"The timing cannot be a coincidence."

In spite of Mr Thorpe's fearless heart and robust countenance, a sense of foreboding settled over her. "Then take Bostock with you if you're going to the docks," she said, knowing Thorpe's companion had fists as hard as mallets. "Indeed, perhaps it is best I come, too." An hour spent waiting for him to return would feel like a lifetime.

Thorpe gritted his teeth. "Have you ever been to a dockside tavern? The only women welcome are those who sell their souls for a penny."

Most places where men drank to excess posed a danger to women, but for some reason, Daphne couldn't cope with the thought of Thorpe going alone.

"I'm familiar with the docks if you remember," Daphne said. "I was the one who lured the guard to the shed so you could punch him on the nose."

Thorpe raised a disapproving brow. "And God only knows what would have happened if I'd not arrived when I did."

"The situation was under control."

"Was it? I recall the guard's wandering hands may have been a problem."

"Must we go round in circles?" she snapped. "Must I boast of my ability to protect myself while you attempt to prove me wrong?"

"I would not advise any further discussion on the matter else you might be inclined to demonstrate your skill in persuasion."

"My skill in persuasion?" Oh, he was referring to the kiss.

Daphne bit down on her lip for the idea of securing his submission was deliciously tempting. "Have no fear, Mr Thorpe. I would not be so presumptuous as to ride roughshod over your delicate sensibilities again."

A sinful smile touched his lips. "Madam, you may ride roughshod over me whenever you please."

CHAPTER 9

"Get out of the blasted road before I run yer man down." Murphy's cries were accompanied by a violent jolt as the carriage ground to a halt.

During the day, the streets around the London Dock teamed with industrious workers going diligently about their business. At night, those with a penchant for vice littered the dirty thoroughfares scouting for a different class of patron entirely. Amid the bustle of drunken revellers, many of them sailors returned to port, half-naked women wandered the grim streets selling their wares.

"Heavens, that woman will catch her death in this weather." Daphne frowned as a buxom wench with breasts bursting from her flimsy gown tapped the window and winked. "Her skin has a mottled, bluish tint. Can she not afford a shawl?"

Daniel smiled to himself. Was Daphne that naive? "Would you buy an apple from a market seller without seeing the produce?"

Daphne shook her head. "A shawl can be removed. I imagine one can use it rather inventively. Would a flash here and there not prove more tempting?"

"Most men who walk these streets are too drunk to notice anything unless it's thrust in their face. Hence the reason she is shaking her flesh at the window."

Taking up most of the seat opposite, Bostock sat forward and waved her away with his chubby fingers. "I think you'll find the grey tint is dirt, Mrs Chambers. Most of them are numb to the cold."

"No doubt they are numb to most things, Mr Bostock," she said with a resigned sigh.

The carriage pulled away again, turned right into Rosemary Lane and rumbled to a stop outside The Compass Inn.

"What are we doing here?" Daphne's head shot between Daniel and the window. "Thomas was last seen at The Mariners, not The Compass. The Mariners is further—"

"I know where the tavern is," Daniel interjected. "But if we're to make any progress this evening, it will take more than a few probing questions to persuade the landlord to speak. The Turners frequent this alehouse and they owe me a favour."

"The Turners?" Daphne wrinkled her nose.

"Businesses pay them a fee to keep trouble away," Bostock replied. "No one wants on the wrong side of the Turners."

Her eyes widened as she searched Daniel's face. "And why would they be indebted to you?"

Bostock snorted. "It has something to do—"

"Thank you, Bostock, I can answer for myself," Daniel said. When speaking to ladies, his friend was incapable of censoring his thoughts. "The Turners like to gamble, boxing mainly. There was a plot to drug their best fighter, to make sure they lost heavily. I was lucky enough to stumble upon the information."

"I doubt luck played a part," Daphne said, her tone conveying a hint of admiration.

"Perhaps not," he replied modestly. "Wait here with Bostock. I shall be but a few minutes." The hairs on his nape prickled to attention. "No one is to leave this carriage, Bostock. Is that clear?"

Daphne huffed. "Trust me, Mr Thorpe. I have no intention of pushing through a crowd of drunken debauchers."

"That's exactly how I feel at the thought of mingling with the aristocracy." Daniel inclined his head. "Don't be alarmed if Murphy moves on. He knows what to do in dangerous situations."

The lady swallowed visibly and bit down on her bottom lip. She had no need to worry and would be perfectly safe with Murphy and Bostock.

"Must you go in there alone?" Mrs Chambers blurted. Her breath came a little quicker. The visible pulse in her neck and her overly bright eyes conveyed fear for his safety. "Can you not take Bostock with you?"

Other than Bostock, no one else cared if he lived or died— not until now.

Without thought, and much to Bostock's surprise, he took hold of Mrs Chambers' hand and gripped it tight. "Bostock must remain with you. I've worked the streets for years. No harm shall come to me here."

The urge to kiss away her fears took hold.

Bloody hell!

Only one person had the ability to hurt him, yet the lady had no clue as to the power she possessed.

"If you have any regard for my welfare, stay in the carriage," he reiterated before opening the door and jumping to the pavement. He waited for Bostock to slam the door shut and then made his way into the inn.

Unlike the air of unruliness out on the street, inside the atmosphere was more subdued. The small, select crowd sat around on crude wooden benches listening to a one-armed man sing a sailor's ballad about riding the rough seas.

As always, the Turner brothers were seated at the round table in the far corner of the room, slightly obscured by a thick, swirling mist of tobacco smoke. Daniel introduced himself to the man blocking his path, a scrawny fellow with a scar running from forehead to cheek. The man glanced behind, received a nod from both brothers and allowed Daniel to pass.

"I trust you received my note." Daniel had paid the errand boy triple the usual fee in the hope of it reaching the brothers promptly. Only one of them could read, but a man was wise not to draw attention to the fact.

"So you want to talk to the landlord of The Mariners," the brother with small lifeless eyes and an oval head said. Some people were known to take on the characteristics of their beloved pets. This brother—no one knew their given names—had a bull terrier who'd bite you before raising a bark.

"As I stated in my note, my friend, Thomas Chambers, drowned in the Thames three years ago. He frequented The Mariners, though I suspect purely on matters of business. New evidence leads me to believe his death was not an accident and so I hoped the landlord would answer a few questions about the night in question."

There was little point lying to these men. In the criminal underworld, relationships were based on trust.

"And if the landlord knows something but never spoke up?" The brother with golden hair and angelic blue eyes—the far more dangerous of the two—smiled. "You'd be asking him to betray his kin."

Daniel shook his head. "I do not see how. If it's a simple case of a mugging gone wrong, then I have no hope of proving it in a court of law. Any information the landlord imparts can be denied."

"And if you discover your friend was murdered?"

"Again, any information given can be refuted. The truth is all I seek." And a means to protect the only person who mattered to him. "You have my word that I will not involve the authorities.

89

But if need be, if matters become complicated, I may have no choice but to take a life to save my own."

The brothers turned away, their heads but an inch apart as they conducted a hushed conversation. Daniel stood patiently and waited. His success as an enquiry agent depended upon knowing when to fight for a cause and when to show restraint and patience.

"Every man 'as a right to defend 'imself," the ugly brother eventually said. "And we understand the need to punish them as wronged you."

"And you did us a great service we can't ignore." The pretty brother gritted his teeth. "That bastard Mackenzie got what was coming to him never you fear." He shook his head, his angry expression suddenly masked by a calm facade. "But you don't need to meet with the landlord."

Daniel cursed inwardly.

To go against the brothers' wishes would be an act of lunacy. But keeping Daphne Chambers safe was his priority and definitely worth risking their wrath. He'd visit The Mariners and accept the consequences.

"Then I must respect your decision." Daniel inclined his head though wanted to knock what was left of their teeth down their throats.

"You don't need to speak to the landlord," the angel repeated, "because we've done it for you. Never let it be said that the Turners don't reward loyalty."

"Or pay their dues," the other brother added.

"You've spoken to him about Thomas Chambers?"

"If that's the name on the note, then yes. It's been a long time, but Jim remembers those patrons with quality. It's not often he's asked to open his best bottle of port. He remembers talk of the tragedy. Your man was a nabob with a golden mop and a beak of a nose?"

Daniel nodded. The beak he referred to was the mark of many an aristocrat. "What did the landlord say?"

They beckoned him closer. "Your man met the same woman there every month or so."

Daniel's throat tightened at the thought of telling Daphne her beloved husband had been unfaithful. Anger flared. Thomas was a bloody idiot for entertaining another woman when he had a gem like Daphne at home.

"When you say Thomas Chambers spent time with a woman are you speaking of the working kind?" The service must have been exceptional to account for the regular visits.

The brothers sniggered. "The beauty's particular about who she takes to her bed, Jim said. Seems she prefers sailors and the like to men of quality."

"Does the landlord know her name?" If she still worked the docks, there was every chance they'd find her. But three years was a long time in the life of a whore. There was every chance she'd caught the pox or been transported for theft. On average two hundred criminals a month were shipped out to New South Wales.

"They say she goes by the name Lily Lawson." The brother puffed on an expensive cigar and blew the smoke in Daniel's direction. "The *Carron* is due in tomorrow. Lily's always hangin' about when the *Carron* docks. Can't promise you'll find her though. Course, your man Thomas travelled back and forth to France on the *Carron* many times according to Jim."

What business did Thomas have in France? His income came from land not trade.

Daphne was right. Had this information been available three years ago, Daniel would have investigated the matter thoroughly.

"One more thing before you leave, Thorpe." The pretty brother stood, the chair legs scraping against the floor. He saun-tered over, and Daniel tensed his stomach muscles expecting a swift blow. The Turners were fair men but often needed to prove a point. "Does that make us even for you givin' us Mackenzie?"

"You owed me nothing for Mackenzie."

The brother chuckled, his pleasant countenance spoiled by the sight of rotten teeth. He slapped Daniel on the upper arm and glanced back over his shoulder. "Do you see where intelligence gets you. Had he said anythin' different he'd 'ave left empty-handed." He turned back and gripped Daniel's shoulders. "Word is there's a pretty price on your head, Thorpe. Someone wants rid of you and quick."

Bloody hell!

As if he didn't have enough problems to deal with. But it wasn't the first time someone sought retribution.

Daniel steeled himself. "There's always a price on my head." Trading information had saved him from many a scrape and scuffle.

"We've spread the word you're one of ours. Never let it be said the Turners don't look out for their friends."

"Then you have my gratitude." Daniel gave a curt nod though he knew the brothers' support came at a price. "And my loyalty should I hear any news that might be of interest."

"That's what I hoped you'd say." The pretty brother exhaled, his sickly sweet breath evidence of a liking for strong spirits. "Now as Jim doesn't know where this Lily lives, you've no choice but to watch The Mariners. Jim'll give you the nod when he sees her, but we swore there'd be no trouble. See as you keep to our bargain."

"You have my word." Daniel stepped back and inclined his head. To linger would be a mistake. "Thank you. Allow me to wish you both a pleasant evening."

"I expect it will be pleasant as long as you keep your head," the pretty brother said. "I'll escort you to the door. Wouldn't want you to have an accident on the premises." The scrawny guard stepped aside to let them pass.

As they reached the door, Turner tapped him on the arm. "You know the *Carron* picks up supplies from the chandler whenever she docks. Always interesting stuff to be found there."

All ships restocked their supplies once they reached port. The fact he mentioned the obvious made it a point of interest. As did the fact he mentioned it out of earshot of his brother.

"I hear some of them shops have rooms to rent," Turner continued.

"Then I'll bear it in mind when I visit the docks."

"Bear it in mind should you ever have to choose a favourite brother." Turner gave a toothless grin, turned on his heels and marched back to his corner.

Once outside, Daniel sucked in a breath for the thick smoke still clung to his throat. Rapid blinking was the only way to soothe his dry eyes. Squinting in the gloom, he noted Murphy parked a little further along the street.

Turner's words echoed in his ears as he strode along the pavement. So Lily rented a room above the ship chandler. It would be a damn sight easier to apprehend her there than at the docks. The visit to the Turners had proved productive and saved them hours of work.

Yet one pressing problem remained. How would he tell Daphne that her husband sought more than cheap ale on his visits to The Mariners Tavern?

CHAPTER 10

THE NEWS THAT THE TURNERS HAD PROVIDED THE INFORMATION necessary to proceed with their investigation—and so there was no need to interrogate the landlord of The Mariners—brought a pang of disappointment.

Daphne sighed.

Not that she wanted to sneak around the filthy docks at night, or jostle with drunken sailors. But the need to discover the truth surrounding Thomas' death burned in her chest, now more than ever.

Since leaving The Compass Inn, Thorpe had said little, other than insist they all return to the modiste shop despite the late hour. Shoulders hunched, he stared out of the carriage window, tugging and reshaping his beard while contemplating heaven knows what. When they reached New Bond Street, he hung back in the shadows and scoured the street with keen eyes before following her into the house.

Perhaps he'd discovered something unsavoury and had important information to impart but required privacy to do so.

Perhaps the near fatal accident with the cart in Covent Garden—an event Daphne banished from her mind every time the memory surfaced—gave him serious cause for concern and so he planned to act as her chaperone, planned to stay the night.

The muscles in her core pulsed at the thought of seeing his huge frame sprawled in her bed. Daphne shook her head. Why on earth had she pictured such a thing? Why had her body reacted instantly?

Three years spent alone had taken its toll. But, truth be told, Daphne had been lonely long before that. Her father's death left a hole in her heart that Thomas failed to fill. A marriage needed more than respect and friendship to satisfy on a deeper level. Consequently, the physical aspects proved awkward, unfulfilling.

So why did she feel a spark of desire in Mr Thorpe's company? Was their relationship not based on respect and friendship, too?

A growl emanated from Thorpe's stomach as he removed his greatcoat and hung it on the coat stand next to the parlour door.

"Heavens, you've not eaten all day," Daphne said, grateful for the distraction. They had been so preoccupied with gathering information they'd not considered food. "Well, you've had nothing during the time we've been together."

"I find I have no appetite when working."

Mr Bostock tutted. "It's important to keep up your strength. A man can't think straight when he's hungry."

Thorpe snorted. "It's not as though those eager for revenge will lure me into a dark alley with the promise of a meat pie."

The mere mention of food roused a grumble from Daphne's stomach, too. "Betsy usually leaves something for me in the kitchen if I've been working late." Indeed, the delicious smell of cooked root vegetables wafted up from downstairs. "I'm sure there'll be enough for us all."

"There's no need to feed me, Mrs Chambers," Mr Bostock said. "I've already eaten. The Cock serves the tastiest beef stew and dumplings for miles around."

Judging by the width of the man's neck, it looked as though he'd swallowed a whole hock of beef.

A loud thud on the door brought Betsy, her hands wrapped in towels as she carried an iron pot. "Sorry, I had no means of knocking and had to hit the door with my foot." Betsy's gaze turned indifferent as it drifted over Mr Thorpe. But her expression brightened as she scanned Mr Bostock's towering frame.

Thorpe's associate rushed forward to offer assistance. "Let me help you with that."

"There's a trivet under my arm." Betsy jerked her head towards her right shoulder. "If you could put it on the table that would help."

Measuring over a foot taller than Betsy, the man's red face revealed his embarrassment at manoeuvring his large hand around her slight frame. In spite of Mr Bostock's robust appearance, the fellow was timid around the fairer sex, more a gentle giant than an ogre.

"You've been out most of the day," Betsy said, placing the heavy pot on the metal stand. "Knowing you, food will have been the last thing on your mind."

Thorpe inhaled deeply and gave a satisfied sigh when Betsy removed the lid and the mouth-watering smell filled the room.

"There's plenty of stew to go around." Betsy brushed her hands down her skirt and moved towards the door. "I'll just nip to the kitchen and fetch the bread."

"I'll come and help," Mr Bostock said.

Betsy's gaze travelled over the man's broad chest. "If you want to," she said with a coy shrug.

"Before you go." Thorpe cleared his throat. "Did you have any visitors this afternoon?"

"Visitors?" Betsy glanced at the ceiling as she considered the question. "Well, Mrs Crowther came for her four o'clock fitting, and Mr Johnson delivered a box of threads." Betsy pursed her lips. "Oh, and a gentleman called and gave me ten pounds to pay for the repair to the window. But I'm sure you knew that already."

"Ten pounds?" Thorpe rubbed his chin. "Is that not a little steep?"

Betsy shrugged. "He said it was for the inconvenience."

"I see."

There was an awkward moment of silence.

Through a series of odd facial expressions, Daphne reminded her friend that Mr Thorpe deserved recognition for the return of the stolen gowns. And for solving the crime of the broken window.

Betsy pursed her lips. "You have my thanks, sir, for bringing the matter to a swift conclusion. Although I'll not be able to sell Miss Cartwright's gown, I can reuse the material. I sent word to Mrs Armstrong-Clarke this afternoon, and she is happy to take receipt of the mourning dress."

Thorpe's expression remained impassive. "And I trust you feel more at ease here at home. A lady's safety is always a priority."

He glanced at Daphne. Strength radiated from every fibre of his being. She wondered if touching him would be akin to caressing the marble statues one found at the museum. Would he respond as her fingers slid over the muscled contours? Or would he be as cold and detached as those lifeless classical figures?

"Well, the stew will be cold before you've taken a mouthful?" Betsy opened the parlour door and jerked her head to Mr Bostock. "We'd best go and get the bread."

The couple left the room and closed the door.

Left alone, the surrounding air in the parlour thrummed with nervous tension. It was not her imagination. Mr Thorpe looked about the room, at the empty grate, at the pot of stew on the table, at anything to avoid catching her eye.

There was something he wished to say, but it was not like him to be hesitant.

"While you made it clear there was no point questioning the landlord, you failed to mention what you learned from the Turners." Daphne watched him intently, in the hope his reaction would reveal something of his inner thoughts. "From your solemn mood, am I to understand it was not good news?"

Thorpe gestured to the chair. "May I sit?"

"Of course."

He waited for Daphne to sit in the chair opposite before dropping into his seat. The wooden legs creaked under the pressure.

"As you rightly said, a gentleman of Thomas' status must have had a reason to drink in a lowly tavern like The Mariners." Thorpe shifted uncomfortably in the seat. "The quality of his bloodline did not go unnoticed. The landlord recalls his visits clearly. The nature of Thomas' death, coupled with his aristocratic breeding, make him an easy man to remember."

Thorpe had never looked so anxious, so uneasy. "Did the landlord share any insight as to why Thomas might have been there? Was he to meet with someone?"

Thorpe dragged his hand down his face. "You're acquainted enough with my methods to know I speak my mind. Before I reveal what I discovered, I want to tell you that while the truth is often painful to hear, the heart is happier for it in the end."

Daphne shuffled to the edge of the chair. "Thomas has been dead three years. The passage of time lessens the blow, makes the truth more bearable. Whatever you have to say, do not spare my feelings."

An uncomfortable silence ensued.

"Thomas met a woman at The Mariners. It was a regular arrangement by all accounts." He sucked in a breath, his broad chest expanding before her eyes. "As to the reason for their business, no one knows."

Daphne chuckled albeit weakly. There were few possibilities to account for Thomas' actions. "There are only a handful of reasons why a man of his quality would spend time slumming at the docks. Smuggling, spying, and seducing tavern wenches. One thing I can say with certainty is that Thomas was not a criminal. Whatever he was doing there had to be legitimate."

"And if adultery was the motive?" He seemed almost sorry the words had left his lips.

"Then I must accept that he sought satisfaction elsewhere." Even though she'd made a tremendous effort to be happy in her marriage, Thomas knew they were not suited in a physical way. "Perhaps I was not enough for him."

Thorpe shot out of the chair. "Then Thomas was a bloody fool. There's not a man alive who'd think you inadequate."

Daphne's throat grew tight at his uncensored outburst. The compliment touched her. Did Thorpe really hold her in such high regard?

"Forgive me," he continued though struggled to hold her gaze. "I spoke out of turn. It is not for me to comment on the nature of your relationship with your husband. He loved you. That much I can attest to."

Daphne could no longer allow ignorance to form the basis of Thorpe's opinion.

"We were not in love, Daniel." His given name slipped easily from her lips, yet she noted the look of surprise in his eyes. "Thomas was my friend, and in a strange way my saviour. He was a good man, and I cared for him deeply." For some reason, she stood too and placed her hand lightly on Thorpe's chest. "But our marriage lacked the soul-deep love that lasts a lifetime. I have never felt an all-consuming passion. Never felt the ache of physical desire."

"Never?" He stared at her lips. "You've never lost yourself in a moment of unbridled lust?"

Heavens, her body reacted instantly to his rich tone. All she could think about was kissing him, running her hands over his impressive chest, taking him into her willing body.

"Perhaps once," she said, recalling the amorous interlude in his carriage, "in a moment of madness when I was eager to prove a point."

"Did this passionate event happen to take place recently?"

"It happened only this afternoon."

His eyes brightened. "Then I must tell you that a single event is not enough to deem a person mad. One must experience the sensation numerous times before a more definitive diagnosis can be made."

Daphne couldn't help but smile. "And so, in your expert opinion, are you suggesting I repeat the experience?"

Thorpe moistened his lips. "I am. Though as with any experiment, the conditions must be the same."

"But I am not in a carriage, Daniel." She liked the sound of his name. "I am not sitting astride your muscular thighs."

"It would take but five minutes to run to The Cock Inn and drag Murphy from his supper."

"You would do that in the name of science?"

"No. I would do it for you."

Those words were like a potent aphrodisiac. Blood flowed through Daphne's veins at so rapid a rate she could hear it thundering in her ears. As soon as she stood on her tiptoes and pressed her lips to his, the spark in her belly ignited.

His hand cupped her neck as he deepened the kiss, his groan of appreciation was perhaps the sweetest sound she'd ever heard. So lost in the magic of the moment, she failed to hear the trudge of Bostock's footsteps coming up the stairs, not until he was almost at the door.

"Bostock …" The word was accompanied by a gasp as Daphne dragged her mouth away and took a step back. "Mr Bostock is at the door."

Betsy burst into the room carrying a loaf of freshly baked bread. "And so Lady Fairweather said the bigger the skirt the better as she needed somewhere to hide her lover should her husband come looking."

Betsy loved to gossip.

Mr Bostock snorted. He placed the knife and board on the table. "Those fancy folk still amaze me."

Daphne glanced up at Thorpe and their gazes locked. Were his thoughts aligned with hers? If this overwhelming need for him continued to grow, it was inevitable they'd become lovers.

But what then?

"Don't stand there gaping. Come and get your supper, else it will be cold." Betsy beckoned them over, took charge and portioned the stew between four plates. Bostock took a plate even though he said he'd not long eaten. "You don't mind if I take my supper here with you?"

"Of course not." Daphne was glad of a chaperone else she was in danger of giving Thorpe more than her opinion on the case. "We're incredibly grateful to you for providing such a hearty meal when you've had Lady Arnshaw's gown to finish."

"Consider it a gesture of my appreciation."

They all took a seat around the small oak table. Daphne tried to focus on her meal but whenever Thorpe opened his mouth or moistened his lips, her stomach performed strange flips.

"Mr Bostock says they're to stay the night." Betsy raised a coy brow at Thorpe's man seated across the table. The man looked down at his stew though a smile touched his lips.

Daphne almost choked on a piece of beef. It was what she'd expected after the accident in Covent Garden. But after yet another amorous interlude with the brooding Mr Thorpe, how would she sleep knowing he was but a few feet away?

Thorpe cleared his throat. "Bostock can sleep on the sofa in the parlour if Madame Fontaine agrees."

"You *can* call me Betsy, Mr Thorpe, or Miss Betsy if you prefer."

Thorpe nodded. "I shall take a chair and sit outside Mrs Chambers' door."

"You can't sit out in the hall all night. Sleep on the sofa in here." Daphne gestured to the small blue damask seat. There would be plenty of room if he dangled his legs over the arm. "It will be far more comfortable."

"Comfort is not a consideration, Mrs Chambers." Thorpe's formal tone revealed nothing of his inner emotions. "I want to be certain no one enters your apartments. The best way to do that is to block the only entrance."

"Why would anyone enter the house?" Betsy frowned. "You said there was nothing to fear now we know who smashed the window and stole the gowns."

When Thorpe caught Daphne's gaze, she hoped the inconspicuous shake of the head would communicate her reluctance to involve Betsy in their current investigation.

"While Miss Cartwright confessed to the theft and returned the stolen goods," Thorpe began, "I have yet to speak to the courtesan's accomplice, Mr Reynolds. Until I have confirmed her story, I prefer to be cautious."

"Oh." Betsy swallowed deeply. "When you came back with the gowns I thought—"

"There is no need for concern," Daphne said. "Mr Thorpe is nothing if not thorough."

They ate the rest of their meal in silence.

"Would you mind helping me move a cupboard before you retire, Mr Bostock." Betsy eyed the man's muscular arms. They were so large the threads on the seam of his shirt were liable to split at any moment. "It's too heavy for me, and I'm tired of seeing clutter lying about the place."

"Of course, Miss Betsy."

"The wooden frame on the back window is swollen, and it gets ever so hot in the dressing room." Betsy was determined to make use of having a man on the premises. "Would you mind seeing if you could open it?"

"Not at all, Miss Betsy."

"Then there's no time like the present." Betsy stood, and Bostock followed her to the door.

"Do you need me for anything else this evening?" Bostock directed his question at Mr Thorpe.

"No, but if you could make sure all the doors and windows are secure before you retire I'd be grateful."

"Right you are."

Betsy and Mr Bostock left the room. Their animated chatter faded leaving nothing but the constant tick of the mantel clock to fill the silence.

"Let me find you a pillow and a blanket," Daphne said, though she doubted either of them would get much sleep. "A draught blows in through a gap in the window, and it can get cold in here at night."

"That won't be necessary. I have no intention of using the sofa."

Oh, this was ridiculous. His sullen mood was beginning to grate. She was a grown woman who managed her own affairs, not a simpering miss naive enough to succumb to temptation. She had no intention of creeping out in the dark to seduce him.

"Mr Thorpe, why is it that whenever our lips meet, you turn into a brooding beast? Why should one simple kiss cause you to fall into a bout of melancholy?"

"Two kisses," he corrected. "You've kissed me twice, Daphne."

Daphne stamped her foot in frustration. "Must you be so pedantic?"

"Minute details are important. Surely you know that. One kiss could be considered a mistake. Two kisses might lead a man to jump to other conclusions." Thorpe tugged at the sleeves of his coat. "But this is a conversation for another time. Now, I ask that you lock the door behind me."

Lord above, the man was as stubborn as a mule. "But you can't sleep outside."

"I have no intention of sleeping."

Daphne jerked her head back. "But you must be exhausted. No. I'll not allow you to sit on a hard chair in a dingy hallway while I sleep in a plush bed."

Thorpe raised an arrogant brow. "Do you know you're the only woman who has ever attempted to tell me what to do?"

"That's because most women are too frightened to approach you."

"But you're not frightened."

Daphne considered the comment. In Thorpe's company, she felt safe. There was no one she trusted more. "No, Daniel. Fear is not the emotion I feel when I think of you."

His dark gaze softened. "Then know you're the only woman I would ever listen to. Indeed, the sofa would be more appealing if my intention was to rest my weary bones. But there is no need for concern because I'm going out."

"Out? At this time of night?" Her tone was that of a jealous wife. "Where are you going?"

"The odd prickling in my gut forces me to go to The Mariners."

"The Mariners?" Now she sounded like Mrs Montague's parrot. She knew better than to question the motive of a man who relied on instinct. "Must you go tonight?"

"No doubt it will be a wasted journey." He took his coat from the stand and shrugged into it. "But I cannot wait until tomorrow."

"But you told Mr Bostock he could retire for the evening." The thought of Thorpe going to the docks alone terrified her.

"Bostock will remain here as instructed."

"Have ... have you arranged to meet someone there?" Was

he intent on speaking to the woman who'd lured Thomas to drink in the sailors' den? The last person to see Thomas alive. Daphne looked him in the eye. "Is it the mystery woman the Turners spoke of?"

Jealousy flared. How odd? She'd felt nothing when she discovered Thomas had met with the wench numerous times.

"Her name is Lily Lawson. The Turners said she waits for the *Carron* whenever it docks. That's tomorrow by all accounts. But the weather can alter the best-laid plans. As I've heard she rents a room in the vicinity, logic says I might find her there tonight." He brushed his hand through his hair. "I can't sit around idle when there's a lead to follow."

"Then I am coming with you. I shall go out of my mind sitting alone waiting for news."

Thorpe smiled. "I'd not have it any other way."

CHAPTER 11

DANIEL HIRED A HACKNEY TO TAKE THEM TO THE DOCKS RATHER than send word to Murphy. The decision had nothing to do with giving the coachman time to finish his supper. Discretion was paramount, and his carriage always drew attention. The black matching pair were such excellent specimens of their breed it was as good as leaving a calling card.

As they approached the London Docks, Daniel leant closer to Daphne seated at his side. "I assume you brought a weapon." He'd make sure she had no need to use it but took pleasure from the spark of excitement in her eyes whenever he spoke to her as an equal.

She smiled. "When working on a case, I'm never without a means of protection."

He glanced right and scanned her from head to toe, wondering whether she had a blade strapped to her thigh, a pistol tucked into her bodice. "Will you tell me where you've hidden this weapon or am I supposed to guess?" Of course, he'd be happy to frisk her, to run his hands over every inch of her body in the hope of finding one.

She turned her head, her mouth but a fraction from his ear. "I have a pocket pistol somewhere on my person, a sheathed blade tucked into my boot and a pot of pepper in my reticule."

"Pepper?" It was obvious why she carried the condiment, but he wanted to feel her breath breeze against the sensitive skin on his neck once more.

"When thrown in a blackguard's face it is most effective."

"I'm sure it is." The image of Daphne wrestling with a fiend in a dark alley filled him with dread. "Remind me never to pick a fight with you. It will do nothing for my reputation if I'm blinded by seasoning."

"The unconventional weapons are often the best." She raised a curious brow. "Please tell me you're armed, too?"

"Of course." The pistol sat nicely in the pocket of his great-coat. "Though I've found my fist to be my most effective weapon."

"Yes," she said with wide eyes. "I recall the little trick you used when on the Harwood case. You put the guard to sleep by simply applying pressure to a point on his neck."

"When one restricts the flow of blood to the brain it is possible to render a person immobile for a short time." It was a skill that came in useful when walking the streets at night. "An uppercut to the chin works just as well."

Daphne glanced at his hands. "Is that how you came by so many scars?"

"No." The question caught him off guard. "Bruised knuckles heal well enough. Broken ones not so."

"But the scar on your hand was made by a blade," she persisted. "The silvery skin on your knuckle looks to be evidence of a burn."

For some strange reason, he held up his hand to examine the marks she mentioned, as though he hadn't realised they were there. But how could he forget? They were the marks that made him the man everyone feared, the man who commanded respect wherever he went.

"The marks were made as you said. A sharp swipe across the fist with a knife. A hand held forcibly over a flame."

Her face turned ashen. "A man who thinks nothing of storming a smugglers' den must be numb to pain and fear." The soft, soothing quality of her voice edged towards pity.

"Mine are the scars of a boy, not a man." God, how he wished he could go back to his school days. If only the boy had possessed the strength and wisdom of the man. "But you're right. What once seemed unbearable now runs off me like rain on a windowpane."

"You were a boy when those terrible things happened?" Daphne put her fingers to her lips and swallowed deeply. "Did… did your father do this to you?"

"No." His father was an honourable man by all accounts. Had Fate not intervened when it did, Daniel's life would have been vastly different. "A few boys at school decided to teach me a lesson." A bastard was no match for the sons of the aristocracy.

"What by slicing your hand with a blade? I hope they were punished severely."

"Oh, they received their punishment." Daniel had waited patiently until they were men with title and the responsibility befitting their station. "But not by the master and not with my fists. The pain of a punch or the whip of a birch is over in seconds. Cuts and bruises last a week or two. Hitting a man in his pocket has repercussions that extend beyond his lifetime."

"I suspect someone with your connections could ruin a man fairly easily."

It had taken years to gather the power needed to take the men down. "With hard work anyone can read Latin or name the great philosophers and their theories. While knowledge can help a poor man rise to greater heights, it cannot rid a rich man of his arrogance."

Daphne sighed. "Conceit is often the mark of the privileged."

"Their belief in their own superiority was their downfall. The self-absorbed often fail to see that which others find blindingly obvious." Daniel could still hear the bitter edge in his voice. "A demanding mistress, an addiction for the gaming tables, an untimely investment or a corrupt man of business can empty one's coffers overnight."

Daphne stared at him, the corners of her mouth turned down. "People believe revenge rids them of past pain." She placed her hand lightly on his arm. "And I suppose it does to a certain extent. But it does not bring peace to the soul. Happiness comes from acceptance."

"To my mind happiness and acceptance are on opposite sides of a coin." Daniel stared at her dainty fingers. Her touch always brought comfort. How could something so small and delicate have such a powerful effect on him? "I can't have the one thing that would make me happy, and so acceptance is all I have left."

Damn, he'd said too much.

She looked deep into his eyes, stared at him as though his darkest fears were evident there. He struggled to gauge her mood. Was she preparing to ask him another probing question? Would she press her lips to his just to torment him all the more?

Thankfully, the hackney ground to a halt on the corner of Burr Street and Nightingale. While Murphy sat atop his box all day without complaining, the cab driver wanted them out so he could find another fare.

"You're to stay at my side at all times," Daniel said, placing her hand in the crook of his arm as they made their way towards the warren of back alleys, home to The Mariners Tavern, brothels, rope-makers and a ship chandler. "Hold on to me like you never want to let me go. Hold on to me as though your life depends upon it."

Daphne gripped his arm. Perhaps it was the anticipation of what their investigation would bring that forced his blood to pump rapidly. Perhaps it was being so close to the only woman who'd ever captured his interest that caused the molten heat to burn inside.

"People will assume we're lovers."

"Good," he snapped as they strode past labourers, watermen and a host of other poor beings who made their living providing services for seafaring folk. "Then it will save me the trouble of beating the life out of every man who dares look your way."

She squeezed his arm affectionately. He contemplated scooping her up and taking her far away from the fog-drenched streets of the city. To a place surrounded by lush green fields, to a house he owned but never wanted to live in.

"I've heard professional thieves prey on drunken sailors in this area," she whispered. "Do you think Thomas fell foul to such men? Do you think that is how he ended up in the Thames?"

"His pocket watch was missing when they found him, but it could have fallen into the water, been stolen by the men who pulled him from the river." Guesswork often led to wasted time and false trails when emotions governed one's thoughts. "In this case, speculation only serves to detract from all potential leads. We must wait until the facts are presented. We must remain impartial."

"You're right."

As they continued along the alley, they came across a man wearing a brightly coloured turban standing amid an assortment of wooden cages. Each one contained an exotic bird: a red parrot with green-tipped feathers, a yellow canary, another with a purple body and white head.

Daphne pulled him closer to study the rare birds. "Oh, Daniel, look. Isn't this one the prettiest thing you've ever seen?"

She was the only thing to steal his breath.

"Don't touch the cage. Like most things around here, they're far more dangerous than they look." The bird squawked and nipped at the bars simply to prove that Daniel's cynical opinion was rarely wrong.

As they moved past the rope and sail-makers, the smell of tar dissipated only to be replaced by the bittersweet scent of ale. From the raucous sounds spilling out into the dank alley, it was evident they were approaching The Mariners.

The tavern was a place where one needed a strong constitution to enter let alone consume a beverage. With not a single brass-buttoned jacket in sight, it was home to those who wished to express their opinion freely after months spent cooped up at sea. Where the downtrodden used drink to forget about their miserable lives. After a few mugs of ale or gin, a man could be anyone he wanted to be. Come the morning, the stark reality only served to send him back to begin the process all over again.

Daniel held Daphne's hand tight to his arm and sauntered past the drunkards who'd taken their merriment out onto the street.

"But I thought we were going to The Mariners?" Daphne glanced back over her shoulder. "I thought we were looking for the woman Thomas met? Although despite what the Turners told you, I doubt she'll still be hanging around the place after all this time."

"Don't stare," Daniel snapped. "Look straight ahead." In this part of town, it took nothing more than a glance in the wrong direction to bring trouble to one's door. "After downing copious amounts of alcohol, these people are easily offended."

"Where are we going?" She quickened her pace to keep up with his long strides.

"To the ship chandler."

"Why, are you in need of twine, rope and a box of tallow candles?" A chuckle escaped from her lips.

"It was something the Turners said—a covert nod in the right direction." Why point him to the chandler if it wasn't relevant to the case? "Nothing about Lily makes sense. If she waits for the

Carron to reunite with a lover or husband, why was she interested in Thomas? If she's involved in smuggling, there are safer places than the London docks to conduct business. Perhaps she supplies goods to those aboard."

"Or information," Daphne added. "Thomas made regular trips to France though said he'd taken work as a translator for a cloth merchant wishing to expand his business."

Thomas had mentioned nothing about his work.

"I was aware his father left the estate with mounting debts." Daniel had dragged the details from his friend after a few glasses of brandy. "That he had to sell the family home and buy a smaller house in London. But I had no idea he needed to work to cover expenses."

"Buy a house?" Daphne gave a chuckle of contempt. "We were left practically penniless once the debts were paid. We didn't buy the townhouse. We rented it. Thomas obsessed over rebuilding his fortune and took paid work to supplement our small income."

Daniel didn't know what to say. Pride had forced his friend to manipulate the truth. "I would have offered assistance had I known you were in financial difficulty."

"The life of an enquiry agent is hard. I should know. I barely earn enough to cover my expenses. Heaven only knows how you afford to keep a carriage in town. Perhaps you charge an extortionate fee for your services."

The lady had no idea as to the extent of his wealth. No idea that he could have given her the life she'd dreamed of if only she'd given him a chance. She had no idea who he was. "And perhaps you're undercharging for yours. You should consider increasing your fee."

"Betsy has said that numerous times. But few people are willing to hire a woman to do a man's work. My price reflects what people deem a disadvantage." She halted and nodded to the small shop with ropes and lanterns hanging from nails on a wooden sign. "Despite the late hour, it seems the shop is still open."

"Places like this rarely close."

"And you think we'll find Lily here?"

Daniel shrugged. "I don't know. The only way to find out is to ask."

CHAPTER 12

THE CHANDLER'S SHOP HAD A MARITIME FEEL THAT HAD LITTLE to do with the assortment of tools, cooking utensils, and other strange metal objects scattered about and more to do with the fact that every wall and surface was wooden. Daphne imagined it was like being below deck on a frigate and at any moment the whole room would shake from the sound of cannon fire.

The smell of tar, tallow and varnish in the air created a not too unpleasant aroma. It was better than the stench of rotting vegetables one found in Covent Garden.

"Can I help you fine folk?" A man with bushy white hair and side-whiskers approached them, wiping his hands on the brown leather apron tied around his waist. The compartment to store tools for ease of access were empty but for a smoking pipe and pouch of tobacco.

"I'm told Lily Lawson lives here," Thorpe said in the stern tone that left most people quaking in their boots. "Would you ask her if she can spare a moment of her time?"

"We have a mutual acquaintance," Daphne added in a friendlier tone.

The man narrowed his gaze. "And who would that be?"

Daphne contemplated saying her dead husband, but that was unlikely to gain them any ground.

"Let's just say our mutual interest spends time aboard the *Carron*." Thorpe looked the man straight in the eye. "I think you understand my meaning."

Oh, Thorpe was by far the better enquiry agent; his mind was quick, sharp. Daphne would have floundered at the direct question.

The trader's gaze flitted between them. "The *Carron* you say. Most people around here are acquainted with sailors. I'll need the name of this acquaintance."

"Names are not to be bandied about lightly. This particular person prefers to spend most of their time in France."

"And he told you to come here?"

Thorpe huffed to show his impatience. He had been deliberately vague about the gender of their supposed acquaintance. Was the chandler's use of *he* a ploy to discredit their claim?

"Tell Miss Lawson we're here," Thorpe insisted, "and let her decide if she wishes to speak to us. Tell her we're here about Thomas Chambers."

Daphne suppressed a gasp. She'd not expected Thorpe to mention Thomas directly.

The chandler frowned. "I know no one of that name."

"It is not for you to know." Thorpe's chest swelled as he sucked in a breath. "But the Turners can vouch for me should you wish to question my intentions."

"The Turners?" The man's face grew as pale as his hair.

Thorpe inclined his head. "Like most people who live and work here, I'm sure you're acquainted with them."

Silence ensued.

Every muscle in Daphne's body clenched tight while she waited for the man's reply.

"I shall take your lack of response as a refusal to co-operate," Thorpe continued. He turned to Daphne. "Come, let's venture back to The Compass Inn and ask the Turners if—"

"Wait!" The man held up both hands. "Lily lives above stairs. I can see if she'll agree to speak to you but ... but that's all."

"I'm sure if you tell her it's about Thomas Chambers she'll not object," Daphne said politely. "I am Mrs Chambers, the gentleman's widow." If Lily was her husband's lover, she must have had feelings for him. Perhaps Lily had spent the last three years wondering what had happened to Thomas, too.

The chandler nodded and scuttled off through a door behind the counter.

A heavy tension hung in the air while they waited for the fellow to return with a reply.

The empty feeling in Daphne's stomach had nothing to do with meeting her husband's mistress, nothing to do with understanding the motive behind Thomas' death. Every step that brought them closer to finding the truth meant less time working with Daniel Thorpe. The thought of going their separate ways, of not seeing him again for years, made her legs weak, her chest tight.

She hoped there was nothing simple about this case, that every lead proved false. She hoped every snippet of information sent them searching in random locations, forced them to travel for long hours in Thorpe's carriage, rent rooms at a coaching inn, dine together in a private parlour.

Daphne cast Thorpe a sidelong glance.

One did not need to be an enquiry agent to know that his broad shoulders carried a heavy burden, something secretive, something from the past. What would it take to break through the hard shell? The only time he'd ever shown any sign of emotion was when she'd kissed him.

What would happen if she took him as her lover? Would the

real Mr Thorpe reveal himself? Would she get to see what he hid beneath his confident facade?

The chandler appeared at the counter to drag Daphne from her musings. "Lily said I'm to show you upstairs. She said she's been expecting you."

The last comment proved worrying. A host of questions flooded Daphne's mind. Had the woman been waiting to speak to them for three years? If she knew something why hadn't she made contact before?

The white-haired fellow led them up a narrow stairway. Thorpe gestured for Daphne to proceed first, yet the feel of his heated gaze on her back made climbing a difficult task.

The chandler left them outside one of two doors on the upstairs landing. "You'll find Lily in there." He rapped on the door on their behalf as though the specific sound conveyed a hidden meaning, and then left them to their business.

With bated breath, Daphne waited to meet the woman her husband had entertained regularly. Would they be similar in looks? Did the lady have the one essential ingredient necessary to please a man like Thomas?

The golden-haired beauty who opened the door was Daphne's opposite in every way: petite in stature, slight of figure with delicate elfin features. The woman cast an admiring glance over Thorpe's masculine frame, and a pang of jealousy hit Daphne hard in the chest. Childish thoughts filled her head. The urge to claim him for herself being the most prominent. Lily had taken Thomas, but she'd not take Thorpe—the only man ever to ignite a fiery passion in her breast.

Lily's attention moved to Daphne. "Mrs Chambers, please come in." Her warm tone sounded sweet and gentle, but wasn't that the way of every temptress? She stepped aside and gestured to the room beyond.

Daphne turned to the object of Lily's fascination. "This is Mr Thorpe, my friend and colleague." The description seemed inadequate. It failed to describe the complicated nature of their relationship. It failed to warn Lily to keep her beady eyes to herself.

Lily moistened her lips. "Good evening, Mr Thorpe."

"Good evening, Miss Lawson." The sudden feel of Thorpe's hand on Daphne's back as he ushered her into the room roused a blush.

With Thorpe at her side, it was becoming more difficult to focus on the case. While she should have been thinking about the link between Lily, the ghostly intruder and Thomas' murderer, her need to learn everything there was to know about Daniel Thorpe had become a priority.

The small room above the chandler's shop was on a par with Daphne's parlour, although this space acted as bedchamber and kitchen, too. It was neat, clean but one glance around the cold, impersonal space confirmed this was a place to rest one's head, nothing more.

Lily moved a wooden chair from around the circular table and placed it near the bed. Thorpe stepped forward to assist in moving the other one.

"Please take a seat," Lily said, gesturing to the chairs. "I shall sit on the bed." The eloquent tone of her voice confirmed that this lady was no backstreet whore. "Can I make tea? I'm sorry to say I have nothing stronger."

"No," Thorpe replied as he waited for them to sit before dropping into the chair. "We will not take up too much of your time."

His blunt response warmed Daphne's heart. She liked that he was cold to everyone but her.

"We would like to ask you about your relationship with Thomas." Daphne felt not the slightest hint of jealousy when she imagined Thomas and Lily together. But if the beauty batted her lashes at Thorpe one more time, she'd have to pull out the pepper pot. "We are aware he met you at the Mariner's tavern on numerous occasions."

"We are aware he travelled with you to France," Thorpe added. "Of the close connection you shared."

It took all the strength of will Daphne possessed not to gasp at Thorpe's speculative comment. Was he not the one who insisted they focus on the facts?

Lily had the decency to avert her gaze. After taking a deep breath, she looked up. "Then you should know that ours was a working relationship. We were not lovers, despite how it might seem."

Daphne did not know whether to be pleased or disappointed. Thomas was a loyal, honest man and she should have known he would never make a mockery of their vows. Yet it would ease the guilt she felt for her inability to love him had he sought solace elsewhere.

"When you say working relationship, I assume your shared venture was legal." Thorpe never took his eyes off the delicate creature.

"Of course." Lily offered a weak smile. "We were not smuggling tea and brandy if that's what you think."

Thorpe leant forward. "Then what were you smuggling?"

"Information," Lily replied confidently. "For the Crown."

Daphne slapped her thigh—it was better than shooting out of the chair and punching the air in satisfaction. "I suspected Thomas worked for the government."

She'd suspected he was a spy to be more precise. She'd never believed his story about the cloth merchant. Spying was the only logical explanation to account for his regular trips to France, to account for the extra income that made life more bearable.

"And you still work for the Crown?" Thorpe clarified.

"Yes, I collect information from a contact who sails on the *Carron*. I pass it on to … well, I'm sure you know I cannot divulge names."

"But Thomas was your partner at one time?" Daphne said,

needing confirmation. This was surely the reason Thomas ended up floating in the Thames.

Lily nodded. "We worked together for eight months before he died."

About the same time Thomas supposedly worked for the cloth merchant.

Thorpe sat back, his expression indifferent yet his eyes held a hint of suspicion. "May I ask why you're still working the same route when your colleague died under mysterious circumstances?"

Lily stared at a point beyond them, her sapphire-blue eyes growing sad, reflective. "Do you think I have a choice? I follow instructions, Mr Thorpe. But you have come here to learn about Thomas, not to hear my sorry tale. And so perhaps it's best I start at the beginning."

"It usually helps," Thorpe muttered.

Daphne nudged him. "Please, tell us all you know."

She looked at them, pursed her lips and nodded. "Thomas believed a colleague of ours was a traitor. He said he had proof. I urged him not to confront the gentleman, to take his information to someone in authority. The night Thomas died we were to meet at the docks, but he never came." Lily bowed her head, the sight of her shaking shoulders evidence of her distress. "Why did he not heed my advice?" she blurted. "Did he not understand that desperate men think nothing of taking a life?"

"Did you love him?"

Daphne turned to Thorpe and frowned, shocked at the nature of his question. Why was he concerned about the woman's emotions instead of demanding to know more about the traitor?

"Well?" Thorpe said when Lily failed to answer. "It is not a difficult question."

Lily looked at Thorpe and then at Daphne. "I loved him as a friend and colleague. The sense of trust and respect we shared was similar to that which evidently exists between both of you."

"But your relationship never progressed beyond friendship?"

"No, Mr Thorpe, it did not."

Daphne caught Thorpe's gaze. He searched her face, but she had no idea what he was thinking.

"Do you think the traitor killed my husband?" Daphne said. It would explain why someone followed her about town, entered her house, yet took nothing. The perpetrator was looking for evidence, for the one thing that would incriminate him, prove he was a turncoat.

Lily shook her head. "That I cannot say. After Thomas' death I was sent to France. I stayed there for a year, forged friendships, secured contacts. When summoned to come back, I begged the powers that be to let me work alone, to use the contacts I'd grown to trust."

"And you use this room merely as a place to conduct business?" Thorpe scanned the bare walls, the empty coal scuttle and grate. A layer of dust covered every surface. Cobwebs clung to the curtains.

"The people around here think I make a living selling my body to the sailors who come ashore. They know I'm a favourite of the crew on the *Carron*. My contact makes it known I'm not any mans for the taking."

And Daphne thought the life on an enquiry agent came with troubles. Why would a woman want to pass secret messages to the government at the risk of death, allow everyone to think her a whore?

"Has anyone ever tried to kill you?" Daphne asked. If the traitor knew that Thomas had confided in Lily, then surely he would have come after her, too? "As a government agent, the traitor must know why you were sent to France."

Lily's face turned ashen. "Thomas would never have betrayed me. He couldn't have, else I would be dead."

Daphne shivered. The image of the horse charging towards her in Covent Garden flashed into her mind. The driver's intention was to run her down with the purpose of breaking bones, causing permanent injury. With her sudden interest in the case, it could not be a coincidence. Yet something didn't fit. Their business in Covent Garden had nothing to do with the investigation into Thomas' death.

"But someone is watching me," Lily continued, the slight tremble in her voice evidence of suppressed fear. "He has entered this room more than once though I have no idea how. The only access is through the shop."

"You're sure of this?" Deep furrows appeared between Thorpe's brow. When Lily nodded, he said, "Did he move anything, take anything?"

"No, nothing."

Daphne's throat grew tight. She knew how it felt to discover someone had entered your private domain, touched your things, invaded your life. The churning sensation in her stomach, the bile burning her windpipe, the imagined film of dirt that clung to her skin, never left her.

"Have you ever seen this man?" Daphne swallowed. She'd pictured someone tall, thin, light on his feet with long nimble fingers and pointed nails. "Do you have a description?"

"I've seen him once." Lily shook her head. "Well, I glimpsed him following me through the alley. But it could have been a drunken sailor, or someone looking to spend a penny for a five-minute fumble."

Daphne sat forward. "Can you remember anything about him? Did he have dark hair? Was he plump or slender? Were his clothes that of a gentleman? Did he leave a—"

"Give her a chance to answer the first question." Thorpe placed his hand on Daphne's arm. The gesture brought instant comfort. This man could ease her fears with a single touch or glance.

"It must be good to have someone so strong to depend upon." Lily stared at the large hand resting on Daphne's arm, and Thorpe immediately broke contact. "In answer to your questions, I don't know. It is like he's a ghost ... there but not there."

"When we arrived, the chandler said you were expecting us," Thorpe said, changing the subject. "It's been three years since Thomas' death, why would you imagine we would make the connection now?"

"In my line of work, information is readily available. We learn every detail of our colleague's background. I'm well aware you're both enquiry agents, know of your connection to Thomas. When Bernard came up, described you both and mentioned Mrs Chambers, it was evident you're working together. What is odd is that it took three years for you to find me."

Thorpe looked to his lap. His shoulders sagged, and he sighed. "I'd always assumed Thomas' death was an accident. There was no reason to suppose otherwise."

"Then I presume you never found the evidence Thomas spoke of?"

"No," Daphne said. "Perhaps he trusted the man he met. Perhaps he handed over the evidence to a person in authority."

Lily tapped her lip as she contemplated the suggestion. "It is a possibility. Had it been with his belongings you would have come across it long before now. Even so, Thomas may have deliberately tried to conceal the information somewhere."

"I can't think of anywhere it could be." When Thomas died, Daphne gave away his belongings—everything except his favourite book.

"Yet something has changed to force you to make enquiries now," Lily said.

Daphne opened her mouth to speak, but Thorpe chose to answer. "Nothing has changed, other than Mrs Chambers and I have recently become reacquainted. She has always had concerns about her husband's death, and I agreed to help her find answers."

"I only wish there was more I could tell you." Lily stood,

which was their cue to leave. "If I remember anything else, where might I find you?"

"At the Museum Tavern on Great Russell Street." Thorpe stood. "Tell the landlord you have ropes for sale, and we'll know where to come."

Lily inclined her head, escorted them to the door and held it open. "Please, I must insist that you do not come here again. Not unless I contact you. In my line of work, it is not wise to rouse suspicion. And would you purchase something from the chandler on your way out? It will account for the time spent in the shop."

"Of course, but allow me to ask one more question before we go." Thorpe turned to face the delicate beauty. "Did you not think to approach Mrs Chambers and tell her what you'd learned from Thomas?"

Lily paused. "Examine your question carefully, Mr Thorpe, and the answer is obvious." She spoke with an air of confidence they'd not witnessed before. But then the lady was a spy. Somewhere within she had to have the mental strength one expected of a man. "To approach Mrs Chambers would mean discussing information about a government agent. I had no evidence. To betray those paid to protect the Crown is treason. Forgive my lack of empathy, but I was too late to save Thomas. And I value my neck more than I desire retribution."

It was a reasonable explanation.

"I understand." Thorpe narrowed his gaze. "So why tell us now?"

Lily opened her mouth, but it took a few seconds for her to reply. "Because I am tired of this life, Mr Thorpe. Because if I turn up dead in the Thames, I hope you'll find the traitor and make him pay for what he has done."

Thorpe remained silent, inclined his head and strode out into the hall.

Daphne lingered for a moment. There were so many questions she wanted to ask. Had Thomas spoken about their marriage? Did he enjoy his work with Lily? But now was not the time to delve deeper into the past, despite knowing the opportunity would never present itself again.

"I am truly sorry about Thomas." Lily grabbed Daphne's hand, squeezed it tight and pressed a small piece of paper into her palm. "He always spoke so highly of you."

Daphne's throat grew tight. Guilt flared. She'd thought highly of her husband, too. She'd just not loved him as she ought.

"Thank you for agreeing to see us," Daphne said, resisting the urge to examine the note. "We should have no need to trouble you again."

"The contents of any missive can be misleading. One must endeavour to find the truth. One must delve deep to find the answers you seek."

CHAPTER 13

THE TIME SPENT WAITING ON THE LANDING WHILE DAPHNE SPOKE privately to Lily Lawson proved informative. From Daphne's calm demeanour, warm handshake and bright smile, it was apparent she bore no malice to the woman who knew her husband far better than she did. The fiery flash of jealousy in Daphne's eyes when Lily first opened the door had gone.

But Daniel was a cynical man and sensed Lily was not completely honest about the depth of her feelings for Thomas.

Daniel purchased a reel of twine from the chandler but waited until they were out in the alley before putting it in his pocket. Daphne placed her hand in the crook of his arm and guided him to the fire burning in the brazier a little further along the narrow street.

"Lily passed me a note as I left." Daphne held up her clenched fist. "I should wait until we're home before reading it but, as Betsy will tell you, I'm not one for patience."

The secret gesture had not gone unnoticed. "The back alleys are not the place to stop and have a conversation." Daniel glanced back over his shoulder. "And you're right. It must wait until we're home."

Just saying the word *home* caused his heart to pound. In an uncharacteristic moment of fancy, he imagined they were strolling back after a night at the theatre. Once there, they would sit by the fire and talk until the early hours, surrender to their wants and desires in bed.

He shook his head to focus, but the loss of his dream left a cavernous hole in his chest.

"Oh, it won't hurt to take a peek." Daphne unfolded the paper before he had a chance to caution her again. "The note's so small it can't contain that much information."

Was she always so damn stubborn?

She stared at the scrawled words, six of them from what he could see over her shoulder.

Impatience got the better of him, too. "What does it say?"

"Nothing. It's just a list of names."

"How many?"

"Three. Three gentlemen."

No doubt they were the men Lily thought might be the traitor.

"Put it away," he whispered, warming his hands over the flame as though that was their purpose for stopping. "We'll discuss the contents once we're away from here."

Her curiosity sated, she slipped the note into her reticule.

"We must investigate the men on the list as a matter of urgency," she said, stopping again despite the fact they'd only taken a few steps. "But I'm to travel to Elton Park tomorrow afternoon and will be out of town for two days."

"Elton Park?" he snapped, resisting the urge to tell her she wasn't to go anywhere without him. "Why are you only telling me now? What business have you there?"

"Elton Park is Lord Harwood's residence. Anthony and Sarah are to be married. Please tell me you remember. They insist the event would not have been possible without our intervention in solving their case." Daphne frowned. "You did receive an invitation?"

"Of course I did."

Lord Harwood had done his best to persuade him to attend. The letter mentioned muggings on the road, and concerns for Mrs Chambers' safety if she were to travel alone. It was all a ploy to lure him there, nothing more, and so he'd not bothered to reply.

Why on earth would he want to go to a wedding?

Mingling with the aristocracy was akin to sitting on the muddy banks of the Thames sifting through the rubbish thrown from passing ships. A dirty task he wanted no part of. A complete waste of time and effort. Besides, making idle conversation was not his forte.

"Then you are coming, too?" Daphne seemed eager for his company, which in itself should have prompted a change of heart.

"I don't see how you can go when we have a job to do here," he said bluntly. The lady took pride in her work and Daniel would use the fact to his advantage. "It is a matter of priority. You are not an heiress with the luxury to do as she pleases. You have responsibilities."

She turned to face him. "There are more important things in life than work," she said, although appeared somewhat shocked that she'd vocalised the fact. "And I promised Sarah I would attend. Perhaps a couple of days away might help us to gain perspective on the case."

"A couple of days!" He gave a contemptuous snort. "I'm not going." Nothing would sway his decision.

She blinked rapidly. "But you must."

"Why?"

"Well, because they're our friends."

"No, they're not. They were our clients, nothing more."

She gasped. "How can you say that?"

"Because it's true." He shrugged.

Two drunken sailors hobbled past them and knocked on a door further along the alley. A buxom woman wearing a tall white wig and red rouge opened the door and beckoned them inside.

The alley was not the place to partake in a heated conversation. Daniel took Daphne's arm and guided her past The Mariners Tavern towards the main street. "If you must go to Elton Park, then I shall continue the investigation without you. You can learn of my progress upon your return."

Daphne stopped and pulled her arm free. "This is my investigation, and you will do nothing without me."

"Did you not hire me to solve your problem for you?" he said with an air of arrogance. "As no money has changed hands, I may do as I please." Perhaps he sounded dramatic, but the thought of her travelling alone scared the hell out of him.

Hands braced on her hips, she glared. But the sudden eerie silence proved distracting. He scanned the alley but saw no one, heard nothing.

"Mr Thorpe," she began as though about to offer a scathing reprimand.

"Hush."

"No. I will not hush. A heavy-handed approach will not work with me."

Daniel ignored her. The feeling of dread swamped him now. With keen eyes he scoured the darkness. He heard the click of the hammer, the sucking sound of a ball discharging. A flash of orange and a puff of white smoke confirmed his worst fear.

With no time for an explanation, he pushed Daphne to the ground as the loud bang echoed through the alley. Distant squeals and Daphne's cries of protest reached him before the ball hit his upper arm.

"Bloody hell!" He dropped to his knees, more from the shock of the impact than from sustaining injury. "You'd better blasted run as I'm coming for you," he called out into the darkness. Well, he was as soon as he found the strength to stand.

He glanced at Daphne, his heart beating so fiercely he could feel it thumping in his throat. Her face was pale, her eyes wide as she crawled to his side.

"Did he hit you?" She ran her trembling hands over his chest, his face, examining her palm as she searched for evidence of blood. "Tell me, Daniel, where does it hurt?"

"My arm … but it's just a graze." He dabbed at the hole in his coat sleeve, relieved to find it was not saturated with blood. Even so, he could feel the damp shirt sticking to his skin. Damn. He knew better than to linger in an alley at night. One way or another, Daphne would be the death of him before the week was out.

"Tell me you're all right?" Her anguish soon turned to anger, and she jumped to her feet, thrust her hand inside her pelisse and withdrew her pistol. "He's escaping. Wait here. I'll be but a moment."

Daniel staggered to his feet as the woman with pea soup for brains darted back down the alley.

"Daphne! Wait!" Of all the foolish, idiotic things to do. Despite the dull ache in his arm, he chased after her, charging through the group of drunken sots stumbling into The Mariners in a bid to find a safe place to hide. "Move," he yelled, trying not to punch those who bumped into him and knocked his wound.

With the advantage of large strides, he was able to catch up with her.

"What the devil?" she cried as he scooped her up off the ground with his good arm and held her tight to his chest. "Put me down. He's getting away." She kicked her legs, the heel of her boot hitting his shin.

"Damn it, woman. Don't make me throw you over my shoulder."

"Quick, Daniel. It's him. It's my mysterious intruder. I'm sure of it."

"Let him go, Daphne." He squinted in the gloom but saw no one of interest. "We'll not find him here. But rest assured, we'll not stop looking until we do." Damn. His arm throbbed, and he needed a drink. "If I don't tend to the wound, it may become infected."

At that, she gasped. Daniel released her, letting her slide down his body slowly until her feet touched the cobblestones.

"Forgive me." She turned to face him, her frantic gaze falling to his arm. "I don't know what came over me. All I could think of was that my silent stalker had finally made his move. I should not have left you." She shook her head and glanced over her shoulder. "We should go to Lily, see if she can help."

From the lack of light in the chandler's up ahead, and the absence of ropes hanging from hooks on the wall, it was evident the fellow had heard the commotion and shut up shop.

"No. We cannot risk hindering her work for the government."

"Then come. Let me help you to the street, and we can hail a hackney."

Daniel snorted. "I can walk, Daphne. I've been shot in the arm, not the leg. And I'm confident the lead only grazed the skin." His attention moved past her shoulder, to the few people who'd found the courage to venture out of The Mariners. "As I said before, the alley is not a place where one lingers."

"A graze to you is probably a gaping hole to someone else." She took his hand rather than his arm and guided him back through the narrow walkway. Another man may have taken umbrage at being treated like a child, but the caring, intimate gesture roused hope in his chest where he'd dared never hope before. "If you're hurt, I'd rather you were honest with me."

"Very well. It might be a little deeper than a graze." Until he removed his coat, he could not give a more definitive answer.

She sniffed numerous times and cleared her throat.

"It's all right," he said as they exited the alley. "There's no need for tears. I'm not going to die." It was said in jest, but she failed to appreciate his humour.

"Don't even joke about such a thing. Of course you're not going to die."

"Would you miss me, Daphne?" Now he'd started, he couldn't help but tease her. Besides, it kept his mind off the pain pounding in his arm. "Would you miss my constant complaining, my constant need to prove this is no work for a woman?"

"Well, I'd not miss that. But I would miss your logical approach and your undeniable courage." She cast him a sidelong glance and her gaze softened. "I'd miss the warmth in your voice when you lose yourself for a moment and forget to be angry with the world."

He stopped walking, stood rigid on the pavement and considered what she'd said. She was right. Only in her company did his troubles seem insignificant. Only in her company was he able to glimpse true happiness. Suddenly, the pain in his arm was nothing compared to the ache filling his chest.

The urge to kiss her took hold.

These overwhelming emotions were the reason he stayed away.

"Come, we can't wait here," she took his arm, "although the man would be a fool to attempt to shoot at us again. Hopefully, we'll not have to walk too far to find a hackney."

The mere mention of the shooter dragged his mind from his fanciful musings. "I think it's fair to assume we were followed here. Unless the chandler keeps a pistol under his bench and is disgruntled because we didn't buy more than a length of twine."

"I told you, someone has been following me about for years."

"Yes, but during that time you've hardly known he was there. And now, in the space of a day, you've almost been killed twice." Daniel considered both events: the accident in Covent Garden, and the shooting in the alley. Was Daphne the target?

Daphne tutted. "When you say it like that it doesn't make any sense."

"There is another explanation." He knew she would over-react when he told her. "The Turners informed me that there's a price on my head."

Daphne stopped abruptly. "A price? You mean someone wants you dead?" Her eyes grew so wide they were liable to burst from their sockets. "Someone wants you dead, and you only think to tell me now!"

"Hush. Keep walking," he said, practically dragging her along the road with him. "Death threats are nothing new to me."

She mumbled something incoherent. "Why on earth would you walk the streets at night when you know your life is in danger?"

"Daphne, if I panicked every time someone threatened to harm me, I'd never leave my bed." He sighed. "Besides, you were the intended victim in Covent Garden, and we cannot know for certain who was the target in the alley."

Daniel cursed. He was missing a vital piece of this puzzle.

They found themselves on Tower Hill and had no difficulty hiring a hackney there. Once safely inside the cab, Daniel tried to use the time to think. But for some reason, the analytical part of his mind could only focus on trying to guess what Daphne was thinking.

A curious hum left her lips, but seconds passed before she spoke. "What if the stalker has no preference over which one of us he kills? What if the point is to force us apart?"

"For what purpose?"

She shrugged. "I don't know. Perhaps together we stand a better chance of finding the truth."

"I need time to think," he said, patting his arm gently to

check his coat sleeve wasn't damp with blood. "Can I look at the list of names?"

"Certainly." She fumbled about in her reticule and handed him the folded note.

He knew two of the men on the list. Marcus Danbury was a friend of Dudley Spencer; the latter was as adept at discovering information as any skilled enquiry agent. To the best of his knowledge, Danbury lived in France and hadn't set foot on English soil for years.

"I've never met any of the men mentioned," Daphne said.

"Lord Gibson I know of, but not Captain Lewis." He handed the paper back to her. "Danbury's not our man. He's a bit of a rogue by all accounts but loyal and trustworthy."

"We should not rule him out of the investigation. People change. Circumstances change."

"You have a valid point," he agreed. "But we'll leave Danbury until last. Tomorrow we'll make some enquiries into Captain Lewis' background."

Daphne sat forward. "But I'm going to Witham tomorrow."

"You're still going to the wedding after what has just occurred?" Was the thought of travelling alone not terrifying? What if the stalker followed her to Elton Park? Damn it. He would have to go too if he could not persuade her otherwise.

"I must."

"What about my injury?" He'd play the wounded soldier if he thought she might reconsider.

"But you said it was just a graze."

"There's too much to do here." Daniel crossed his arms in defiance, the wound throbbing just to aggravate him some more.

"Time out of town might help give us a new perspective on the case." Daphne smiled at him sweetly. Oh, this lady was skilled in manipulation. "Time in the country might rejuvenate our spirits."

Two days and nights spent alone with her would leave him

fit for Bedlam. It was becoming increasingly more difficult to keep his rampant thoughts to himself. But what choice did he have?

"Are you certain I cannot persuade you to stay?" he said, clutching the last thread of hope.

"I made a promise, Daniel. But I understand if you want to remain here."

"No," he groaned. "I shall accompany you to Elton Park."

Her emerald-green eyes brightened. "You will? It will mean an overnight stay in a coaching inn and then a night mingling with the aristocracy."

"I can hardly contain my excitement." Was there anything he wouldn't do for this woman?

"Excellent." She clapped her hands together. "I hired a post-chaise, but we can meet at the coaching inn."

Did she honestly think he would allow her to travel in one of those ramshackle vehicles? "We'll travel in my carriage."

"But I've already paid Mr Butteridge. He insists on payment in advance. Only last month, he took a man as far as Stratford and the blighter absconded when they stopped to change the horses."

"Butteridge can keep the money." Daniel smirked. "Don't worry. I'll not charge you to ride with me."

"Perhaps I should charge you for the pleasure," she countered playfully.

"And I would gladly pay."

A blush touched her cheeks. She struggled to hold his gaze and glanced absently out of the window. "We've just turned into New Bond Street."

Good. The conversation had served as a distraction, but he was eager to see the extent of the damage to his arm.

The cab rattled to a halt outside the modiste shop. Daphne alighted first and pulled the key from her reticule while Daniel paid the driver.

"Betsy can heat some water while I look at your wound," she said as they entered the shop. Noting a flicker of light from the parlour she called out to the modiste. "Betsy! Betsy!" Mild panic infused her tone. "Mr Bostock, are you here?"

Both people burst from the parlour as though the drapes had caught fire, although they looked guilty rather than concerned.

"What is it?" Betsy patted her golden locks and brushed the creases from her dress as she walked over to Daphne. "What's happened?"

"It's Daniel ... I mean Mr Thorpe. Don't worry. He's fine. But he's been shot."

"Shot!" Bostock boomed. "Bloody hell!" The man turned to the ladies. "Forgive a fellow for cursing." Two large steps and Bostock was at Daniel's side, his frantic gaze searching for evidence of the injury.

"It's my right arm," Daniel said, gesturing to the tear in his coat. "But it's nothing serious. Just a graze I suspect but find Murphy and take me home."

"Home?" Bostock frowned. "To Rainham Hall?"

"No," Daniel snapped. If only Bostock would engage his brain before speaking. "Take me to the house on Church Street."

"There's no need to leave." Daphne straightened. "I can tend to the wound here."

"No." To feel her warm hands on his bare skin would be the end of him. Besides, there was a chance it needed a stitch or two, and he'd not put her through the agony of doing that. "Bostock will see to it."

Daphne placed her hands on her hips in defiance. "I have seen a man's bare chest before if that's what concerns you. Granted, it may not have been one so large and impressive but—"

"Bostock knows what he's doing, and I need a change of clothes. If we're to go to Witham, there are some matters I need to attend to."

While his explanation appeased her somewhat, the two lines were still prominent between her brows. "But how will I know if everything is all right?"

"Bostock will return within the hour." After what had occurred in Covent Garden and the alley near the docks, Daniel could not leave her without protection. "And he'll stay here with you until I return tomorrow."

Betsy's beaming smile meant she was either glad to have Bostock for company, or glad to be rid of *him*.

Daphne sighed. "Very well. We must leave at noon." She glanced at his arm. "Now go quickly. Heaven knows the extent of the damage beneath that coat."

"Lock the door behind us and do not open it until Bostock returns." It crossed his mind to kiss her cheek, to do something to ease the sudden ache in his chest caused by his impending departure. Instead, he reached into the pocket of his greatcoat and handed her the pistol. "An extra precaution. Perhaps use the time to teach Betsy how to wield a weapon."

CHAPTER 14

THORPE WAS LATE.

Daphne stared at the busy street below and scanned numerous parked carriages in the hope of spotting a black unmarked vehicle.

Panic flared.

Had he misled her over the wound to his upper arm? Was he too weak to send a note? Was he lying stretched on a chaise in a pool of blood, the life draining from him drip by drip?

After charging off into the night, Bostock and Murphy had returned without him. Under strict instructions to ensure no one entered Betsy's premises, and with pistols half-cocked, both men remained at their posts until sunrise.

Murphy left at nine o'clock. After visiting Mr Butteridge to cancel the post-chaise, he was to return to Church Street to collect Mr Thorpe. Bostock was to stay with Betsy until Daphne returned from Lord Harwood's wedding. Grateful for the company and even more grateful to have a man about the house, Betsy had made a list of jobs to keep him busy.

The clock on the mantel struck one, the single chime more like an ominous warning.

Damn the man.

Where the hell had he got to? She'd specifically said they were to leave at twelve. Did he not think she'd be worried?

The journey to Witham took five hours, assuming there were no accidents on the road, and she wanted to reach the coaching inn long before nightfall. The thought of sitting alone with Thorpe for such a length of time proved just as unnerving. Would their petty quarrels turn to passionate kisses? Would she be able to keep her ever-growing need for him at bay?

Another fifteen minutes had passed before she noticed the pair of muscled black stallions pulling an equally intimidating carriage.

Relief surged through her when it stopped outside the shop and the occupant vaulted to the pavement. Daphne pressed her nose to the window, hardly recognising the gentleman in a black billowing coat marching towards the front door. She turned and listened to the thud of booted footsteps mounting the stairs and coming to a halt outside her door.

Thorpe knocked once and opened the door when she called for him to enter.

"Forgive me, I had every intention of arriving on time but had a few errands to run first. It appears Lord Gibson's estate is near Chelmsford, some sixteen miles from Witham. If we stop at the coaching inn at Great Baddow, we'll have time to pay Gibson a visit."

Open-mouthed, Daphne stared at him. The fluttering in her stomach raced up to her throat. "What … what happened to your beard?"

Thorpe stroked his clean, chiselled jaw as the corners of his mouth curled up into a half smile. "It was time for a change." He was a handsome man with the beard. Without it, he stole her breath.

He looked younger, not nearly as sombre. The dimple on his chin only heightened his appeal. "It's a vast improvement. And I see you've tied back your hair." The dark locks that skimmed his shoulders were held back in a queue.

"I cannot mingle in society looking like a man who's been lost at sea for six months."

Daphne chuckled. "There is to be a small gathering, nothing too formal. I doubt you'll have to make polite conversation with pompous lords and ladies."

Thorpe raised a challenging brow. "You could have told me that before the barber sharpened his blade."

"I'm rather glad I didn't," she said, noting the fullness of his lips. Everything about his countenance appeared brighter. Then it occurred to her that she'd not asked about his arm, or why he'd decided not to return to her last night. "How is your arm? I suppose you took to your bed as soon as you got home. Did Bostock stitch the wound?"

Thorpe shook his head. "It wasn't deep enough to warrant a stitch. Two large gulps of brandy helped numb the pain."

"I never thanked you for pushing me out of the way last night." A grazed hand was better than a lead ball in the back. "Everything happened so quickly. I didn't hear the shooter approach. Thank heavens you responded so quickly."

"Had we kept walking as I suggested he would have found it difficult to take the shot." Thorpe sighed and rubbed his eye with the pads of his fingers. "We were like sitting ducks on a pond. But come, we are already late. On the journey, we can discuss how we intend to confront Lord Gibson."

Intrigued by the proposition, she nodded. "But if we find Lord Gibson at home, he can't be the man who shot at us in the alley."

"A man of Gibson's status hires people to do his bidding." Daniel glanced at the mantel clock and then the floor. "Do you need help with your luggage?"

"Oh, Bostock carried my trunk downstairs."

"Trunk? Lord help me, Daphne, I won't stay more than a

night at Elton Park." He seemed flustered. The man was not afraid of a gang of knife-wielding smugglers yet the thought of spending time with the aristocracy filled him with dread. "One night at a coaching inn and one night at Harwood's estate," he clarified. "You gave your word."

"And I shall keep it. Obviously, you know nothing of a lady's wardrobe." Then again, he might have sisters, most definitely had a mother. Educated at the best school, he knew of the complex rituals otherwise known as etiquette. "I shall need at least three dresses for one overnight stay at Elton Park, not to mention petticoats and fripperies."

"All the unnecessary fuss is one reason I decided not to attend. The pomp and ceremony turns my stomach. There is every chance I'll say something derogatory and offend a guest." Thorpe mumbled something incoherent. "Be warned. Should anyone attempt to discuss the merits of a racing curricle or offer advice in the art of driving, I'm liable to punch them on the nose."

Thorpe made no secret of his disdain for the privileged.

"Why do you despise them so much?" she asked.

"Because they'd sell their offspring rather than suffer a stain on their precious reputation."

Daphne gave a challenging smirk. "They are not all like that. You speak of a minority."

"I speak from experience," he snapped. It was evident from his wide eyes and pursed lips he wished he'd not let the words fall.

How interesting?

To press him further on the matter would mean being met with a wall of silence. No. She would bide her time, wait for an opportunity to discover more about the elusive Mr Thorpe.

"Well, we cannot stand here all day exchanging quips," she said. From his relieved sigh, it was clear he was grateful she'd not pursued that particular line of enquiry. "And you know what happens whenever our emotions get the better of us."

"You mean you might kiss me again?"

She refused to lie. "Now you've lost that ridiculous beard it's a possibility."

He rubbed his chin again. "Then your emotions must have been running high when you kissed me so passionately before."

All this talk of kissing left her mind muddled.

"I think we have more important things on our mind than kissing." She tried to sound confident, but her conflicting feelings for Thorpe dominated her thoughts of late. "After the shooting last night, it's obvious we're on the hunt for a murderer. A clear head is a must if we have any hope of catching the culprit."

This time the smile almost reached his eyes. "I've not had a clear head since the day I met you."

CHAPTER 15

THEY'D TRAVELLED THREE MILES ON THEIR JOURNEY TO Witham, and still Daphne couldn't tear her gaze from Thorpe's square jaw. There was something superior about his countenance now, dare she say something aristocratic.

Lord, he'd curse her to the devil if she ever said that aloud.

Seated opposite with his eyes closed, Thorpe exhaled deeply. He seemed so content in sleep, not nearly as intimidating. Not that she found him to be so anymore. During the last two days he'd mellowed, his tone conveying warmth and humour whenever he spoke to her. With others, he was still abrupt and cold of manner. The beard had served to enhance his menacing aura. Would he behave differently now stripped of his disguise? Would he still use arrogance as a shield?

Would the real person reveal himself?

Occasionally, and for the purpose of work, Daphne had worn a wig. And it was true. A mask of any sort gave one a sense of invincibility, gave them licence to be daring, to be someone new. Did Thorpe don his disguise to help with his work? Or did it stem from a need to distance himself from the man inside?

Perhaps he'd loved someone once, and the lady had broken

143

his heart? It would certainly explain his obsession with duty, his need to ease his frustration with women paid to give pleasure rather than seeking commitment.

It all proved puzzling.

Even Lily Lawson failed to attract his attention. What did Daniel Thorpe dream about if not a golden-haired beauty with porcelain skin?

Daphne stared at his handsome features. He had incredibly long lashes for a gentleman.

"Is there something you wish to say?" His voice startled her. The corners of his mouth curled up although he didn't open his eyes. "I can feel the heat of your penetrative gaze."

Thank heavens he'd not got the ability to read thoughts. In a moment of fancy, she'd imagined running kisses along that smooth jaw.

"I was just thinking …"

"Is that not a dangerous pastime?" he teased.

Daphne sighed. "Do you think there was more to Lily's relationship with Thomas than she led us to believe?"

Thorpe's eyes flew open. "Yes, it's possible, although that would make Thomas a fool."

A fool for finding love elsewhere? Or a fool for choosing Lily? Could Thorpe not see the woman's merit?

"But you must admit, Lily possesses all the attributes men desire in a woman. You must have thought her attractive."

"Me?" He pointed to his chest. "I thought this conversation was about Thomas."

"As he is not here to answer, you may do so on his behalf."

Thorpe raised an inquisitive brow. "Despite being his friend, I cannot presume to comment on his preferences."

"Then comment on your own. Did you find Lily Lawson attractive?"

He seemed confused for a moment. "And you want me to answer truthfully?"

"Of course." Thorpe had never lied to her. "You have no need to spare my feelings."

"Very well." Tugging the sleeve of his coat, he straightened. "Yes, Lily possesses a certain beauty I imagine most men drool over. But while she has the face of an angel, she has the body of a child."

"Oh, I see." Daphne didn't really see at all.

"To please me, a woman must be curvaceous." His heated gaze skimmed the length of her body, travelled slowly back up to linger on her breasts. "I have large hands and prefer them full. To please me, a woman must have hair as dark as night, possess intelligence, and a tongue as deadly as a blade."

"Oh."

"In short, you are the most attractive woman of my acquaintance."

A hard lump formed in Daphne's throat. A molten heat pooled between her thighs. She wasn't sure how to respond and so the truth was the only option open to her.

"And it would be fair to say you are the most handsome gentleman of *my* acquaintance."

He inclined his head. "Is that with or without the beard?"

"Both."

They were silent for a moment. Daphne's mind was engaged in trying to decipher what that meant. They shared a mutual attraction, a hidden passion that once released burned with ferocious intensity.

"I remember the first time I met you," Thorpe suddenly said. "I'd missed the wedding, what with it being a small family affair, and Thomas brought you to London."

"We went to the theatre, I recall." Daphne had fond memories of the evening. She'd found Thorpe friendly, charming. A true gentleman. "A wealthy merchant lent you his box even though you hate opera."

"I despise any expression of sentimentality."

"But Thomas told you I'd always wanted to go." The emotive performance had stolen her breath, surpassed all expectation. "It was kind of you to take us. From what I remember you were thoroughly bored."

"The opera holds no fascination for me. Watching the look of joy and wonder on your face proved to be far more captivating."

Heat crept up her neck to warm her cheeks. He had studied her without her knowledge. "The music carried me away. The beauty in their voices brought a tear to my eye more than once."

"I remember," he said softly. After averting his gaze for a moment, he looked up at her. "There is no need to be jealous of Lily. Whatever happened between them must have had something to do with the nature of their work. Thomas was a loyal man. I cannot imagine him ever having a reason to hurt you."

Thorpe could not have said anything more damning. Thomas had every reason to despise her. Tears formed, and the silly things trickled down her cheek before she could wipe them away.

"You must miss him," Thorpe continued.

"It's not that," she said, searching in her reticule for a handkerchief.

"Then what is it?" He reached across the carriage and handed her a navy-blue cotton square embroidered with his gold initial. "Here, take mine." Seeing the solitary letter *D* reminded her that Thorpe was but one of many names he used to protect his identity when working. But he'd always been Daniel.

Daphne brought his handkerchief to her nose and sniffed. The aromatic scent of nutmeg, wood and lavender flooded her nostrils. It was a smell she would never forget.

"They are tears of guilt, not sorrow," she said.

"There was nothing you could have done to save him."

"Oh, there was." It didn't matter what she said or did, Daniel believed her capable of nothing but good. "If I'd loved him as he'd wished perhaps he might have confided in me." It felt good to confess her sins. "I married him because that was what my father wanted. I made a promise to him on his deathbed, agreed to honour the pledge he'd made to Thomas' father many years before. Our parents knew that once they were gone, we were both alone in the world, without siblings and cousins to support us. It brought our fathers peace to know that Thomas and I had each other. Sadly, love was never a factor in our decision to wed."

Daniel sat back in the seat. "Did Thomas know that is how you felt?"

"He did, but he always hoped our friendship would grow into something deeper, more profound. As did I. But it wasn't to be." Daphne hung her head in shame. She'd let Thomas down. Wiping the tears away she looked up at the man she'd grown to trust. "Not all friendships blossom into love. Not all lovers become friends. We both soon realised that the secret ingredient was missing. That no matter how hard we tried we could not force the feeling."

Daniel scratched his head. "But when Lily opened the door, I saw the way you looked at her. Jealousy is a trait most people struggle to hide. And from your questions earlier, one would assume the thought that Thomas was attracted to Lily bothers you."

What was she supposed to say? That she was so heartless she cared not for the husband she'd lost, only for the man who caused passion to flame in her chest?

"As always your instincts are correct. But Thomas was not the cause of my unease or my resentment towards a rival." Her cheeks felt so hot they must surely be glowing. "I was jealous because of the way Lily looked at you. I asked the questions to gauge *your* reaction to her. Do you find her attractive? Do you want to kiss her the way you kissed me?"

There was a moment of silence as they stared into each other's eyes. The sound of their laboured breathing filled the air.

"Then I defer to my earlier answer." Daniel sat forward. "You are the most attractive woman of my acquaintance. I have no desire to kiss anyone but you."

The sudden rush of excitement clouded her vision. She felt drunk, a little dizzy. The fluttering in her stomach sent shivers shooting through her body. Only in Daniel's arms did she feel at peace, and she so desperately needed to banish the ghosts of the past.

"I seem to recall talk of an experiment," she said, the need to lose herself in Daniel's sinful mouth her only thought now.

"An experiment?" A sinful smile touched his lips. Lord above, it was the most spectacular thing she'd ever seen. He crossed the carriage to sit at her side. "And what might it involve?"

"Well," she began but her hands were shaking, and she struggled to form a word. "We ... we must determine if physical desire always leads to a moment of madness."

"As any man of science will tell you, when it comes to experiments all working conditions must be the same." He cupped her cheek and ran the pad of his thumb over her lips. Molten heat pooled between her thighs. "Sit astride me, Daphne."

Those words were her undoing.

Without another thought she gathered her skirt to her knees and did as he asked. Heavens. Never had she experienced the urge to take a man into her body.

"Purely for scientific purposes I will let you kiss me first." His rich drawl sent tingles down her spine and she almost jumped when his large hands settled on her hips.

Daphne stared at his smooth jaw, leant down and pressed her lips to the cool skin. The exotic yet utterly unique scent filled her head.

Daniel's head fell back against the leather headrest and he closed his eyes as Daphne ran kisses along his jaw and nipped at the sensitive skin below his ear. Anticipating what was to come was more than she could bear. But she craved a reaction. Only his unbridled response had the power to unleash the passion buried within.

"To create a moment of madness, there must be two willing partners," she whispered in his ear.

"Oh, trust me. I'm willing."

"Then kiss me, Daniel."

"With pleasure."

The atmosphere thrummed with suppressed desire: a vibrant energy desperate to burst free. And so when Daniel claimed her lips she'd expected him to devour her mouth, for his movements to be urgent, frantic, unrestrained.

But no.

He cupped her face gently between both hands and closed his eyes as their lips met. The tender kiss spoke to her in a way words never could. He kissed her as though she was the answer to a question that had plagued him for so long. He kissed her as though the memory had to last him a lifetime.

The kiss was slow, soul-deep, heaven-sent.

The waves of pleasure rippling through her body were so profound she felt them deep in her core. Only once he'd sated some deep-rooted need, savoured every second, did she notice a change in mood and tempo.

One hand moved to cup her neck. The other caressed her thigh beneath her skirt as his tongue penetrated her mouth. Pure carnal lust burned in her veins.

"Daniel," she moaned against his mouth and pressed her body to his, desperate to satisfy the undeniable craving. The first soft, passionate kiss had left her feeling bare, exposed. This wild, erotic dance awakened every fibre of her being.

Things progressed quickly then. His hands were everywhere all at once. Caressing. Stroking. Daphne couldn't get deep enough into his wet mouth to taste him as she needed to. The urge to run her hands over his bare skin took hold. Clothing became an annoying encumbrance, and she pushed his coat off his shoulders.

"Bloody hell," he cursed, dragging his mouth away, "my arm."

"I'm sorry." Daphne gasped. "I forgot all about it." She tried to slide off his lap, but with one strong arm he held her there.

"Don't move." A wicked smile touched his lips. "If you wish to undress me, just have a care."

Excitement bubbled in her chest. "Does that mean you want me to continue?"

The hand on her thigh slid up past the ribbon securing her stocking, up to the intimate place where she'd never thought to feel a man's touch again. Daphne gasped as his fingers brushed the sensitive spot between her legs.

"Do you want to continue what we've started, Daphne?" His voice had a husky tone that spoke of decadence and sin. It was a sound she'd not heard from him before, but it was one she would never tire of.

"Continue?" Brazenly, she moved her hips to rub against his hand. A soft moan left her lips. "I'll not stop until I've had everything you have to give."

A growl resonated from the back of his throat. "Damn, why could we not have the luxury of a bed?"

"Where is the madness in that?" she said, divesting him of his coat. He continued to stroke her, offered a grin of satisfaction when her breathing grew ragged. "Where … where is the spontaneity, the … the danger?"

"You want impulsive?"

"Yes," she panted as he slipped a finger inside her, and then another. Nothing had ever felt so wonderful, and she bore down until he could go no deeper. "I want you."

"Love, you're so wet."

"Oh, Daniel. Don't tease me. Don't make me wait."

"Make you wait?" He sighed. "You wouldn't believe how long I've waited for this moment." He withdrew his fingers, and a groan left her lips. With his strong arm he anchored her to his body while he leant forward and drew both blinds. "Now, where were we?"

The urge to taste him was upon her again, and she devoured his mouth, sucked his tongue, licked his earlobe. Heaven help her. Never had she wanted anything as much as she wanted him. Had her luggage been accessible, she would have torn her dress to shreds so that he could run his hands over her bare skin.

"Touch me," she said, though it didn't sound at all like her voice. "Claim me."

"Please tell me you just said that, and it wasn't my rampant imagination." He fumbled with the buttons on his breeches, his solid manhood bursting free.

Good Lord! She'd always known he was a big man, but …

"Oh, this is real," she said, recovering from the shock. "Like I said, touch me and see."

She didn't need to ask a second time.

He cupped her breast, his thumb brushing over the nipple aching beneath the material. "Next time, I intend to worship your naked body for hours."

"Mmm … then let us hope that is sooner rather than later." Feeling far bolder than any other time she could remember, she reached down and wrapped her fingers around his impressive shaft.

It was his turn to groan and jerk his hips as she pleasured him until he covered her hand. "Stop, else this will be over too quickly."

Shuffling forward and raising herself up on her knees, Daphne positioned him at her entrance. "Then join with me," she whispered. Every nerve in her body tingled at the prospect. She lowered herself down slowly, took every hard, thick inch and sheathed him fully.

The sound of their laboured breathing filled the carriage. Their gazes locked. His dark eyes were warm, brimming with desire. His large hands edged under her skirt, gripped her bare buttocks and held her there.

"Love, you feel so good," he hissed through gritted teeth.

Just those few words caused the muscles in her core to pulse around him. When he moved ... well ... the coil in her stomach wound tighter and tighter as each slow, delicious slide became vigorous thrusts.

Daphne clutched his shoulders, writhed in his lap and rode him hard.

"Damn," he complained as he struggled to touch her and thrust inside her at the same time. "I'd give everything I own for a blasted bed right now."

"I can turn around."

"No. I want to watch you."

Daphne leant back, allowing him easier access to the place throbbing for his touch. "Then we shall just ... just have to work harder."

Daniel's fingers found her sweet spot. A few expert strokes, coupled with the movement of him filling her full, brought her to the point of release.

"Oh, Daniel," she cried as her muscles tightened and she drew him deeper inside. "Say we'll do this again."

"Give me a minute and I'm game." He thrust twice, withdrew and finished the job with his hand. "Forgive me," he panted. "Had I known you were going to ravish me, I would have been prepared."

Daphne was still riding high on a wave of euphoria to understand his meaning. As her breathing settled, she looked down at his handsome face. The grin stretching from ear to ear was the most marvellous thing she'd ever witnessed.

Exposed, and needing the use of his handkerchief, the

moment should have been awkward, embarrassing, but it felt as natural as taking a breath.

She reached down and grabbed the blue cotton square lying on the seat. "Here, take this. You have more need of it than I."

"Had we the luxury of a private bedchamber," he began, taking the cloth and gesturing for her to look away, "we might have been more adventurous."

With interest, she watched him go about his ministrations. The dusky pink head of his manhood glistened in the dark confines of the carriage. "Would you like some assistance?" She'd never taken a man into her mouth. The idea had never appealed to her until now.

"Another time," he said with a chuckle. "Perhaps tonight."

"Well, our experiment certainly proved effective. It's fair to say that passion in a carriage leads to moments of madness."

"I'd spend a month in Bedlam for another chance to bury myself inside you." He stared at her mouth and moistened his lips. "Next, we should test the theory that the power of one's release is more profound in different positions."

With his erection diminishing, he tucked the object of her desire back into his breeches.

"What a fascinating theory," she said, eager to experience all the wonders of her newly awakened passion. She kissed him once on the lips and moved to the opposite side of the carriage. "We must test your hypothesis at our earliest convenience."

"The next two nights might give us ample opportunity." The smile that had been a permeant fixture for half an hour faded. "But first, we must pay a visit to Lord Gibson's house. It's approximately two miles from the coaching inn in Great Baddow."

Daphne sighed. She'd been so engrossed in her amorous liaison with Daniel Thorpe she'd almost forgotten about the case.

"Well, we'd be foolish not to take advantage of the opportunity." She yawned and settled back against the squab. Partaking in such vigorous activity had left her weary. "How long until we reach the inn?"

Daniel leant forward, raised the blind and peered out of the window. "Another hour at best."

"Good. I'm struggling to keep my eyes open." She covered her mouth and yawned again. "The events of the last few days seem to have caught up with me."

A smirk touched his lips. "Perhaps it's the events of the last few minutes that have taken their toll. Use this time to sleep. I doubt you'll have an opportunity later."

CHAPTER 16

It was a two-mile walk across a field to reach Lord Gibson's manor house. Using the carriage would only alert the servants of their arrival, and it was easier to make a hasty retreat when on foot. Besides, Daniel had called at the house an hour earlier, and the staff were sure to recognise his coachman and unmarked carriage.

"You're certain Lord Gibson is not at home?" Daphne clutched his hand while trudging through the long grass. In the dark, one could twist an ankle while attempting to navigate the uneven ground. "What if he was simply too busy to receive visitors?"

"The housekeeper said he's in London on business." Business that no doubt involved shooting at them in a dim alley. "I'd have known if she was lying. After slipping the stable boy a coin, he confirmed the woman's story."

"So if you have no intention of knocking the front door, how do you propose to gain entry?" Her breath came quicker now, the white mist breezing from her mouth evidence of over-exertion. His thoughts were drawn instantly to their amorous interlude in the carriage—when she'd panted, clutched his shoulders and cried his name.

Damn it all.

The intimate moment they'd shared did nothing to satiate his craving, only fed it all the more. Nothing would ever compare to that one perfect moment. Even now, while holding Daphne's hand to steady her balance, desire coursed through him like a fast-flowing river in danger of bursting its banks.

"We'll enter through the window in the study," Daniel said, forcing his mind back to the present. "Did you bring a candle and tinderbox as I asked?"

"Of course. They're in the concealed pocket of my pelisse."

"You have a hidden pocket in your coat?"

From her soft hum, he imagined her nodding but couldn't see clearly in the dark. "Betsy made a few alterations for me. Depending on the circumstances, it is often better than carrying a reticule."

"Perhaps I might ask her to sew a holster for a pistol inside my greatcoat. It would certainly make life easier."

Daphne chuckled. "I'm sure if Mr Bostock asked her she would do anything. Betsy does seem rather enamoured with your associate."

"Or rather enamoured with his carpentry skills." Daniel chuckled as he imagined his friend rearranging furniture and repairing cupboard doors.

"Bostock told me how he met you," she suddenly said. "By all accounts, he's always been skilled with his hands."

For all the saints. Were his friend not made of stone, he'd punch him on the nose. "If there's one thing Bostock detests it's an unfair fight. He offered his assistance despite knowing nothing about me. It was during one of my first cases as an enquiry agent. Try as I might, the man has refused to leave my side ever since."

There was much more to the story than that. But now was not the time to dredge up memories of the past.

"He said you declined an education at Cambridge in favour of working for yourself," Daphne continued. Bloody hell. Bostock needed a lesson in curbing his tongue. "When Thomas said you met at school, I assumed that was where he meant."

"I met Thomas at Eton. While he continued with his studies, I chose another route." His blunt response conveyed his desire to change the subject. The urge to run took hold, the urge to do something other than reveal the extent of his tragic upbringing.

"Wait. I'm struggling to keep up with your long strides." Daphne tugged on his hand forcing him to stop. "Just give me a moment to catch my breath. Do you always walk so quickly?"

"Trust me this is a slow pace." The lie fell easily from his lips. "Perhaps it would have been best if you'd stayed at the inn." He'd tried to persuade her to do just that, but logic said the safest place to be was at his side—even if they were about to enter Lord Gibson's house without permission.

"Two people searching is quicker than one." She was right. The least amount of time spent in Lord Gibson's house the better.

But did she really think he would allow her to enter the lord's premises unlawfully?

"You'll wait outside while I search the study." Robbery carried a more severe sentence than loitering. Not that he would get caught. "Should we be discovered, we may have no option but to run."

Daphne failed to reply, which meant she'd do what she pleased regardless of his opinion.

They continued in companionable silence. The night was cool, calm, peaceful. Yet the refreshing breeze on his face brought no relief to his chaotic thoughts.

For a man who'd spent his childhood living in a fantasy world of his mother's creation, he'd come to realise daydreams were for the misguided. Dreams were for those too weak to face the harsh reality of life. So why did fanciful notions of love, marriage, and a family home in the country continually fill his head?

"Look, over there." Daphne's voice broke his reverie. She pointed to the grey shadow in the distance. "That must be Lord Gibson's house."

"When we get a little closer, there's a stone wall around the perimeter, but it's low enough for me to lift you over." Touching her without his body flaming would be the greater task.

The distinct lack of light spilling out from the tall windows on the facade suggested no one was home. They followed the gravel path around the house, though were careful to walk on the grass verge. After peering through the windows in the east wing and discovering the drawing room and then the ladies' boudoir, it became apparent that the masculine rooms were located in the west wing.

Once they'd passed the billiard room, common sense told him the next room was sure to be the study.

"This is it," Daphne said, cupping her hands to her face and pressing her nose to the glass. "How are we to get inside?"

Daniel scanned the frame. "Breaking one of the small panes is an option." It had to be done with skill and precision to avoid waking the household.

"With their master away, the servants will be in their beds, or playing cards around the kitchen table while drinking his port. Either way, I doubt they'll hear a thing."

While examining which pane to remove, he noticed the brass catch had been left open. "There's no need to break the window. Some fool forgot to lock it." Daniel used the heel of his palm to push up the sash. "Wait here. Once I'm inside, pass me the candle and tinderbox."

He climbed through the gap, padded over to the door which he presumed led into the hall, and turned the key in the lock. The sudden sound of flint striking steel captured his attention, and he swung around to see Daphne leaning over the empty grate, trying to light the charcloth in the tinderbox.

"I told you to wait outside," Daniel whispered as Daphne blew on the piece of glowing fibre. "Be careful. Blow too hard, and a speck of cloth might fly up and catch the drapes."

"Why do you think I'm lighting it down here? I've done this a hundred times before." She blew a handful of times as a cloud of smoke wafted into the room.

"You're blowing too hard." Daniel fanned his hand in front of his face for fear of choking. "We're liable to alert the whole household with our incessant coughing."

As the cloth ignited, she took the candle from the inside pocket of her pelisse and dangled the wick in the flame. "Here," she said, handing him the candle as she blew out the flame in the box. "Find a holder."

Daniel did as she asked. With the room cast in a golden glow, he scanned the mahogany desk as it was always the best place to start. He placed the holder on top and tried the drawers only to find them locked.

"Gibson may have taken the key with him." Daniel moved the chair and ran his hand under the wood in the recess. Nothing.

Daphne came to stand in front of the desk, brushing ash from the grate off her hands. "Why take it with him when something so small could be easily lost." She examined the ink pots on the desk, removed one of the gilt lids and picked out a small key from inside the glass holder. "This might be what you're looking for."

Daniel jerked his head back. "How did you know it would be in there?"

"No one would lift the lid on an ink pot without just cause in case they got ink on their hands." She offered him a sweet smile. "And a man doesn't need four pots on his desk."

"Indeed."

Trying not to show his slight embarrassment for not finding the key first, Daniel unlocked the middle drawer and peered inside. Other than a quill knife, a magnifying glass and a leather pouch full of sovereigns, there was nothing of interest. He moved to the row of drawers on the right, relieved to find the same key worked in the lock.

"I've found nothing so far," he said.

"I'm not really sure what we're looking for." Daphne wandered about the room, picking up books and flicking through the pages, examining the tiny door on the rear of the mantel clock. "Gibson would be a fool to leave written proof of his duplicity." She moved to the row of rosewood bookcases lining the far wall and sniffed.

Daniel found a pile of papers in one drawer including a legal document pertaining to land the lord had recently acquired in France. There was a vowel for the price of fifty pounds owed by a gentleman named Biggs. A copy of a supplement from *The Gentleman's Magazine* dated 1820.

"This might be of interest." Daniel flicked through the pages until he got to the section on domestic occurrences. "There are details of a trial for libel, a riot in Greenwich and—" He stopped abruptly, scanned the document again to be certain his eyes weren't playing tricks.

"And?" Daphne did not look at him but continued to sniff in the vicinity of the bookcase.

"And brief details of the coroner's inquest into Thomas' death."

"What?" Daphne rushed to his side and glanced over his shoulder. "The jury brought a verdict of accidental death due to drowning." She muttered the words as she read the article. "Why would Lord Gibson keep a copy of a magazine that's three years old?"

"As a token perhaps." As Daniel turned the page, a leaf of paper floated to the floor.

Daphne picked it up and held it near the candle. "It's a list of times and dates the *Carron* docked in London. They go back three years or more."

"May I see it?" Their fingers touched as he took the note, sending a shiver of awareness shooting up his arm. Regardless of where he was or what he was doing, his desire for her always simmered beneath the surface. "There's no mention of Lily or Thomas. But Gibson obviously has a vested interest in following the *Carron's* movements."

"Perhaps Lord Gibson is not the traitor." Daphne glanced left and right and sniffed the air again. "Thomas might have sent him the list for some reason."

"But why would he send it to Gibson?" Daniel frowned when Daphne rubbed her nose. "Are you ill? Has the walk across the damp grass given you a chill?"

"No." Chin in the air, Daphne turned away from him. "I caught a whiff of something familiar." She walked over to the bookcase, sniffing like a hound eager to latch on to a scent. With a sudden gasp, she bent down and opened the first in a row of cupboards underneath. "The smell is stronger over here, far more potent."

Daniel should have continued searching the drawers, but he couldn't drag his eyes from Daphne's round derriere as she worked her way along the row. "Perhaps Gibson spilt brandy or port and the scent still lingers."

Daphne gasped. "That's it. The scent lingers." She knelt on the floor and rummaged through the cupboard. "It's the same musky odour the intruder leaves behind at home."

"Are you sure?" Daniel placed the paper back inside the magazine, slipped it into the pocket of his greatcoat and moved to stand next to Daphne.

"Positive." She pulled out a small wooden box and opened the lid.

There was a lengthy pause while she stared at the objects inside.

"What's wrong?" Daniel crouched at her side.

A gasp left her lips when she picked up the plain, glass bottle of French cologne and removed the stopper. "This is the scent worn by the intruder." All colour drained from her face as she inhaled deeply. "This is the smell he leaves behind." With a quick shake of her head, she pushed the stopper back into the bottle and dropped it into the box as if it might burn her fingers.

"There's another item in the box." Daniel knew she'd seen the object wrapped in a soft red cloth, but she seemed reluctant to examine what was hidden inside.

"You take it out and see what it is."

Daniel picked up the item. From the shape and weight, he had an idea what it was before he peeled back the cloth. He glanced at Daphne, but her eyes were closed.

"What is it, Daniel?" The tremble in her voice spoke of apprehension, not excitement.

"It's a gold pocket watch."

Pain flashed across her face. She opened her eyes slowly and stared at the metal case sitting in his palm.

"May I see it?" she said, her fingers trembling as she held out her hand.

"Of course." He placed it in her palm and for a moment feared she lacked the strength to hold it.

She grimaced as she flicked open the case, sucked in a few sharp breaths and tried to regain her composure. "This ... this watch was given to Thomas by his father." Her finger came to rest on the dent on the lid. "He dropped it once when we were out walking and cursed himself the whole way home. Many times, he said he would get it repaired, see if a watchmaker could smooth out the metal."

A tear trickled down her cheek, and Daniel placed his hand on her arm. Rage burned in his chest at the thought of confronting Lord Gibson with the evidence. Sorrow pained his heart for there was nothing he could do to bring Thomas back.

"I suppose he thought there was no rush," Daphne continued. "That he would get around to it, eventually. But fate intervened."

"Thomas did not deserve to die like this." Anger was the only emotion evident in his voice. "Killed by a coward who'd sell his own mother to the devil."

A whimper left her lips as she closed the lid and clutched the watch tight in her hand. "I'm not leaving it here. I'm not leaving it in a dusty old cupboard."

"No, we'll take the box and cologne with us, too." Daniel came to his feet and held his hand out to her. "Come, we must leave this place before we're discovered."

Daphne nodded and slipped her tiny hand into his.

After climbing out of the window, Daniel closed the sash gently, and they trudged back across the field towards the coaching inn. They walked the two miles in relative silence. A wistful melancholy settled around them, dragging them deeper into the depths of despair. Images of Thomas' last moments flashed into Daniel's mind: eyes wide with terror as he fought the urge to breathe water. Had it happened quickly? What did one think about when they realised death was inevitable?

They arrived at the coaching inn to find a new coach in the courtyard. The small family-run establishment operated with minimal staff and consequently, the innkeeper and his wife were too busy with the late arrivals to pay them any heed.

"Do you want to keep the box with you in your room?" Daniel said as they stopped outside the door to Daphne's bedchamber.

The lines between her brows grew prominent as she searched his face. "Stay with me," she whispered. "Don't leave me to sleep alone, Daniel. Not tonight."

The words tore at his heart. He'd give everything he owned

to ease her pain. "What if someone should see me entering your room?"

"No one knows us here. Discretion is a skill we've both mastered." She touched his arm, and it took all the strength he possessed to suppress his desire.

"Very well." He glanced left and right. "Open the door before someone sees us."

Once inside the private space his body reacted instantly. But one did not need to be a skilled enquiry agent to know that she wanted something else from him tonight.

Not really knowing what to do or what she expected, he followed her lead. They removed their coats and boots, washed their face and hands in the bowl of cold water on the washstand.

"I'll sleep in my clothes," she said as she climbed onto the bed.

And that was his cue to do the same. Stripping off his waistcoat and pulling his shirt loose from his breeches, Daniel settled down beside her.

They both lay there staring at the oak beams on the ceiling for a few seconds though it felt more like an hour.

"So what do we do now?" She turned on to her side and looked at him.

The ambiguous question left him floundering. "In what regard?"

"Now we've found evidence of Lord Gibson's involvement, how should we proceed?"

What they'd found proved nothing. But he needed time to think. "Let's get some sleep. We've a long day ahead of us tomorrow. There'll be plenty of opportunity to discuss the case."

Once at Elton Park, Daniel would make himself scarce. Long walks in the garden would give him the perfect excuse to be away from the main house, from the guests who had nothing better to do than pry and ask impertinent questions.

Daphne sighed. "Would you do something for me?"

Daniel cast her a sidelong glance. Did the woman not know he'd do anything she asked? "That depends on what it is you're asking?"

"Hold me."

It was remarkable how two simple words had the power to render him helpless. He put his arm around her and gathered her closer. Damn. If his heart continued to beat so fast, it would burst from his chest.

Daphne snuggled into him, placed her head in the crook of his arm, her hand flat on his chest. Needing to find a way to distract him from all amorous thoughts, he held her close and stroked the hair from her brow.

Exhausted from the events of the day, she drifted off to sleep in a matter of minutes. He stared at her for the longest time, buried his face in her hair, closed his eyes and inhaled the unique scent that had a magical ability to soothe his soul.

That was the moment he finally admitted the truth he'd spent years denying. He was in love with the woman sleeping in his arms. So in love with her it hurt.

CHAPTER 17

THE WEDDING TOOK PLACE IN ST. BARTHOLOMEW'S, A QUAINT medieval church less than half a mile from Elton Park. While Daphne's eyes welled upon hearing Anthony and Sarah recite their vows, Daniel kept his head bowed and stared at the ancient flagstones. With his sombre expression, one would think they were mourning the dead not celebrating the joining of two people in love.

"What's wrong?" Daphne whispered, giving him a little nudge to get his attention.

"Nothing."

"Can you not try to look happy for them?"

"I am."

Daphne sighed. He'd been cold and distant since leaving the coaching inn. Hostility radiated from every fibre of his being. Heaven help the person who made eye contact or dared strike up a conversation.

What had happened to the kind, considerate gentleman who'd held her in his arms, soothed her fears and banished her nightmares? Where was the passionate man who made her heart skip a beat?

He was buried, hidden, lost beneath this austere shell. But why?

As they followed the procession from the church, he kept his head bowed. Outside, the sun shone. The birds sang a pretty tune. A gentle breeze rustled the leaves on the trees. Nature chose to celebrate, too, yet Daniel looked like Satan waiting for a perfect opportunity to spoil the party.

While Anthony and Sarah rode in a barouche with the collapsible top down, the rest of the party, all except the elderly matrons, strolled back to Elton Park. As expected, Daniel insisted they walk at the back of the procession, a good ten feet behind the stragglers.

"Are you going to tell me why you've suddenly developed this black mood?" Daphne placed her hand in the crook of his arm as they continued along the winding country lane. "It's going to be a long day if you continue to sulk in the corner."

He shot her a sidelong glance. "Sulking is something people do to gain sympathy. Trust me, that's the last thing I want from these people."

These people? Of course, he meant the aristocracy.

"Why do you detest them so? Is it because of what happened to you at school?"

"I find their morals lacking." An ugly sneer formed on his lips. In that brief moment, he appeared as a stranger to her. "To them, money and status prevail over love and loyalty."

Could he not hear the hypocrisy in his words? His income came from the very people he despised. Then it struck her. Daniel played the peers like pawns in a game. He used and manipulated them for information, enjoyed playing master and having them at his mercy.

"There are good and bad examples of people in every tier of society," she said, still struggling to understand his motive. "To judge a group as a whole based on past experience is ... well, it's foolish and ignorant."

"I have my reasons." The bitter words told tale of a secret. "It is difficult to focus on anything when we have work awaiting us at home."

Finally, an explanation she understood. "Last night sorrow filled our hearts. Finding Thomas' watch opened old wounds. But we must move forward. We must find the person responsible and learn to put the past behind us."

"And conversing with these people will make a difference how?"

Lord above. If it were possible to shake stubbornness from a man, she'd grab his lapels and not let go. But the complex nature of his character could not be unravelled through conflict. She had to break down the wall, speak to the passionate, sensual man inside.

"Despite all your attempts to disguise the fact, you're a gentleman, Daniel, not a cutthroat with a grudge. Integrity and logic form the basis of your actions in everything you do except for this."

"Like most people, I lack the capacity to be consistent."

The odd backward glances from the people walking in front told her now was not the time to pursue the matter. A different approach was necessary if she had any hope of dragging him out of his depressed mood.

"Then let us pretend we are the only people here." Daphne squeezed his arm, caressed the bulging muscle she longed to see in the flesh. "Let us use the opportunity to further our acquaintance."

Daniel glanced at her, his raised brow and half smile roused optimism. "After what occurred between us yesterday, I'd say we are more than mere acquaintances."

The fluttering in her stomach returned at the thought of being intimate with him again. "Then perhaps I did not make myself clear. While here, there will be plenty of opportunity to indulge in a few private moments of pleasure, to pursue our obvious connection."

"A few?" This time his smile reached his eyes. "Madam, I shall be grateful for one."

"Then you understand that a lady must be mentally stimulated if a gentleman is to receive the reaction he desires." That should give him something to contemplate. "Conversing with a grump hardly leads a lady to have amorous thoughts."

Daniel raised a brow. "Are you bribing me?"

"Of course not. I catch criminals not imitate them. No, I am merely offering insight into the workings of a woman's mind." And if the idea of bedding her didn't drag him from his melancholic mood, she didn't know what would.

"To succeed as an enquiry agent, one must be a master of manipulation." From his playful tone, it was evident she'd achieved her goal. "And you, I believe, are the best."

"Does that mean you'll smile and partake in mindless conversation about the weather?"

"It means I shall make an effort simply because you've asked me to."

They turned through the impressive sandstone piers and wrought-iron gates—the main entrance to Elton Park—and followed the guests up to the house.

"Lord above," Daphne gasped as she surveyed the giant Doric columns that were almost as tall as the house itself. "Lord Harwood's home is rather stately and majestic. The effort required to maintain such a grand place must be great indeed."

Thorpe scanned the rows of windows on the facade. "Running an estate of this size takes considerable work, time and money."

"Good heavens, Mr Thorpe. Did I catch a hint of admiration in your tone?" She enjoyed teasing him. "Are you saying that not all peers sit around idle?"

"The viscount and his brother, Lucas Dempsey, are exceptions. I respect any man willing to fight for a cause." His gaze softened. "I respect any man who dedicates himself to one woman. And if one thing is abundantly clear, both brothers are in love with their wives."

So, fidelity, honour and integrity were traits Daniel Thorpe valued. What more could a woman want from a man? What more could a woman want from a husband?

Love!

"Experience has taught me love is vital in marriage," Daphne said. Without love to bind a couple together, everything fell apart. "Duty is important, but a partnership based on deep affection and shared passions is necessary if one wants to be truly happy."

Daniel's gaze travelled over her face. "I could not agree more."

"Were your parents in love?" Daphne's father grieved the loss of her mother every day for ten years. "Do you think it is better to love for a short time than never at all?"

He ground to a halt and turned to face her. From his dull eyes and empty stare, she expected him to say no.

"My parents were deeply in love. To them, nothing else mattered." He put his hand to his throat as though the words pained him. The gravel crunched under his feet, and he shuffled awkwardly.

"And what of my second question?" Her heart raced as their eyes locked.

"In answer to that, I believe love is all there is."

Daphne stared at him. The man was baffling. Why make her an offer a few years ago? Why cite duty and responsibility as good reasons to marry if he wanted something more?

She glanced over her shoulder and noted the guests entering the house. They were alone on the drive. At any moment someone would come to escort them inside. But she was desperate for an answer to a burning question.

"If love is everything, why offer to marry me out of a sense of duty? Love played no part in your decision."

Daniel's gaze dropped to his boots. Sucking in a deep breath, he glanced up. "Daphne, I offered marriage because I wanted to bed you. There, that's the truth of it. I offered marriage because you fascinate me. Because I hoped our friendship would develop into something more."

He wanted to bed her? She had no idea he felt that way.

"Then why did you not say so?" Would her answer have been different if he'd made a more passionate appeal? Probably not. Her heart had been too full of guilt, too full of grief. "Why did you not try to explain your position?"

Daniel removed his hat and pushed his hand through his hair. "Because I thought you loved Thomas, that you'd never love another. Foolishly, I thought you needed someone to take care of you. A life companion."

"You would have made that sacrifice?"

He exhaled slowly, but before he could answer the butler hobbled over to greet them.

"Good day, sir, I'm Chadwick, the butler." The old man pushed his spectacles up to the bridge of his nose. "As it's such a pleasant day, we're to serve drinks on the terrace. If you'd care to follow me."

"Thank you, Chadwick." Daniel inclined his head. His tone conveyed a hint of relief rather than frustration. "A drink would be most welcome."

It appeared Daniel's fears were unfounded. The wedding was an informal affair, with the viscount the only peer in attendance. Thank the Lord he didn't have to look at Pulborough's pathetic face or listen to his jibes and taunts. One wrong word from the arrogant marquess and the celebration would have turned into a brawl.

The wedding breakfast, too, was a casual event. Various breads, buttered rolls, meats and cheese covered the long table which sat twenty without the fear of one banging their neighbour's elbow. The addition of chocolate and a wedding cake were the only things to mark the special occasion.

Daniel sat next to Miss Hamilton, a friend of the bride who barely raised her gaze from her plate, let alone sought meaningful conversation. The opposite was true of the elderly matron to his left who raised her monocle more than a handful of times to study him.

"What did you say your name was?" The white-haired lady frowned as her curious gaze scanned his face. Why could she not leave him alone? There were other guests to prod and poke. "My memory is not what it was."

"Mr Thorpe," he replied respectfully before popping a piece of ham into his mouth. There wasn't a person alive who could lay claim to a family connection when using that name.

"Are you family?"

"No, simply a friend of the happy couple." It was a slight exaggeration but better than saying he was the person responsible for catching Lord Harwood's blackmailer.

"I could have sworn you were a relative. You look so familiar." The lady's shrill voice sent a shiver shooting through him. She muttered his name to herself and shook her head numerous times. "Have I seen you before? Who is your father?"

"Bloody hell," he whispered. He suddenly wished Pulborough was here. At least he could punch the pompous lord when he refused to be quiet.

The matron cupped her hand to her ear. "Sorry, who did you say your father was?"

"My father died before I was born."

The evasive reply was sure to rouse pity and distract from

further prying. He glanced across at Daphne. From what he could hear of the conversation, she was educating the bride's brother-in-law, Max Roxbury, in the telltale signs often displayed by liars. She looked so comfortable in the grand house. The country air had brought a glow to her cheeks. The lines often apparent between her brows had disappeared in the relaxed environment. Daphne deserved to live a peaceful life full of love and laughter. She did not deserve to be cooped up in a room above a shop, too scared to sleep at night.

"Was it an accident?" The matron at his side continued to probe him. "For he must have been in his prime when he died. Tragedy often strikes the young."

Daniel swallowed down the lump in his throat and took a sip of wine. "He fell off his horse and broke his neck."

The matron gasped. "Monstrous beast of a thing, was it? Forever chomping at the bit?"

Did the lady not know when to change the subject? "I believe the blame lies firmly with the arrogance of the rider." It wasn't true. But resentment was easier to live with than regret.

"Your poor mother." The lady tapped his arm. "So tragic to lose a husband at such a young age."

"Indeed." His mother lost a lover, not a husband. And therein lay the problem that had plagued him his entire life.

"And she died young too I fear. When one suffers loss, pain is always evident in the voice. It doesn't matter how long…" The matron continued talking, but Daniel stopped listening.

This was precisely the reason he'd refused to attend. Someone was bound to recognise him. Someone was bound to remember the scandal. One derogatory word about either of his parents and he was liable to bring the house tumbling down around them.

It was much easier to stay away. In the back streets of London, no one bothered him. No one cared. He controlled events. They did not control him.

Daniel stared at the pristine tablecloth, at the polished silver cutlery, the lavish gilt fruit bowl, at all the fancy trimmings that spoke of wealth and excellent breeding. The blood that flowed through his veins was as good as any of the men seated at the table. But not everyone saw it that way.

"You don't have to answer." The elderly woman at his side placed her frail, wrinkled hand on his arm. "You'll find your way out of the darkness. We all do eventually."

"In the darkness, we can be anyone we want to be," he murmured.

The lady smiled. "No matter how hard you try, you can never run away from yourself."

Daniel swallowed down the lump in his throat. How the hell had he ended up having this conversation? Thoughts of the past swamped him. He'd spent a lifetime running, and the past was yet to catch up with him. Thoughts of the future left him equally dazed. His feelings for Daphne robbed him of breath, made running that much harder.

He turned to the matron. "If you'll excuse me, I'm in need of air."

Before he had a chance to drag his napkin off his lap, Anthony stood and hit his crystal goblet with a knife. The high-pitched *ching* caught everyone's attention. "As it's a little early for port, gentlemen, and because I have no intention of letting my wife out of my sight, I suggest we all retire to the drawing room."

Relief coursed through Daniel's veins. Moving to another room would give him an excuse to sneak outside. The grounds were vast. One could easily get lost. Even if he couldn't persuade Daphne to accompany him, he'd go alone.

"Move?" the matron grumbled. "Oh, can that boy not sit still for five minutes. I've hardly touched a morsel." Had she not spent so much time talking it might have been a different matter. She grabbed Daniel's arm. "Help me up. There's a good fellow.

Now where did I put my walking stick? The staff always offer to take it," she said, gesturing to the liveried footmen standing as still as statues by the sideboard, "but I feel better knowing it's at my side."

Though the urge to flee was still upon him, it would be rude not to offer the lady assistance. And he was a gentleman, even though he frequently denied the fact.

"Your cane is propped against your chair." Daniel stood and helped the elderly lady to her feet.

"Now, give me your arm." She held on to him. "And don't hunch your shoulders. Stand up straight else they'll think I'm not able to support myself." Beneath hooded lids, she looked up. "Your father was a tall man I suspect. One rarely inherits their height from their mother."

"I believe so."

"You're not a man of many words," she said as they crossed the entrance hall and walked towards the drawing room. "One would almost think you had something to hide."

"Then perhaps I should leave you to sit with the ladies." Daniel escorted her to the gilt-framed sofa in what was the most exquisitely furnished room he'd ever laid eyes on. "You have a way of extracting information from a most unwilling party."

The matron gave his arm a friendly squeeze and chuckled. "Curiosity helps keep the mind young."

"Then that explains why you're sprightlier than the rest of us."

The lady used her stick as support as she eased herself down into the seat. "I like you, Mr Thorpe. I hope we have the opportunity to talk again."

"Should that be the case I ask you give me fair warning, and I shall be sure to wear my armour."

"Your father had a sense of humour too no doubt."

All this talk of his father unsettled him. It was only a matter of time before the lady made the connection. A woman of her years would remember the scandal.

Daniel inclined his head. "I shall leave you to ponder the possibility."

Moving away from the group of people assembling, Daniel found a quiet spot near the window, next to a statue of a Greek god who looked equally as bored. Daphne entered the room and noticed him standing alone. She was about to walk over and rescue him when Lady Harwood clutched her arm and dragged her to the sofa to meet her sister.

Minutes passed.

He knew he was scowling. Numerous times he considered pulling out his watch to check the time. Weren't the guests supposed to leave after the wedding breakfast? Why the hell had the Harwoods insisted people stay the night?

Memories of the past crept into his mind. Did the father he imagined bear any resemblance to the real man? A painting of his father hung in the gallery at Pulborough Hall, though now it had probably been relegated to the attic. Even so, he'd be damned before he'd set foot in that house.

A weary sigh left his lips.

How in blazes was he supposed to think about the case when the matron's meddling had given him a thousand and one other things to think about?

He glanced over at the white-haired lady as she stood and wandered over to the viscount. They stared at him. At one point she raised her cane and waved it in his direction. No sooner had she walked away than Lucas Dempsey joined his brother and they continued ogling.

It crossed his mind to march over and demand to know what they found so interesting. Instead, he looked out of the window at the manicured lawns, which was why he failed to notice Lucas Dempsey approach.

"Don't tell me you also have an irrational fear of peacocks."

Lucas Dempsey grinned and slapped him on the upper arm where the skin was cut and bruised.

"Peacocks?" Daniel said, swallowing down the pain.

"Have you not seen the wallpaper in your room? Blasted peacocks are everywhere. It's enough to make a man want to sleep in the barn. Why else would you be standing here with a dour face?"

"During the time you've known me, have you ever seen me wear a different expression?"

Lucas cupped his chin and gazed at him with a look of thoughtful contemplation. "It was hard to tell what was going on beneath that beard. But while your lips are always drawn into a thin, ugly line, your eyes often forget to be angry. I noticed it just now when you were salivating over Mrs Chambers."

Bloody hell. What was this? Poke the miserable man in the corner until he bears his soul?

"I was not salivating over Mrs Chambers." He was drooling, but his personal affairs had nothing to do with Lucas Dempsey.

"There is no need to sound so defensive." Lucas chuckled. "I'm on your side, Thorpe. Though you may find the thought abhorrent, we are similar in many ways. I too had to work to build my fortune. You're not nearly as handsome, but we share the same disdain for society."

The memory of Lucas charging at Mr Weston in a fit of rage drifted into his mind. "You used to despise everyone as I recall. Had it not been for Bostock's timely intervention, you would have beaten Weston to a pulp."

"The weasel almost ruined my life," Lucas said, animosity still evident. "A good fight is the best medicine when resentment festers."

"In that, we are agreed." A fight was a way of releasing years of suppressed frustration and anger. "I find hypocrisy hard to stomach."

"As do I." Lucas nodded. "The same people who once refused to speak to me now invite me to dinner."

"And do you go?" The answer would speak volumes as to the nature of Mr Dempsey's character.

"Hell, no." The corners of Lucas' mouth turned down. "There are those who preach that forgiveness is good for the soul. That a man cannot love when there's hate in his heart."

"But you don't agree." This was quickly becoming an enlightening conversation.

Lucas held his hands out. "I am proof that the theory is nonsense. While my heart bursts with love, I cannot pretend that the past doesn't matter. I cannot break bread with those who thrust a knife in my back."

The Marquess of Pulborough, Daniel's estranged cousin, had begged for clemency, begged for the return of his vowels, for a way out of the debt sucking him under. Daniel could forgive the taunts and jibes at school. The scars on his hand mattered not. But he could never forgive what the family had done to his mother.

"Do you ever feel the urge to seek revenge?" Daniel asked. The need for retribution was the one thing that made him strive for better things.

"Revenge?" Lucas scoffed. "Have you not heard that happiness is the best revenge?" He glanced over his shoulder at Mrs Dempsey. It took but a few seconds for her to look up and meet her husband's gaze. "Damn. There's not a day goes by when I don't give thanks to fate."

"And if someone hurt those you love?"

Lucas clenched his jaw. "Then I'd hound them to the gates of hell."

"Then you're right. We have more in common than I realised."

CHAPTER 18

THE MATRON, WHO INSISTED DAPHNE CALL HER LAVINIA, frowned. "I am telling you that boy is the son of the Marquess of Pulborough."

Helena put her arm around her great-aunt and guided her into the seat. "While Mr Thorpe has the manners of a gentleman, he is not the son of a marquess."

Daphne's heart went out to the elderly matron. At the ripe old age of eighty, one was bound to get confused when their head was brimming with memories.

"Mr Thorpe is my colleague," Daphne said, sitting in the seat opposite. "We work together in London." Granted, Thorpe was a fictitious name used for business, but the idea that Daniel could claim such a connection was preposterous.

"Work?" Lavinia looked aghast. "That boy has no need to work. What about the estate Tobias bought the boy's mother?"

The boy? After witnessing Daniel's impressive form first hand, he was a man in every sense of the word.

Helena glanced at Daphne and raised a frustrated brow. "Aunt, we have no idea who Tobias is?"

Lavinia sighed. "Tobias is the boy's father. They have the

179

same brooding look, the same olive skin and dark hair. All the girls swooned when Tobias entered the room."

Daphne glanced over her shoulder at Daniel Thorpe, relieved to find him in the company of Lucas Dempsey. The men had been talking for half an hour. Mr Dempsey's charismatic charm obviously worked on gentlemen, too, as an uncharacteristic chuckle escaped from Daniel's lips.

"I'm sure Mr Thorpe will be pleased to know you hold him in such high regard." Helena patted the lady's hand affectionately.

"Everyone loved Tobias," Lavinia said with an air of melancholy. "Such a good man. Such a tragedy. And the boy lives in London, you say?"

Daphne nodded. "Yes, we rode up together yesterday." While Daniel used numerous houses in the city, she had no idea which one he considered his permanent residence.

"And he's not married?" Lavinia asked a lot of questions.

"No, he's not married." Daphne could not imagine Daniel with a wife and family. A jealous pang filled her chest at the thought. Like a vine, the feeling grew and twisted around her heart.

"Didn't Sarah look beautiful in her new gown?" Helena said in a bid to change the subject.

Lavinia frowned. "Who's Sarah?"

Helena breathed deeply, and whispered, "Anthony's wife."

"Oh, for the life of me I have no idea why, but I thought her name was Susanna." Lavinia shook her head and chuckled. "You shall have to keep reminding me, dear."

Lucas' hearty laugh captured their attention, and they turned to find Daniel laughing, too. His dark eyes were alight with amusement. Lord, he was handsome when he wasn't frowning.

"Finally," Lavinia said. "I thought I'd never see that boy smile. If anyone can pull him from his black mood, it's Lucas. I know I'm not supposed to have my favourites, but I do like a man with spirit. Tobias had spirit. Heavens, that man could raise the temperature in an ice house with one glance."

"Lucas prefers the country air to the grime of the city," Helena said, attempting to steer the conversation away from Lavinia's fanciful musings. "Green fields and large gardens bring out the child in him."

Lavinia nodded. "As it does to us all. A spell in the country will soothe any man's soul." She turned to Daphne. "Despite living in London, I assume the boy still owns the country estate?"

Daphne wasn't sure how to answer without offending the matron. Perhaps pleading ignorance was the best policy.

"Mr Thorpe—"

"Of course, Rainham Hall is not nearly as vast as Pulborough Hall," Lavinia continued. "But it has a certain charm that encapsulates the theme of love. The garden boasts lavish fountains and statues of nymphs and satyrs."

"It sounds wonderful," Helena said.

Rainham Hall?

Was that not the place Mr Bostock mentioned when Daniel had asked to go home?

Good Lord. Daniel Thorpe couldn't possibly be related to a marquess. He despised the aristocracy.

"I'm confused," Daphne said, intrigued to hear more. "If you believe Mr Thorpe is the son of the Marquess of Pulborough, then what reason can there be for him not inheriting? Why would he own Rainham Hall and not Pulborough, the family seat?"

Lavinia leant forward. "It's the scandal, my dear. The boy confirmed his identity when he told me his father had died before he was born. The likeness is uncanny. It cannot be a coincidence."

Daphne knew Daniel's parents were dead and that a guardian

had paid for his education. "Mr Thorpe has never mentioned anything about a scandal."

"As with any gossip," Helena began, "it is wise not to give the tale too much merit."

"Oh, this isn't gossip." Lavinia's eyes widened. It was evident the matron enjoyed talking about the past. "Most people my age remember the tragedy."

Tragedy? Daphne's heart ached before she'd even heard the sad recount. "What happened?"

"Tobias was supposed to marry the daughter of the Earl of Holden, but he fell in love with Maria, the daughter of his father's man of business."

"Love considers not one's fortune or position," Helena said, appearing much more interested, too. Her gaze drifted to her husband. "Love is blind to all prejudices."

Lavinia nodded. "Of course, the union was forbidden by his father and Maria loved Tobias too dearly to see him lose everything. For months, she rejected his suit. But as the great poets say love finds a way."

The matron waved to the maid who was passing with a tea trolley. Daphne and Helena sat patiently waiting to hear the rest of the story.

"Talking gives me a croaky voice if I don't moisten the cords," Lavinia continued. They waited another minute or so while she sipped the beverage.

"And so were Tobias and Maria able to be together?" Daphne asked, her impatience getting the better of her. She recalled Daniel's comment that his parents loved each other dearly. Yet there was a sad end to this story. Was that why love was so important to him?

Lavinia placed her cup and saucer on the side table. "Tobias bought Maria and her father a small manor house. He visited them often. When he inherited, he offered marriage, and she accepted. Maria would have been happy to elope, but

Tobias had a point to prove. So a lavish wedding was arranged."

"I suspect those in society made derogatory remarks about the lady he chose to marry," Helena said with a hint of bitterness.

"There were some who were happy to make an exception for a love match. Some whose black hearts sought to cause the couple nothing but pain."

"And did they marry?" Helena said.

Daphne knew the answer. Thomas had told her Daniel was illegitimate. He'd just never mentioned he shared a bloodline with a marquess.

Lavinia put her hand to her chest. "Two days before the … the wedding, Tobias fell off his horse and broke his neck." Her expression turned sour. "And that pathetic excuse for a brother inherited everything. He's dead now, of course, and his wastrel son took the title."

"So Maria was with child when Tobias died," Helena clarified. She placed her hand on her slightly swollen stomach and rubbed gently. "How dreadfully sad."

Lavinia gestured to Daniel. "And there stands the man who would have made a far better marquess."

Daphne glanced at Daniel who was still engaged in an animated conversation with Lucas Dempsey. The story had to be true. Why else would he despise the aristocracy? Why else would he create a new persona, one who possessed power and strength, the ability to ruin men overnight?

Just when Daphne thought the story could not get any worse, Lavinia said, "Of course, the family denied Tobias was the child's father. There was nothing they could do about the house he'd bestowed. They spread false rumours about Maria's many lovers. Painted her as a harlot."

"Society can be cruel." Once more Helena's eyes drifted to Mr Dempsey. "It does not take much to ruin a fragile reputation."

"And what happened to Maria?" Based on Daniel's often cold countenance, Daphne suspected things had not ended well.

"Maria spent years trying to prove the paternal connection. She never married. When a lady loves a man like Tobias, no other could ever compare. Maria died when the boy was young. I'm not sure what happened after that."

Daphne had an idea what happened. The dark, brooding Daniel Thorpe was born. The boy had grown into a man, set to wreak havoc on the landed gentry and pompous peers. He took power from the privileged. He sought justice for those incapable of doing so for themselves. And so he used his disguise: no fixed place of abode, a false name, altered his physical appearance, all in the hope of doing what? Protecting his true identity, or running away from it?

If only Tobias had eloped with his love, married her before their child was born. Why were men so terribly foolish and stubborn?

With a wistful sigh, Lavinia stared at the floor, her mind lost in memories of the past. Daphne's thoughts were drawn to the schoolboy who no doubt bore the brunt of his parents' misfortune. Helena's glum face only brightened when Mr Dempsey approached, took her hand and brought it to his lips.

"Aunt. Mrs Chambers." He inclined his head, his captivating blue eyes settling on Daphne. "How do you find Elton Park, Mrs Chambers?"

"It is everything a grand house should be and more," Daphne replied, grateful for the distraction. "Your great-grandfather built it, I hear."

Mr Dempsey nodded. "While the house boasts many elegant features, the gardens give it a sense of grandeur. Thorpe is planning a walk outdoors this evening. There's a picturesque spot by the lake that's not to be missed."

Daphne smiled. "I shall bear that in mind should the gentleman invite me to walk with him."

"Oh, I am assured he will. With the garden being so vast, no doubt he has a full evening of entertainment in mind." Mr Dempsey leant down and whispered, "I do hope you like peacocks?" Offering a confident grin, he turned to his aunt. "Heavens, this is a wedding, not a wake. Why do you all look so miserable?"

"We were talking about the old days," Lavinia said. "Remembering that not everyone is as lucky in love as you and your brother."

"Well, while you've been sharing sad stories, Thorpe has kept me highly entertained," Mr Dempsey said in his usual rich drawl. "Had I known he possessed such a wicked sense of humour I'd have sought his company earlier."

Daphne turned to catch another glimpse of the man who monopolised her thoughts, but the space was empty. Daniel Thorpe was nowhere to be seen. "Indeed, Mr Thorpe is full of surprises."

CHAPTER 19

WHEN DAPHNE FINALLY DRAGGED HERSELF AWAY FROM LAVINIA, she went in search of Daniel. She had no idea what she would say to him. The man had always been a conundrum, so opaque, so complex. Now she could see that every action stemmed from a need to right the wrongs of the past.

But nothing could repair the damage done.

Surely a man of his intelligence knew that.

Daphne wandered out onto the terrace, descended the stone steps and followed the gravel path only to find the garden deserted. She returned to the house, searched the library and billiard room, but they were empty, too.

Walking back out into the hall, she stood at the foot of the grand staircase. Searching the bedchambers was the only other option. And she considered racing up the stairs before any of the guests noticed.

"Do you need any assistance, madam?" Chadwick appeared at her side, squinting through his poorly fitted spectacles.

"No, thank you, Chadwick." Daphne had been so lost in thought she'd not heard the butler approach. "I was looking for Mr Thorpe."

"Are you referring to the tall gentleman with dark hair you were walking with earlier?"

"Yes. Have you seen him?"

"I believe he went upstairs, madam. Shall I see if he is available?"

"No. Thank you, Chadwick. You've enough to do looking after the guests. After the long journey yesterday, Mr Thorpe is probably in need of rest." Either that or the thirty minutes spent laughing with Mr Dempsey had taken its toll.

The butler inclined his head and ambled away down the hall. Daphne returned to the drawing room and made polite conversation with Prudence Roxbury, the bride's sister. Numerous times she'd been forced to ask the lady to repeat her question. While Daphne's body was in the drawing room, her mind was somewhere else entirely.

When Prudence went to the aid of her grandfather, who often confused people's names and insisted Mr Dempsey was a gentleman called Captain Lawrence, Daphne found herself alone.

So much had happened since leaving London. They'd discovered Lord Gibson's involvement in Thomas' murder. Daphne now knew of Daniel's past, his motivations. She knew his desire to avoid the aristocracy stemmed from a fear of being recognised. Which was probably the reason he'd made himself scarce at the first opportunity.

Of course, the most life-changing moment had occurred in his carriage. Taking Daniel Thorpe as her lover had only made her want him all the more.

"Remind me to give Thorpe a good shaking for leaving a lady alone," Mr Dempsey said, disturbing her reverie. "Lord knows where he's disappeared to."

She should go to him. Had she known the story of his past, she would not have forced him to come.

Daphne leant closer to the handsome gentleman. "I need

your help, Mr Dempsey. Thorpe has retired to his chamber, and I've no idea where that is."

A sinful grin formed on Mr Dempsey's mouth. "And you want to join him there? Is it not a little early in the day to be … cooped upstairs?"

The only way to deal with men who enjoyed teasing was to play them at their own game. "You do not strike me as a man who requires a blanket of darkness to enjoy life's pleasures, sir. You're the last person I'd think to call a prude."

"Prude?" Mr Dempsey laughed. "You're as amusing as your colleague, Mrs Chambers. Thank heavens you're both here else I might die of boredom."

"Does that mean you will help me?"

"I gave you a clue earlier. I'm surprised a woman with your skill for deduction missed the sign." When she frowned, he said, "Peacocks. Thorpe is in the room plagued by the ugly creatures." He turned, caught his wife's attention, and she came to stand at his side. "Mrs Chambers needs your help, Helena."

Helena turned to Daphne and smiled. "Wonderful. Is it a question about a case?" she said with some excitement.

"Unfortunately not," Mr Dempsey said. "I know how you enjoy a good mystery. But no, this requires the utmost discretion."

Feeling somewhat impatient, Daphne whispered, "I need you to take me to Mr Thorpe's room. Or at least tell me where it is."

Helena smiled. "Of course. Who am I to stand in the way of two people in love?"

"We are not in love," Daphne protested. "We are friends and colleagues, that is all." And occasional lovers, she thought, but no one need know of that. "I've had an idea about the case and need to speak to him before it slips my mind completely."

"Forgive me," Helena said softly, "if I spoke out of turn. Come with me, and I shall point you in the direction of his room."

"If you find your .... discussion becomes a little heated, Mrs Chambers, have no fear." Lucas Dempsey gave her a knowing wink. "There'll be plenty of time to cool down as dinner won't be served until six."

Helena tutted. "Pay Lucas no heed," she said as they walked out into the hall. "He is fond of Mr Thorpe and credits him with saving his reputation. There's not a man he respects more. Without your friend's intervention, Mr Weston might never have confessed."

Pride blossomed in Daphne's chest. "Thorpe is an exceptional enquiry agent—the very best. It's not often in our line of work one hears such praise."

"After everything you both did for Anthony and Sarah, we want you to be happy."

They climbed the grand staircase. Once at the top, Helena pointed to a door further along the corridor.

"It's the third door on the right," Helena continued. "I shall wait here to make sure no one sees you."

"Thank you." Daphne's stomach fluttered at the prospect of entering Daniel's chamber. The sensation was akin to thousands of butterflies bursting from their chrysalises.

With a quick glance over her shoulder, Daphne hurried to the room Mr Dempsey insisted was plagued by peacocks. After rapping gently three times on the door, Daphne breathed a sigh of relief when Daniel finally answered.

"Here you are," she whispered, noting that he'd removed his coat and boots. It was obviously his intention to remain upstairs as long as possible. "I've been looking for you everywhere. Can I come in?"

"Did anyone see you come up here?" he snapped.

"Only Mrs Dempsey."

Daniel popped his head around the jamb. Helena smiled, waved and continued to a room along the opposite corridor.

Daniel shot back into the room, wrapped his fingers around Daphne's wrist and yanked her inside.

"It is not wise to enter a gentleman's bedchamber."

The cold look in his eye eradicated all the progress they'd made over the last few days. He stood before her as the old Thorpe: stiff stance, tart tone, and stony expression. The need to keep his secret pressed heavily on his shoulders. Lavinia had talked to him constantly through the wedding breakfast. Did he fear the matron might have more questions? Was that the reason he'd sought the privacy of his room?

"Then perhaps you should shut the door, Daniel, before someone walks past and sees us." Daphne searched his face. She understood it all now. A wealth of pain lay buried beneath his facade. "Sneaking in fully clothed in the afternoon is hardly the same as being caught leaving at midnight wearing nothing but a nightgown."

He closed the door and came to stand before her. "Is there something wrong?"

"Wrong?"

"That you felt the need to seek me out."

This was going to be extremely hard work. Breaking Daniel Thorpe was the most difficult case she'd ever taken.

"I came to ask if you wanted to return to London." Daphne smiled. How could she make him stay knowing Lavinia would continue to pry until she'd gained a confession? "We could say we've had a breakthrough in the case and leave after dinner."

He tilted his head and squinted. "But don't you want to stay?"

Not if it roused painful memories of his past.

"Anthony and Sarah are too absorbed with each other to miss us." She shrugged. "Mr Dempsey might be sad to see you go. Helena said you're one of the few gentlemen her husband respects."

The corners of Daniel's mouth twitched. "We do have a

190

remarkable amount in common. There are not many men who will admit to thinking the way I do."

"We don't have to leave. If you enjoy Mr Dempsey's company, we can stay. The choice is yours."

"I came here for one reason only—to keep you safe. And so the choice is yours to make not mine."

He'd come to Elton Park for her, knowing one of the guests might reveal his secret. Leaving was the least she could do for him. "Then we'll leave after dinner. With luck, we'll make it home sometime after midnight. We can discuss how we want to proceed with Lord Gibson on the way."

"It's probably for the best." His shoulders relaxed, and his frosty countenance thawed. "I can't think about the case while here. My mind is too occupied with other things."

Daphne glanced around the room. The peacock wallpaper hit her immediately. Why had she not noticed the hundreds of ugly creatures before?

"I agree. Perhaps it's best we do go home," she said. Her mind was made up. Sarah would understand. "Sleeping in this room would be like spending a night in a cramped aviary. I doubt you'll get a wink of sleep. And we must be bright and refreshed if we expect to solve this case any time soon."

"One's bed should bring relief from a busy mind and a hard day," he said, scowling at the birds, "not add to the stress and confusion."

A pang of sadness filled her chest. What did go on in that marvellous mind of his? Too much thinking, she feared. Perhaps a distraction might help soothe him.

Daphne wandered over to the window. The views of the garden were spectacular. "No doubt the monstrous wallpaper is a ploy to lure you to the window. I've never seen a landscape as beautiful."

He came to stand at her side. "I've spent the last ten minutes admiring the shaped topiary."

"I thought you found the hustle and bustle of the city more appealing? The incessant noise, the fog-drenched streets, the constant stench from the river."

There was a long pause before he replied. "The city keeps me busy. Dealing with other people's problems, helps me to forget about my own."

She understood that. "My work is the reason I've remained sane these last three years. I had no time to think about the mysterious intruder. But then maybe that is not a good thing. We cannot use work to run away from our problems."

Daniel stared deep into her eyes. "You know, don't you?"

Daphne cleared her throat. "Know what? That you're the son of the Marquess of Pulborough? That you own a country estate but choose to rent a townhouse in London?" That you're running away from your past, she added silently.

He squeezed his eyes shut and inhaled deeply. "Yes."

While Lavinia's story sounded convincing, hearing Daniel's confirmation sent Daphne's heart racing. That one word proved powerful. Perhaps now he would be more open. But she didn't want to press him further, didn't want to bombard him with questions.

A distraction was needed. A means to pull him out of his black mood.

She placed her hand on his chest, and he opened his eyes. His heart was beating so hard she could feel it pounding against her palm. "Do you want to talk about this now?" With a quick glance at the bed, she smiled. "The only problem with leaving early is that we'll never know what it's like to sleep next to one another in such a large bed."

A sinful smile replaced his grim expression. "That is one problem we can rectify." He bent his head and kissed her softly on the lips.

The slow, sweet melding of mouths caused her desire for him to burst to life in her belly. The warm tickling sensation soon spread. Needing something more to ease the ache in her chest, her tongue penetrated his mouth, brushed against his gently at first.

Daniel wrapped a strong arm around her, pulled her tight to his chest and devoured her mouth with a hunger that stole her breath.

"Lock the door," she panted breaking contact. "Quick. Hurry."

He smiled, kissed her once more and then strode to the door and turned the key. "What's the rush, love? We have hours until dinner. I'm determined to study every inch of your naked body. All in the name of science, of course."

Oh, he was so different now than when she'd first entered the room. Relaxed and carefree, his countenance was so bright it was almost blinding. This was the man she loved, the man she adored.

The thought forced her to jerk her head back in surprise. She loved him. Good Lord. Her heart swelled in confirmation. She loved him.

Daniel beckoned her over to the bed. "If you're going to stand there gaping, this experiment may run into the night."

A nervous chuckle escaped from her lips. It had nothing to do with his amusing comment and everything to do with the feeling of hope that sprang to life in her breast.

He held out his hand by way of a prompt, and she ran into his arms, eager to rejoice, to celebrate the wonderful feeling inside.

"I can't wait to touch your skin," she said as he ran kisses along the line of her jaw, leaving a hot molten trail in their wake. She tilted her head as he nipped at the sensitive spot below her ear. "I can't wait to feel your hard body pressing me down into the mattress."

Daniel growled. "Damn, love, keep talking like that, and this will be over before I've unbuttoned my waistcoat."

"Then undress me." It was like her addiction for him had found its own voice.

"Undress you? I'm so impatient I'm liable to tear the dress from your body." He spun her around, ran his hand over her back. "Where the hell are the buttons?"

She giggled, the sound of an innocent young woman, not someone whose world had been tainted by all the terrible things she'd witnessed. "They're at the side." She turned back to face him and raised her arm to reveal the row of small pearl buttons. "Betsy made this dress for me."

"Does she not know that a man struggles to say his own name when consumed with desire?" He held out his hands, and she noticed them tremble. "Do they look like nimble fingers to you? Even a child would struggle to open such tiny fastenings."

"Then allow me." Holding his greedy gaze, she undid the buttons, dragged the dress over her head and stood before him in her petticoat. She threw the garment at him, and he caught it with ease.

"I'll have your undergarments, too."

Daphne enjoyed playing temptress. All her married life, she'd felt so hopelessly inadequate. She unthreaded the cords of her petticoat, lifted that over her head and threw it, too. This time she aimed for his face and laughed when it covered his head like a veil.

"I think I can tackle the stays," he said, throwing her clothing onto the chair by the bed. He stepped forward. His fingers grasped the end of the cord and pulled gently. Poking one finger through the laces, he tugged until they were all free of the eyelets. He pushed the straps off her shoulders, his hands skimming her breasts in the process.

Daphne sucked in a breath. "For a man with large hands, you're incredibly tender." Her skin tingled in response. Blood pounded in her ears as loud as thunder. Her erect nipples pressed against the thin fabric of her chemise, eager for his touch.

Wearing a wicked grin, Daniel knelt before her. "Now for the moment I've imagined many times over the years." He clutched the hem of her chemise, slid the garment up over her thighs, over the curve of her hip, higher still.

"You must forgive me," he whispered, holding her chemise at her waist. "The need to taste you is too great." He buried his face in the hair at the apex of her thighs, his tongue pushing between the folds.

Lord above!

The action sent a jolt of pleasure shooting to the tips of her toes. She choked down her embarrassment, parted her legs to give him easier access.

"Daniel ... I ... heavens." She stumbled back and fell onto the bed. Grabbing the ends of her chemise, she dragged it over her head and threw it onto the floor.

"Bloody hell," he hissed between clenched teeth. "You're so damn beautiful."

For a woman who'd never shown a man her naked body, she was surprisingly calm.

"What about my stockings?"

"Leave them on."

He settled between her thighs, the tongue that was just as skilled as the rest of him continued to tease her, to lick and suck the tiny bud. Lord, she could not wait to take this man into her body, to feel full, stretched tight.

"Undress for me," she managed to say, though struggled to relinquish her grasp of his hair, to stop thrusting her hips up to meet his wicked mouth.

Daniel jumped up, fumbled with the buttons on his waist-coat, practically ripped the shirt as he yanked it over his head.

Her wide eyes feasted on the impressive breadth of his chest, on the bulging muscles in his arms. But then she noticed the wound. On his upper arm, the skin was red and swollen. The graze was oval in shape, a brighter red.

"You were lucky," she said, a sudden sense of panic taking hold as she pointed to the inflamed area that was sure to leave a scar.

"Had I not been wearing such a thick coat the damage would have been far worse."

Swallowing deeply as his gaze travelled down the length of her body, he undid the buttons on his breeches. When his solid manhood sprang free, Daphne gulped. The muscles in her core pulsed in anticipation.

She shuffled a little closer to the end of the bed and beckoned him closer. The cool air breezed across her sensitive nipples just to add to her torment.

Stepping out of his breeches, he climbed onto the bed and settled on top of her aching body. Daphne wrapped her legs around him tight, determined to anchor him there for all eternity.

The feel of his warm skin against hers flamed her desire. With eager hands she caressed the hard planes on his back, arched and grasped his buttocks when he entered her in one long, fluid movement.

The deep groan resonating from the back of his throat was music to her ears. He kissed her, withdrew almost fully before pushing slowly back inside.

"Hmmm…" The soft sound of satisfaction left her lips as he buried himself deep. She could feel the coil inside tightening, pulling her towards her release. She liked it slow. Liked watching the satisfaction etched on his face when she sheathed his thick shaft and held him there.

"Lord knows what we'll do once we're back in London," he said, thrusting a little quicker, grinding his hips to rub against her intimate place.

"What … what do you mean?" Waves of pleasure rippled through her body.

"This needs to be … to be a regular occurrence," he panted, pumping harder now. Trickles of sweat ran down his back. The bed creaked from the sudden urgency that drove them. "Damn it all, Daphne. Loving you makes life worth living."

Loving her? Did he mean joining with her in bed?

Before her mind could dissect and probe his statement, he rubbed against her once more, and she exploded around him. Her legs shook as she panted for breath. Her whole body sang his tune.

"We'll have to … have to do this again," she said, as he filled her over and over. She gripped his buttocks to prolong the moment. "We can try other positions … purely … to satisfy our experiment."

"Precisely." The word was accompanied by a guttural groan. "Relax your grip. I need to withdraw."

She had failed to conceive in the two years she'd been married to Thomas. Then again, intimate moments were rare and had always been beneath a mound of sheets and under the cover of darkness.

"Tell me you want me," he said, slowing his pace and holding the base of his shaft as he pulled himself free of her body.

"I have never wanted anything more." It suddenly occurred to her that a man born on the wrong side of the blanket would not wish to repeat history. Daniel Thorpe would not want to father a child out of wedlock. In a moment of fancy, she pushed at his chest. "Sit up."

"What?"

"Sit up."

"Why?" He came up on his knees, and she did, too. Without considering her lack of experience, she bent her head and took the man she loved into her mouth. The sensation was oddly liberating. She felt in control as she mimicked the motion of their joining.

"Your mouth is divine." He caressed her back in soothing strokes as his hips jerked violently. "Stop now, love."

But she ignored him. Continued pleasuring him until his seed burst into her mouth, wet and warm. He shook from the power of it, stilled and gasped for breath as the tremors subsided.

Daphne sat up and moistened her lips. For a woman who lacked experience when it came to passionate encounters, she was quite pleased with herself.

"You did not have to do that," he said, still struggling for breath.

"Did you not enjoy the experience?"

"Enjoy it? I've never felt anything so damn good."

"Excellent." She drank in the look of contentment on his face. Tried to ignore the faint battle scars on his shoulder and chest. Nothing would spoil this moment of utter bliss. "Now you can do something for me."

He raised an arrogant brow. "I thought I just did."

Daphne gazed at him. The overwhelming sense of love and longing in her chest must surely be apparent. "Lie with me. Hold me in your arms. Let's forget about the rest of the world for a while."

"By now you must know I would do anything you asked," he said, taking her hand and lying down next to her on the bed.

She turned to face him and buried her head in his chest. With his strong arms wrapped around her she closed her eyes, drew comfort from the smell of his unique scent.

Daniel Thorpe was her match in every way. Why had she not seen it before?

CHAPTER 20

IT WAS ONE O'CLOCK IN THE MORNING WHEN DANIEL'S conveyance rumbled to a halt outside the modiste shop on New Bond Street. After yet another passionate interlude in his carriage, they'd spent more than half the journey asleep. Daniel turned to the woman whose head was resting on his shoulder. The soft, rhythmical sound of her breathing confirmed Daphne slept so deeply she had not realised the vehicle had stopped.

He watched her for a moment, marvelled at the rise and fall of her chest, in the warmth flooding his body whenever he stopped and acknowledged the depth of his feelings.

Once they'd gained a confession from Lord Gibson—which Daniel did not expect to be an easy task—his mind would be free to consider what to do about the captivating lady at his side.

The physical relationship they shared had done nothing to ease his craving. But why would it? He'd fallen in love with Daphne the first night he met her. The intense longing had sparked to life in his chest as he watched her enjoy the opera. Despite lengthy times apart, his feelings never changed. It was the reason he avoided the couple during their two-year marriage.

"Are … are we home?" Daphne sat up, rubbed her eyes,

stretched her arms and craned her neck. "How long have I been asleep?"

"Since you fell back in the seat exhausted from our recent activities," he said, unable to prevent the smile forming.

He could not recall another time in his life when he'd felt so elated. Yet they could not continue like this. They'd been careful up till now. But it was only a matter of time before he lost himself in her body. The last thing he wanted was to father a child out of wedlock.

"Being cramped in a carriage forces one to work a little harder," she replied with a giggle.

God, he loved seeing her smile. She looked so happy now compared to the first night she'd let him into her parlour to explain about the theft.

"It did not seem to bother you at the time." Daniel glanced out of the window at the modiste shop. "Do you think Betsy will be in bed? The place is in darkness."

"Not if she's behind in her work. But we'll be quiet, just in case."

"We?" Daniel grinned. "Does that mean you're inviting me inside?"

Daphne leant forward and pressed three soft kisses on his mouth. "I assumed you'd stay the night."

Damn. His cock pulsed to life at the erotic image her words evoked. "I suppose we do need to decide how to tackle Lord Gibson."

They'd both narrowly escaped death during this investigation. Their lives were still in danger. Yet it was the case of seduction that occupied his thoughts.

"Then come inside," she whispered softly. "We can devise a plan while you rub the knot in my neck."

"You know as soon as I touch you my mind turns to mush." By the time they eventually got down to the matter of business, the traitor would have fled to France. And he still hadn't visited

Mr Reynolds. It was not like him to be so lax. "We'll discuss the plan first else I doubt we'll ever solve this damn case."

With no sign of light coming from the parlour, they crept through the house and up the stairs. The faint hum of silence convinced him the modiste was in bed though he expected Bostock was hiding somewhere in the shadows waiting to pounce. The boards on the landing creaked every time they took a step no matter where they placed their feet.

"These boards are as noisy as the bed at Elton Park," he whispered.

"My bed's not noisy, but it's not nearly as comfortable," she replied as she opened the door to the small parlour and stepped inside. "And as it only half the size—ouch!"

"Hush."

"What the devil!" She knelt down and felt about in the darkness. "The chair is upturned and blocking my path."

"We need to light a candle." Daniel squinted and scoured the room. It took a few seconds for his eyes to grow accustomed to the scene of devastation before him. The odd grey shapes on the floor amounted to broken furniture, strewn garments, the contents of drawers.

"Good Lord!" Daphne cried as she gazed upon what looked like a mound of rubbish and not one's prized possessions.

"Hold your bloody hands up high where I can see them." Bostock's gruff voice boomed through the room as he cocked a pistol.

Daniel froze as Bostock dug the end of the barrel into his back. "I'd think twice before you shoot lest you'll be out of a job."

"Thorpe? Is that you?"

"We've come home early, Mr Bostock," Daphne said, turning slowly to face his associate. The tremor in her voice spoke of her anxiety at discovering the shambles in the parlour. "What on earth happened here?"

"There's been a robbery."

"I can see that," Daphne countered.

"For-forgive my disgraceful appearance, Mrs Chambers," Bostock stuttered. "Had I known it was you I would have worn a shirt."

With his hands held high Daniel turned, too. One did not need the luxury of a candle to see that his man was barely dressed. "Do you normally keep watch wearing nothing but your breeches?" Daniel said, lowering his hands. "Does it not get a little chilly?"

Bostock mumbled to himself and eventually said, "A man has to sleep."

"Indeed." Daniel inhaled the sweet smell of jasmine lingering in the air. It was not Daphne's scent. He would know her potent fragrance anywhere. "And is it necessary to wear a woman's perfume while carrying out the task?"

Bostock bent his head and sniffed at his bare shoulder. "I've been helping Miss Betsy sort out the dressing room. Smells like a ladies' boudoir in there."

Daphne gave a disgruntled sigh. "Will one of you gentlemen please light a candle. In case it has escaped your attention, my home has been ransacked."

"Of course," Daniel said apologetically. He looked at Bostock. "Does the modiste have a lit candle in her room?"

Bostock nodded. "Miss Betsy's kept one burning by her bedside tonight. Since finding the mess in here, she's frightened to sleep."

Daniel suppressed a grin. How did Bostock know what Miss Betsy did in her bedchamber? He was about to suggest Bostock fetch the candle when the floorboard creaked, and a golden glow appeared in the doorway.

"Daphne? Are you home?" Wearing a dressing gown and a shawl wrapped around her shoulders, Betsy padded barefoot into the room. She handed Bostock the brass candle holder and grabbed Daphne's hands. "Oh, forgive me. I wanted to tidy up the mess, but George—" She stopped abruptly and cleared her throat. "Mr Bostock said I was not to touch a thing."

"Mr Bostock is right, Betsy. Thorpe and I will want to observe things exactly as the thief left them."

"Would you hold the candle aloft, George," Daniel said with some amusement as he stressed the use of his friend's given name, "so we might gaze upon the devastation."

Bostock nodded and raised the light.

Daphne sucked in a sharp breath and put her hand to her chest.

Daniel came to stand at her side as he surveyed the room. The oak dresser was upturned, the drawers scattered across the floor. Stuffing from the slashed seats on the sofa lay dotted about the place. Broken gilt frames from the paintings, feathers from ripped cushions, and numerous items of clothing created a scene of chaos and disorder.

This was not a robbery.

The culprit was looking for something—proof as to the identity of the traitor.

"It's the same in the bedchamber," Bostock said solemnly.

"Everything is ruined." Daphne's high-pitched tone conveyed her distress. "The landlord will expect me to replace anything that's damaged. I'll have to work day and night for months."

Daniel put his hand on her arm. "You have no need to worry about money."

She smiled at him albeit weakly. "I suppose we could make a list of repairs as we tidy up. But where on earth shall we start?"

"I'm sure I can repair the sofa and cushions," Betsy said.

"And a nail and hammer should right the picture frames," Bostock added.

Daphne turned to them. "You're both very kind."

"As you've not apprehended the man responsible," Daniel said, "I assume neither of you were here when it happened."

Bostock shook his head. "We went to an inn for supper." Guilt flashed across his face. "You never said anything about staying indoors."

Daniel raised a hand to ease his friend's fears. "I am simply trying to establish what time this occurred. Someone must have been watching the house."

The person hired to monitor their movements must have sat outside for hours. Such a determined effort spoke of desperation.

"How long were you gone?" Daniel asked.

Bostock glanced at the modiste and shrugged. "More than an hour. Two at most."

Lord Gibson's house was but a ten-minute walk. There would have been plenty of time for him to enter the shop, search the rooms and leave unnoticed. Daniel made a mental note to speak to the pawnbroker. The man had an eye for detail and monitored all the comings and goings on the street.

"And I trust your rooms were untouched?" Daniel directed his question to Miss Betsy.

Betsy nodded.

"It is no surprise that I am the target," Daphne said with an air of despondency. With a vacant stare and down-turned mouth, she appeared so different from the vibrant woman he'd witnessed at Elton Park.

"I promise you this will all be over soon." The anger in his voice was evident. Not since the death of his mother, had he felt so damn helpless. "Come the morning I shall expend time and energy finding the person responsible."

Betsy cleared her throat. "Why don't I go downstairs and make some tea?" She looked up at Bostock. "Come on, Mr Bostock, you can help me. Let us leave them to their work, and then we can help with the repairs."

Betsy took Bostock by the hand, but he waited for Daniel's

nod of approval before placing the candle holder on the small dining table and leaving the room.

"Oh, Daniel," Daphne said with a weary sigh once they were alone. "Will this nightmare ever end?"

He pulled her into an embrace, caressed her back, stroked her hair, whispered words of comfort. When she looked up at him, the sorrow in her eyes tore at his heart. He tried to kiss her worries away but the intense passion they shared only sought to distract them from the work that lay ahead.

With some reluctance, Daniel dragged his lips from hers. "If we have any hope of solving this case, we must do our utmost to focus. One kiss and all sense and logic abandon me."

She smiled though her eyes were red, a little watery. "When I'm with you I find it hard to concentrate, too." She sucked in a determined breath and squared her shoulders. "But we are nothing if not professional, and so let us pay closer attention. Let us put every ounce of strength we have into solving this quickly."

"Agreed." Daniel was relieved to see her smile again. "What is your opinion of what happened here?"

Daphne stepped back and scanned the room. "This is the work of the traitor made to look like a robbery," she said confidently.

"And how do you know?"

"Because a thief would not slash the seat of a sofa. A thief wouldn't rip apart cushions. In my professional opinion, the traitor is looking for the evidence Thomas mentioned." She put her finger to her lips and tapped gently. "I can only assume that he knows we are working together. That he fears we are close to discovering his identity and so is searching for the only thing he believes is proof of his duplicity."

"Then we are of the same opinion," he said, his chest swelling with admiration, pride, and love for the woman standing before him. "Now I want you to think carefully. If such a piece of evidence exists where would Thomas have hidden it?"

After a few silent seconds, she shook her head. "We sold everything we owned to pay his father's debt from the failed shipping venture. We sold the paintings, all the books in the library, bar one. I've moved house so many times, all I truly own are the clothes on my back."

Daniel rubbed his temple as he tried to think. "Did Thomas say anything to you that seemed odd? Anything that seemed trivial?"

"No." Daphne frowned. "He joked about his favourite book being the only thing of value he had left. The night he died he made a strange comment about it."

"The night he died?" Surely it could not be a coincidence. "And you did not think to mention it to me before?"

"It was something said in passing," she said defensively. "An expressed opinion, nothing more."

"What did he say?"

"He spoke of Shakespeare's wisdom. That his work was for all time. That studying the text provides insight into today's society not just that of the past." She shrugged. "As I said it was an odd thing to say."

"You must have said something to prompt the conversation."

"No. It was while he was dressing to go out."

"Well, we must examine everything that occurred on the night Thomas died." Daniel stared at the damaged furnishings. "Did you say you kept the book after he'd died?"

Daphne nodded. "Yes, it was on my night stand. Thomas mentioned your love of Shakespeare, too. He spoke about gifting you the book, said you would appreciate the sentiment."

Daniel jerked his head back. "I have no love of Shakespeare. Thomas knew that. He knew I found some plots implausible." It was a debate they'd had many times. "We need to find the book."

"With any luck, it should still be in my bedchamber."

"Then help me lift the dresser to make a walkway." He gestured to the obstruction. Clambering over furniture in a dimly lit room had no appeal.

Daphne grabbed one side, and together they lifted it up onto its base.

As soon as Daphne opened the bedchamber door, she gasped. The bed sheets were in a crumpled heap on the floor next to the top mattress. The night table lay on its side, the glass candle lamp smashed to pieces.

"Stay where you are," Daniel instructed. "There are shards of glass all over the floor." The pieces crunched under his boots as he moved to straighten the table. He found the green leather-bound book underneath, picked it up and shook it.

Nothing fell out.

"Thank goodness." Daphne put her hand to her heart. "I think the fact it's still here confirms this was not a robbery. That book is worth five pounds."

Clutching the book to his chest, Daniel stepped over the strewn covers, and they moved into the parlour. After straightening the chairs, they sat at the table to study the pages in the candle light.

"If memory serves, *Julius Caesar* and *Macbeth* were his favourite tragedies." With the book laid flat on the table, Daniel flicked to *Macbeth.*

Daphne leant forward. "What are we looking for?"

"I have no idea."

He studied the pages to find nothing of interest. However, when he turned to *Julius Caesar*, one passage from *Act III* was underlined boldly in ink.

Daphne pointed at the marks. "Only certain words are highlighted."

Daniel tried to swallow down the hard lump in his throat. "I think you were supposed to give me this book three years ago."

The feeling of regret weighed heavily in his chest. "When read together, the words say, '*Then I ... fell down ... Whilst bloody treason flourish'd over us'.*"

"Good Lord." Daphne covered her mouth with her hand as she stared at the text. "He must have known his life was in danger. But why did he not confide in one of us? Why leave a clue in a book knowing we'd only find it once he was dead?"

But they hadn't found it once he was dead. They'd found it three years later. And this was not the only clue Thomas had left.

"I saw Thomas the week before he died." Daniel's stomach churned. Now he understood the relevance of his friend's flippant comment. "I was leaving Hobley's coffee house in Covent Garden as Thomas was entering. He made a comment about our school days, about the master's love for the birch. We laughed, but he put his hand on my shoulder and said that he'd come to learn that the master was right."

"Right about what?"

Daniel cursed inwardly. How could he have been so blind?

"On flogging day, the master quoted Cicero to those boys caught lying. It's a passage about treason and how an enemy at the gate is less formidable than the enemy within." A stab of guilt hit him in the chest. "Although you were not working as an enquiry agent at the time of his death, you've always had an inquisitive mind. Thomas must have presumed we would come together and discover the truth. Perhaps on that last night at the docks, he hoped to apprehend the traitor, hoped never to involve either of us."

The sound of Daphne's ragged breathing mirrored his feelings of frustration.

"Why is it we are both adept when it comes to solving other people's problems and so lacking when it comes to solving our own?"

"It is not your fault," Daniel said, as he recalled Lord Gibson had been drinking in Hobley's coffee house on that particular day, too. "You tried to tell me something was amiss, and I ignored you." After she'd refused his suit, he'd kept his distance, lacked the strength necessary to deal with rejection.

The thud of Bostock's heavy gait on the stairs drew Daniel's gaze to the parlour door.

Betsy appeared carrying a tea tray. "Sorry we were so long. We couldn't find a box to light the candle and didn't want to disturb you."

Daniel closed the book, and the modiste placed the tray on the table.

Betsy pursed her lips as she considered Daphne's forlorn expression. "Don't worry. We'll have this place cleaned up in no time. Won't we, Mr Bostock?"

"In no time at all," Bostock replied, looking far more respectable in a shirt.

"We'll begin with the bedchamber," Daniel said with a renewed sense of determination. "The parlour can wait. It's imperative we get some sleep tonight as we've a long day ahead of us."

While Daphne slept, Daniel would form a plan. Judging by the state of Daphne's apartments, the traitor was desperate to find the proof Thomas bragged about. They'd escaped death twice. Time was of the essence. And they were yet to locate the other man on the list, Captain Lewis.

CHAPTER 21

DESPITE THE URGE TO WATCH DAPHNE WASH, DRESS AND NIBBLE on her toast, Daniel gave her some privacy and moved into the parlour. Betsy had gathered the loose feathers into a basket and taken the cushions to her sewing room for repair. Judging by the loud banging coming from below stairs, Bostock had already set to work on the picture frames and broken drawers. A little more sweeping and the room would be presentable, almost as it was before.

Daniel yawned. He'd not slept a wink. Thoughts of the past came to haunt him. Daphne had not pressed for a more detailed explanation of his lineage since discovering he was the son of a marquess. But while he had no desire to recount the tragic tale, she deserved to know the truth.

"I've thought about it, and I'm not comfortable with you going to visit Lord Gibson alone." Daphne came to stand before him. "Can you not take Mr Bostock?"

Daniel sighed. "Bostock is to accompany you," he said, trying to ignore the heat from her palm when she placed her hand on his chest. "How many times must I tell you? Gibson is no match for me. I intend to ask a few questions that is all."

Only a fool would accuse a peer of murder and treason based on nothing more than a bottle of cologne and a pocket watch. Doubt crept in. As a spy, no doubt Lord Gibson possessed an inner strength that made him immune to a verbal attack. They would need more evidence if they hoped to gain a confession. Still, he'd prod the peer a little, follow him for a day or two in the hope he would make a mistake.

"It's likely Lord Gibson is responsible for what happened in the alley," Daphne said, struggling to maintain her composure. "Do not underestimate him, Daniel."

"Daphne, I've been working these streets for years." Admittedly, he had come close to losing his life on a number of occasions.

"Yes, and you almost died."

"It's a superficial wound and only occurred because my mind was engaged elsewhere. Had you not insisted on going to Elton Park, we'd have had no need to linger in the alley."

She raised a brow, and her lip curled. "And do you regret your decision to attend?"

He knew exactly what she was referring to. The memory of their passionate encounter in the bedchamber flooded his mind. "You know I don't regret a single second. I'd even partner Lavinia at dinner for the chance to spend an hour in a private room with you."

She smiled. "I can't help caring."

The comment touched him more than she would ever know. "I want you to care." He cupped her cheek. "But I need to work. Gibson must be held accountable if we've any hope of moving on with our lives."

She sighed. "Promise me you'll carry a weapon."

He gave a weak chuckle. "When on a case, I never leave home without one."

Daphne's gaze travelled over his face. "Whatever happens, I can't lose you."

"You won't." His heart swelled. It took all the strength he possessed not to confess his love, not to press her to explain the depth of her feelings, too. But a mind filled with tender thoughts was no good to either of them. Sentiment was the enemy of logic. And the longer he lingered, the harder it would be to leave.

"We'll meet back here this afternoon," he said, placing a chaste kiss on her lips. "Bostock will accompany you to the circulating library so you may return your book. Then you will stay with him while he makes discreet enquiries about Captain Lewis." Fearing she'd take the matter into her own hands should she discover any new information, he added, "We cannot presume Gibson is guilty. If you uncover anything of interest regarding the captain, you're to come straight home to discuss it with me."

She struggled to hold his gaze. "If we locate the captain, could I not simply strike up a conversation—"

"You'll do nothing without speaking to me," he snapped. Fear was the basis of his anger. He softened his tone. "I can't lose you either."

She pressed her warm lips to his cheek. "Then hurry home. Let's pray we confirm the identity of the traitor before this day is out."

Daniel inclined his head and strode towards the door. He stopped, turned to face her. "I hold Bostock personally responsible for your safety. Remember that, if curiosity gets the better of you."

Murphy dropped him at the house on Church Street and was to wait while Daniel shaved and changed his shirt. As a man who preferred to dress himself, eat in taverns and make his own damn bed, Daniel had no need for servants. Daphne was right.

Servants were a liability: loose-tongued, easily bribed. Indeed, the house was merely a place to store his clothes and to sleep.

Daniel was about to put the key in the lock when he noticed the scratches on the brass plate and hole. They were fresh. The mark of a tool used to pick locks.

With caution, he entered the premises. The drawing room was a shambles. Broken ornaments, pictures, even the decanter and glasses were scattered over the floor. In the study, there wasn't a book left on the shelves. The desk drawers were open, empty. No doubt the other rooms were the same.

He snorted to himself. The scoundrel would be lucky to find a scrap of bread in the house, let alone the evidence to convict him of treason. However, the fact someone had entered the house illegally raised a very important question. If Thomas' murderer had stalked Daphne for three years, why had he not stalked him? Why wait until now? Whoever it was must have only recently learnt of their connection.

Daniel was still contemplating that point while he changed his shirt. With a mind engaged in reconstructing Thomas' last movements, he nicked his chin while shaving. Thomas was a strong, healthy man. Whoever pushed him into the Thames, must have been of similar build and stature. He recalled seeing no defensive wounds on the body, so perhaps Thomas was caught unawares.

During the journey to Lord Gibson's house on Brook Street, Daniel rehearsed what he would say. Make no accusations, he told himself, though he already deemed Gibson guilty despite the logical part of his brain battling for him to remain impartial.

"I'm here to see Lord Gibson." Daniel spoke with confidence as he handed the butler his card.

The willowy figure kept him waiting at the door, his graceful movements conveying no sense of urgency.

"I'm afraid his lordship is otherwise engaged," the butler replied upon his return.

Daniel took a step closer. "Tell your master I have important news from the *Carron* that might interest him." When the butler opened his mouth to protest, Daniel added, "If you do not tell him, I shall barge my way in. I would prefer to deal with this like gentlemen. Tell Gibson I have news from the *Carron*."

"Show the gentleman in, Cuthers," a masculine voice boomed through the hall.

"Certainly, my lord." Cuthers stepped back for Daniel to enter. The butler took Daniel's hat and gloves and escorted him to the study. Gibson stood in front of his desk. The man was of medium height, average build with equally nondescript features. His dull brown hair lacked lustre. When questioned, it would be difficult to give an accurate description of the man, which no doubt proved useful in his line of work.

"Mr Thorpe." Gibson gave a curt nod. "While we have never met, I have heard good things about you."

Daniel inclined his head. "I only wish I could say the same about you, my lord."

Gibson did not appear fazed by the comment. He gestured to the chair in front of the desk. "Won't you sit down?"

They both took their respective seats, the large rosewood desk acting as a barrier.

"You say you're here to bring news from the *Carron*," Gibson reminded him. "May I ask how you know I have an interest in that particular vessel?"

"A man in my position stumbles upon all sorts of information." Daniel observed the lord's blank expression. He gave nothing away. "You keep a log, I hear. Of the times and dates the *Carron* has docked over the last three years."

"What of it?" Gibson tried to sound nonchalant, but his slight hesitation spoke of a hidden anxiety. Confusion flashed in his eyes if only for a second.

"You must know my friend, Thomas Chambers, made regular trips on the *Carron*. That his work for the Crown meant securing sensitive information and passing it to the appropriate authority."

"I am aware that Mr Chambers made regular business trips to France before he died," Gibson said in his monotone voice.

"And I am aware that you also share an interest in his business." It was a covert way of telling Gibson he knew he was a spy.

"Then you are an extremely informed man, Mr Thorpe." Gibson sat forward. "Let me advise you to keep that information close to your chest."

"Protecting the Crown is the responsibility of us all."

Gibson's shoulders relaxed. "I'm pleased you feel that way. Now, why are you here?"

The easiest way to catch a rat was to use bait.

"Thomas discovered there was a traitor among his colleagues. I believe he was murdered while confronting the suspect." Daniel spoke slowly, read the silent language of Gibson's every muscle twitch and eye movement. "The person responsible for his murder has spent the last three years secretly stalking his widow. All in a bid to find where Thomas hid the evidence of the blackguard's crimes."

"Evidence?" Gibson made no effort to hide his surprise. "Chambers had evidence naming the traitor?" The lord appeared thrilled rather than frightened. The reaction raised doubt over Lord Gibson's guilt.

"So I am led to believe."

"Then we must find this evidence as a matter of urgency." Again, his wide eyes conveyed excitement. "I must speak with Chambers' wife."

"Mrs Chambers is not in possession of the evidence. That I know for a fact. With all due respect, Thomas has been dead for three years. What good is the information now?" It was only worthwhile if the traitor was still operating.

"Acting on false information makes the Crown look foolish.

Wars are often fought based on nothing more than lies and manipulated facts. The person cannot go unpunished."

While the feeling in Daniel's gut said that Gibson was innocent, there were a couple of questions that needed answering.

"I was there the night Thomas was pulled from the Thames." Daniel had been tracking the movements of a gang of river pirates. "His pocket watch was missing. The item has never been recovered, but I've been told his murderer stole it and hid it somewhere."

Gibson narrowed his gaze but said nothing.

"I believe the same person has entered Mrs Chambers home numerous times in a bid to search for the evidence. While the intruder leaves no trace of his movements, he leaves a distinctive smell that is attributed to French cologne. Can you shed any light on the theory?"

Gibson narrowed his gaze.

A prolonged silence ensued.

"Then you should know that I am in possession of both items mentioned," Gibson eventually said as he brushed his hand through his hair and sighed. "I don't know why, but my instincts tell me I can trust you, Thorpe. But to repeat what I tell you now will be considered an act against the Crown."

Daniel nodded. "I understand. You have my word."

"The items you mentioned were sent to me in a box. Anonymously. It came with a note that said they belonged to Thomas Chambers. When we prised the back off the watch case, we found a tiny strip of paper containing various images though we have been unable to decipher them."

"Can you describe the images to me?" Daniel's throat grew tight. At school, Thomas had developed a secret language, a way of communicating messages without the master's knowledge. Years later, whenever responding to Daniel's letters, Thomas used the symbols purely as a means of amusement.

"I don't have the paper here. If you give me a day or two, I can ask permission to study it."

Judging by the devastation left in Daphne's apartment and at the house in Church Street, the traitor was growing more desperate by the minute.

"Very well." Daniel sighed.

Gibson rubbed his chin. "Do you think you might be able to decipher these images?"

"If they're what I think they are, then yes." His eagerness to translate the cryptic message burned in his chest. "Can you remember any of the symbols?" Even the first one would help.

"Let me think for a moment." Gibson pulled a leaf of paper from the desk drawer, dipped the nib of his pen into the ink well and scratched away. He crossed something out and tried again. "I recall this symbol was used twice in the first word."

Gibson turned the paper and pushed it across the desk.

Daniel leant forward, observed the small triangle with a tail curling from the bottom left point. His heart raced. The thumping in his temple proved distracting.

"And if memory serves," Gibson continued, "the second symbol looked like the pattern made by a bird hopping through snow."

Daniel struggled to maintain his composure, but pretended the heavy frown weighing down upon his brow was that of a man deep in thought. "Hmmm. Without seeing the symbols written together it's difficult to be certain," he lied. To reveal his suspicions now would be a mistake. "It would be lapse of me to make a judgement when one wrong flick of the pen might convey a different meaning entirely."

"I understand."

Daniel stood. "Send word to the address on my card when you receive the document." The urge to leave was too great to sit and partake in unnecessary conversation.

Lord Gibson cleared his throat. "As it is a question of

national security, I must ask how you came to know of my involvement in such matters."

"All will become clear when I return." Daniel inclined his head. He would discover the truth about Thomas' killer before the government could intervene. Once he'd spoken to Daphne, he'd visit the ship chandler. Based on the information given by Gibson, he suspected the first word spelt Lily.

CHAPTER 22

"WOULD YOU MIND IF WE STOPPED HERE?" DAPHNE TAPPED MR Bostock on the arm and gestured to the quaint book shop. "I'll be no more than a few minutes."

Mr Bostock glanced back over his shoulder and then up at the shop's facade. "I don't see as it can hurt."

"I doubt I'll make a purchase," Daphne said as Mr Bostock opened the door and stepped back for her to enter. "But there's something comforting about the smell of books. I could sit in a chair and read all day, time and money permitting."

"Well, I've never seen the attraction myself." Mr Bostock frowned as he scanned the rows upon rows of books lining every available wall space. The varying hues of the bound covers: reds, golds and greens, reminded Daphne of an autumn scene.

"But you do read?"

"I can read if that's what you're asking. Thorpe taught me everything I need to know to get by." His expression turned solemn, and he heaved a sigh. "Without Thorpe's guidance, I'd be robbing pies from the market, not dressed in finery and dining with ladies."

The men had formed a close bond over the years. Any fool could see that.

"And without you, he might have been beaten to a pulp the night you met."

Mr Bostock snorted. "Oh, he'd have saved himself somehow. He always does."

Daphne truly hoped that was the case as she couldn't imagine a life without Daniel now. "Have you ever been to Rainham Hall?" she said casually, feigning interest in a selection of books near the door.

Mr Bostock's mouth fell open, and he blinked rapidly. "You know about that?"

"Yes, though I don't understand why Mr Thorpe lives in the city when he has such a beautiful home in the country." Why did he move from place to place, never really having anywhere to call home?

"Perhaps it's because he has a point to prove." Mr Bostock shrugged. "Or maybe the big house reminds him too much of the past."

Or maybe he didn't know how to stop running.

"Do you think there'll ever come a time when he'll live at Rainham Hall?" Daphne hoped he would. But he enjoyed his work, and as he'd said himself, people in the shires had no need for an enquiry agent.

Mr Bostock shook his head. "Can't see him ever leaving the city while you're still here."

"Me?" Daphne put her hand to her chest. "Thorpe has hardly spoken a word to me these last few years. Had we not worked together to help Lord Harwood, I doubt he'd be speaking to me now."

The thought caused a sharp pain in her chest. Things were so different since they'd been working together. But once they'd discovered who murdered Thomas, what then? Perhaps he would agree to a business partnership. It would make working cases far more appealing.

"Just because you don't speak to him, doesn't mean he's not there," Mr Bostock replied. "He knows about your cases, always intervenes when necessary."

Daphne drew her head back. "Intervenes?" The word burst from her lips. The few people milling about the shop turned to stare. "What do you mean?" she whispered.

Mr Bostock shuffled uncomfortably. "It's not for me to say."

Daphne placed a hand on her hip. "Mr Bostock, you will explain the comment."

He muttered something to himself. "Don't say I was the one who told you."

"You have my word."

"My objective is always to keep you safe," he said defensively. "Like the night you were searching Mr Mason's office looking for proof his client had exaggerated his wealth."

"What of it?" The Suttons had heard rumours about their prospective son-in-law and hired Daphne to prove the man was nought but a fortune hunter. "Nothing untoward happened that evening."

Mr Bostock offered a weak grin. "Mr Mason came back to the office while you were still inside. My job was to stall him so you could make your escape without being seen."

Daphne could barely catch her breath. "And how long have you been offering your assistance?"

The poor fellow glanced at his boots. "For more than two years. But I've only had to help a few times."

"I see." Her cheeks flamed. Daniel must have thought her a fool for boasting of her ability to care for herself.

"He cares about you that's all," Mr Bostock said in Daniel's defence. "The last thing he would want to do is hurt you."

"But he should have been honest with me." Daphne wanted

to be annoyed with Daniel, but his actions had nothing to do with control or needing to belittle her efforts. It had nothing to do with him thinking her incapable. She knew it was because he cared.

Mr Bostock met her gaze. "And if he'd have told you, what would you have done?"

"I have no idea." She would have cursed him to the devil. Been more secretive. Varied her route in an attempt to lose his associate. "Well, I came in here to look at books not spend the morning discussing Mr Thorpe." She leant closer. "The Gothic horrors are up those three stairs, hidden at the back. I only want to browse through the collection." And read a few pages of any that took her fancy.

"Take a few minutes, and then we'd best be on our way." Bostock folded his arms across his chest. "I'll wait here."

Daphne left him to stare out of the window. Perhaps he thought perusing books meant he had to buy one. After offering the shopkeeper a warm smile, Daphne climbed the small flight of stairs at the rear of the shop. Had she been alone, she would have sat at one of the tables and passed a few hours, her mind lost in the fanciful tales.

"Mrs Chambers." The whispered words drifted past her ear. "Mrs Chambers."

Daphne glanced at Mr Bostock who was still watching the people passing by the window.

"Mrs Chambers."

Daphne looked back over her shoulder. The door leading out to the back yard was ajar. She walked over, was but an inch away when a woman grabbed her by the hand.

"Thank goodness you heard me." The petite woman appeared highly agitated.

"Miss Lawson?" Daphne narrowed her gaze. Lily Lawson wore a pretty bonnet and fashionable pelisse. "I hardly recognised you. What on earth are you doing out here?"

"There's no time to talk. We must leave now. Heavens. Please listen."

The woman was rambling.

"I fear Mr Thorpe is in grave danger," Lily added. "I should never have given you the list."

"Thorpe? Does this have something to do with Lord Gibson?"

"Lord Gibson cannot be trusted." She tugged Daphne by the arm. "Come. I have a hackney waiting. If we do not hurry, Mr Thorpe is sure to face the same fate as Thomas."

All the air dissipated from Daphne's lungs. "Then let me fetch Mr Bostock, Thorpe's associate. He's here with me and will know what to do."

Daphne turned, but Lily refused to relinquish her grip.

"You will leave with me now, Mrs Chambers." The click of metal drew Daphne's gaze to the pistol pointed at her stomach. "Don't test my patience. Besides, if I shoot you, how will you be able to rescue Mr Thorpe?"

CHAPTER 23

DANIEL RACED BACK TO NEW BOND STREET. FINDING THE front door of the shop locked, he rapped several times. Panic flared. Betsy had said nothing about going out. He waited and rapped again.

The shuffling of feet on the tiled floor in the hall beyond caught his attention. "It's Mr Thorpe, Betsy," he said when the footsteps stopped and he sensed the modiste's hesitation.

"Good Lord," Betsy cried as she peeked around the jamb. "Give a lady a chance to reach the door." She ushered him inside. "You'll bring the house down if you knock any louder."

His thunderous bangs on the door mirrored the wild thud of his heart. Since discovering it was Lily's name on the strip of paper, he'd been forced to acknowledge his error. Lily played the victim as well as any consummate actress gracing the stage. He should have followed her, gathered more information before tearing off to Witham on a fool's errand.

"Do you normally close the shop during the daytime?" he snapped.

"No, but with all the commotion this week I'm behind on my

224

work. I closed the shop so we could concentrate on Lady Balthrome's trousseau."

The sound of feminine voices carried through from the parlour. "Has Mrs Chambers returned?" He craned his neck and stared down the corridor.

"No, not yet. But George ... Mr Bostock said they're calling at the circulating library and knowing Daphne she'll take hours to choose a book."

"Is there someone here with you?" Suspicion formed the basis of all his thoughts now. Of course, there was every chance the message on the paper was a warning for Lily and not a means of naming her as the traitor. "I assumed you worked alone."

"Alone?" Betsy gasped. "Heavens, no. I have a contact in Spitalfields who hires girls by the hour. But I only use the service when I have to."

"I see." Daphne had said nothing about having strangers on the premises. Along with means and motive, opportunity was a key factor necessary for a person to commit a crime. "And you're happy to vouch for the women you have working with you today?" He would take a list of their names later once he'd spoken to Daphne.

Betsy appeared a little confused. "I've worked with them all numerous times if that's what you're asking."

He wasn't sure what he was asking. "Then I'll trouble you no further. I'm sure Mrs Chambers won't mind if I wait for her upstairs."

"I'm sure Mrs Chambers won't mind you anything." Betsy gave a coy grin.

There was nothing he could say to that, and so he inclined his head and walked away. He supposed he could make an amusing comment about Bostock, but he had more important things on his mind.

The high-pitched voices drew his attention back to the

parlour. This time they were loud enough for him to make out the odd string of words. The women were discussing which one of them would make tea, and it brought to mind his earlier thought that a seamstress had the freedom of the house.

"Just a question if I may, Betsy," he said, turning back to the modiste. "Do you choose the girls you hire or are they sent to you?"

"Mr Buchanan decides who to send. If I find their skills are poor, I can request he not send them again. But I've only done that once before."

"And are the girls you employ free to roam the house?"

Betsy frowned. "Oh, there's usually too much to occupy them down here. We tend to work together in one room. Except when one of us nips to the kitchen to make tea." Betsy pursed her lips. "Why, is something wrong?"

To search Daphne's room thoroughly, the intruder would need more than the ten minutes it took to boil water.

"I'm simply trying to establish if one of your seamstresses could have entered Mrs Chambers' room unnoticed."

Betsy shook her head and scrunched her nose. "But why would they want to do that?"

"Just humour me." Daniel sighed. "So you're saying no one would have had time to explore the upper floor?"

"Well, no. When you pay by the hour, you tend to keep a close eye on what they're doing. The only time I've ever let a girl into my private room was when one pricked her finger on a needle and fainted."

He imagined such a mishap was a regular occurrence. "And this was when?"

Betsy shrugged. "A few weeks ago."

"And did you leave her alone?"

"Yes, she slept for almost an hour. The rest of us had to work our fingers to the bone to make up for lost time."

Daniel dragged his hand down his face. "Let me guess. Was this girl petite, with golden hair and an angelic face?"

"Why, yes." A smile touched Betsy's lips, and she nodded. "The other girls thought we were twins."

Bloody hell!

In all his years as an enquiry agent, he'd never been duped to this degree. Lily had batted her eyelashes and offered a pretty pout all in the hope of throwing them off the scent. Daniel had to give the woman some credit. Even he'd been convinced by her protestations.

The sudden thud on the front door startled them both.

Betsy gasped. "Lord above. What is it with everyone today?"

"Open the damn door," Bostock cried. "Quick."

Betsy hurried over and had barely turned the key in the lock when the door burst open.

Bostock stood before them, his eyes bulging as he struggled to catch his breath. Perspiration trickled from his brow.

Daniel looked beyond his friend's shoulder, his heart ready to explode from his chest when he realised Bostock was alone.

"Where's Daphne?" Daniel marched over and gripped Bostock's arm. "Why isn't she with you?"

"I ... I don't know."

"You don't know!" Daniel shook the man's arm, desperate for an answer. "What the hell do you mean?"

"We were in the book shop. She wandered to the back shelves while I waited near the door." Bostock scratched his head and mumbled to himself. "I'd have seen her if she'd left the shop."

"Were you followed there?"

"No. Not that I noticed." Bostock's hands clenched into fists at his side. "I should have paid more attention. I should have stayed at her side. One minute she was there, the next she'd disappeared."

"People do not simply disappear," Daniel replied through clenched teeth.

Betsy moved to pat Bostock's arm. "Think, George," she said. While her eyes looked fearful, her voice was calm. "Did anyone speak to you? Did Daphne mention going anywhere else? Was there another exit that you failed to notice?"

Bostock shook his head. "No. There was a door leading to the back yard, but Mrs Chambers wouldn't have left without telling me. I'd have heard raised voices if someone had tried to lead her astray." Bostock turned to Daniel, his expression slack, his eyes dull. "I've let you down."

Feeling a wave of compassion, Daniel gripped his friend's shoulder. "It's not your fault, Bostock. We have been chasing our tails for the last few days. Looking in all the wrong places."

Indeed, he was just as much to blame. A man of his skill should have questioned Lily's word, but his thoughts were not his own. Love, an intense craving, and a profound sense of longing had captured him mind and body. The only puzzle he was interested in solving related to his future with Daphne.

Daniel let out a weary sigh and then straightened his shoulders. "You're to come with me to Wapping, Bostock." Daphne would not have left the shop with a man; he was convinced of it. Which meant Lily had lured her away from Bostock. "We have a traitor to catch."

"What about Captain Lewis?" Bostock asked. "We know nothing about his motives."

"He's not our man," Daniel replied with some certainty. "The list of names were just a ruse to throw us off the scent."

The sudden knock on the door sent a wave of relief surging through Daniel's body. Betsy rolled her eyes, but Daniel rushed to the door and flung it open.

"Daphne." The word died on his lips as he stared at the boy's dirty face.

"Are you Thorpe?"

Daniel nodded. "I am."

The boy thrust the note at him. "I've been told to give ya this."

As soon as Daniel's fingers gripped the paper, the boy ran off down the street. With a sense of trepidation, Daniel peeled back the folds and read the few lines written inside. Fear clutched him by the throat, the lack of air to his lungs making him dizzy.

"What is it?" Betsy hugged Bostock's arm, and they both stepped forward. "Is it news of Daphne?"

"Yes." Daniel took a moment to compose himself. He was no good to anyone if he let his emotions rule him. He needed the old Thorpe. The cold, detached gentleman who followed logic not his heart in cases such as these.

"Is she all right?" Betsy snivelled.

God, he hoped so. The world would feel the full wrath of the Devil if anything happened to her. "Lily Lawson is holding her at the docks. I'm to meet her there tonight at eight o'clock, in Lower Shadwell, south of the basin." He whipped his watch from his pocket and checked the time. He had hours to prepare.

"What can we do to help?" Bostock asked solemnly.

"I'm to go alone. Should Lily catch sight of anyone else she will kill Daphne."

Bostock squared his hunched shoulders. "But tell me you don't intend to do as she says?"

"I'm not sure what I'm going to do yet. I need time to form a plan."

CHAPTER 24

THE SHED WAS DARK, THE WOODEN FLOOR DUSTY. THE SCENT OF rum hung in the air, sweet yet sickly. A scurrying sound from somewhere in the far right-hand corner near the mound of old sacks caught Daphne's attention. She flexed her fingers though her hands were secured in front of her body by a pair of shackles, the words *Newgate Prison* stamped into the cold metal. The rope tied tightly around her ankles prevented her from pulling the knife from inside her boot, and so she could do nothing but sit and wait for Lily to return.

Lily Lawson had fooled them all. Poor Thomas. To discover his partner was a liar and cheat must have hurt him deeply. Yet he'd said nothing, given no indication of the stress he must have suffered as a result.

Daphne suppressed all feelings of guilt. Now was not the time to dwell on the past.

Lily had made no mention of her plans. Even so, her failure to provide food and water suggested Thomas wasn't to be the only victim on Lily's list. The fact that Daphne was still alive raised certain questions. Yet the answer always came back to the cryptic comment Lily made when she'd forced Daphne from the book shop.

If I shoot you, how will you be able to rescue Mr Thorpe?

What was her game? Was Thorpe her prisoner, too? Is that why she'd left Daphne in the shed and not returned? Regardless of the mess they'd made of the case so far, Thorpe was too clever to fall for Lily's tricks. Then again, the woman seemed comfortable playing a damsel in distress. And they had been so convinced of Lord Gibson's guilt they'd been blind to Lily's involvement.

Daphne closed her eyes.

The faint sound of lapping water reached her ears. But the absence of muffled voices or the rumble of a cart proved worrying. She listened for a while, was still wondering if anyone would find her in the musty old shed when the rattle of a key in the lock drew her gaze to the door.

The glow from the lantern held aloft illuminated the person's face.

"Good evening, Mrs Chambers." Lily came into the room, placed the lantern on the floor and pulled the pistol from the leather satchel slung over her shoulder beneath her cloak. "Thank heavens for safety catches." She pointed the pistol at Daphne. "I trust you've not been too cold in here."

"Have you come to kill me?" Daphne's tone brimmed with contempt. She had no desire to partake in meaningless conversation.

"Kill you? Oh, I can't kill you yet," Lily said with a snort. Her once sweet voice was filled with bitterness and loathing. "You're the bait."

"Bait?" Daphne stared at Lily's face. It had lost its angelic appeal. Now Daphne had glimpsed the rotten core inside, the rest proved equally unappetising.

"Surely you don't imagine I could drag Mr Thorpe here for any other reason than to save you? With his lack of options, I'm hoping that logical brain of his will soon realise he has but two choices. Either I'll persuade him to join me, or I'll use you as bait to kill him."

The words conjured a vision of Daniel lying lifeless in the water.

"There is no need for any of this," Daphne pleaded. She wasn't afraid to beg if necessary. She'd sell her soul to save Daniel's life. "Despite what Thomas told you, he had no evidence you were the traitor. We've searched high and low and found nothing."

"Thomas was too clever to make idle threats. He'd been monitoring my movements for weeks, knew I was selling information to the French and lying to the Crown." There was a hint of admiration in Lily's tone when she spoke of Thomas. "I offered him many incentives to join me." From the seductive lilt in Lily's voice, the woman had used her charms to tempt him. "The man was loyal to a fault which was to his detriment in the end."

A sudden wave of sadness swept through Daphne, the emotion pooling at the base of her throat. Pride swelled in her chest for her husband, her friend. Thomas was a good man who deserved so much more. Despite Lily's devious plots, he had remained faithful to his wife, and to the Crown.

Daphne shuffled on the cold, hard floor. "Did you care about Thomas at all?"

Lily took a step closer, bent down and stared into Daphne's eyes. "Care about him? I loved him. Despite the fact he didn't love you, he refused to love me in return."

Perhaps Lily expected the comment to shock. But regardless of the other problems Daphne had in her marriage, they'd always been honest.

"We loved each other," Daphne corrected. Thomas had been her dearest friend. "Only not in the way a husband and wife should." Not in the way she loved Daniel.

"We shared a kiss once," Lily boasted. "I knew then I had to have him and tried to persuade him to assist with my plan." With an ugly look of disdain, Lily's gaze travelled the length of Daphne's body. "But you always seemed to get in the way."

"A woman does not kill the man she loves," Daphne countered.

Lily jumped to her feet. "Do you think I wanted to see Thomas dead? I added a tincture to his ale, something said to loosen the tongue and banish inhibitions." She waved her pistol about mindlessly as she told her tale. "We walked along the wharf while he attempted to reason with me. Traitors hang, I told him, while I waited for his mood to mellow."

To hear of Thomas' final moments caused a host of horrifying images to flood Daphne's mind.

"And then you killed him because, in spite of your efforts to corrupt him, Thomas remained true to his cause."

Lily shrugged. "We argued. I pushed him, tried to grab his waistcoat when he tumbled back into the river but caught hold of his watch instead. The effects of the tincture took hold, and the cold water froze his muscles. I was forced to stand there and watch him drown."

Daphne's throat grew so tight she could barely breathe. Tears welled in her eyes. "You could have called for help. You could have saved him if you'd wanted to."

"Perhaps. Had my crimes carried the penalty of transportation it might have been a possibility. But we both know I'd have swung by the neck until dead." Lily gave an impatient huff, waved the pistol to gesture for Daphne to stand. "Now, get up. We're to meet your colleague, and we can't be late."

"You've tied the rope around my legs so tight it's impossible to stand." Daphne had tried numerous times but to no avail.

Lily reached into her satchel, removed a knife in a leather sheath and slid it across the floor. "Cut the ropes." She aimed her pistol at Daphne's head. "One wrong move and I will pull the trigger."

For a spy, the woman lacked logic.

Daphne raised her shackled hands. "And how am I supposed to do that?"

Lily scowled. "Hold the knife between your palms."

"It's in a sheath."

With another huff of impatience, Lily placed the pistol carefully on the floor, picked up the knife and pulled the blade free. Daphne watched Lily intently as she cut the fibres with a sawing motion. In a moment of fancy, Daphne imagined kicking the traitor to the floor once her legs were free. Imagined punching her hard with her clasped hands.

But Lily had nothing to lose. And Daphne knew the odds of escaping were slim. She stood a much better chance once they were outside.

Lily cut the bindings, recovered her pistol and dragged Daphne to her feet. The hours spent lying on the floor, and with the circulation to her toes restricted by the tight rope, it took a moment to keep her balance.

"You're to walk by my side," Lily said, threading her arm through Daphne's. "One word from you, or one move in the wrong direction and I'll shoot." Hiding the pistol beneath her cloak, Lily pressed the end of the barrel into Daphne's side. "This will blow a hole so big your innards will spill out onto the wharf."

Keep calm. Keep calm.

There would be ample opportunity to escape, Daphne told herself. For now, she would follow Lily's plan.

After blowing out the candle burning in the lantern on the floor, Lily escorted Daphne out of the shed and along the narrow wharf. The night was clear, the wind barely a whisper. The waning moon cast a modicum of light. There were other ramshackle buildings to the right—none of them occupied. To their left, the river looked like an inky black sheet of glass.

They'd walked for no more than a minute when a dark shadow appeared to block their path. From the shape of his shoulders and breadth of his chest, Daphne knew it was Daniel. He wore his over-sized greatcoat, the collar raised to his chin.

Lily hesitated, scanned the area and muttered a warning before stepping closer.

"Mr Thorpe, you will show me your hands, sir." Lily waved the pistol in Daniel's direction.

Daniel raised his hands slowly. "Allow Mrs Chambers to leave, and we'll talk."

"You know that is not possible," Lily sneered. "Now stop playing games. I trust you've used your time wisely and have managed to locate the proof of my duplicity."

"I have. I also spent my time interrogating Mr Brown, the pawnbroker. It seems you have an interesting relationship with the gentleman. How else would you have known of my involvement? How else would you have known our every move?"

Lily gave a hapless shrug. "Mr Brown will do anything to earn a shilling. He's been spying on Mrs Chambers for months."

Daphne swallowed down her surprise. No wonder the man had been so helpful. "And so that's how you knew when it was safe to enter my private rooms."

"That's not how she knew," Daniel replied. "She played the role of seamstress to gain Betsy's trust."

"I hoped to find the evidence Thomas spoke of," Lily replied. She focused her attention on Daniel. "Indeed, I hope you've had more success, Mr Thorpe."

"Let us just say I stumbled upon interesting information," Daniel said though Daphne suspected he was lying. Despite numerous conversations they'd shared on the topic, they'd found nothing to implicate Lily. "But if I give you the only evidence linking you to the crime, what then?" Daniel added.

"Then you have found it?" she asked not bothering to hide her desperation.

Daniel lowered his hands. "Answer my question first."

"Keep your hands high where I can see them. You are in no position to bargain."

"Oh, but I am." Daniel gave an arrogant smirk although Daphne could sense his unease. "Allow Mrs Chambers to step a few feet to your right, and I shall tell you what you want to know."

Lily looked at Daphne and hesitated. She pushed the barrel of the pistol into Daphne's side while she decided what to do.

"What if I told you that you'd held the proof of your involvement in your hand only to let it go?" Daniel continued by way of an incentive.

Lily frowned, but then recognition dawned. "The pocket watch?"

"Yes." Daniel nodded. "The one you sent to Lord Gibson hoping to convince us he was the traitor. That is why you gave us the paper with his name on it? With Danbury living in France, you knew we'd have no way of investigating his activities. Today, I discovered that Captain Lewis is in India, which no doubt you already knew."

In the hours Daphne had sat helplessly on the floor of a shed, Daniel had been extremely productive.

"What doesn't make any sense is the time frame." Daniel sighed. "You feared that once Mrs Chambers and I became reacquainted, we would discuss the events surrounding Thomas' death, which in turn might prompt us to visit The Mariners. But Lord Gibson received the package days before I began sitting outside the pawnbrokers to guard Mrs Chambers' house at night."

Daphne had not even considered that point. Daniel's insight was remarkable.

"In my line of work, one must prepare for every eventuality."

Lily's tone conveyed her arrogance. "I've followed you both for years. A few weeks ago, I saw you together at the docks. Based on her flimsy clothing, I wondered if Mrs Chambers had taken a new profession. But then you boarded the *Falcon*, and I knew you were working together on a case."

So Lily had seen them working the Harwood case, and all the while they had been oblivious to her interest in them.

"Now I have done your work for you and answered your questions, give me the pocket watch."

"I'm afraid you'll have to shoot me in the heart," Daniel said, "for I will tell you nothing more until you've released Mrs Chambers from your grasp. You have a pistol, and I doubt there's much the lady can do while her wrists are bound."

It took Lily a moment to consider the suggestion. "Very well." Lily pushed Daphne away. "Take three large steps. That is all."

Daphne did as she was told but hoped to heaven Daniel had a plan to save them.

Lily pointed her pistol at Daphne. "If she moves, I'll shoot her. Now, Mr Thorpe, give me the proof I seek. I assume you stole it back from Lord Gibson."

"Of course." Daniel gestured to his pocket. "May I?"

"Retrieve the item slowly." Lily's eyes grew round as Daniel lifted the watch gently from his coat pocket. He threw it to her, and she caught it with her free hand. "I trust the proof is hidden somewhere inside?"

"It was." Daniel shuffled backwards as Lily examined the gold case. With a discreet jerk of the head, he gestured for Daphne to move further back. Then he placed his hands on his head, even though Lily had lowered the weapon and had not instructed him to do so. "But it is not there now."

Lily's frantic gaze shot up. "Do you not value this woman's life? Give me what I ask."

"I can't." Daniel took another step back. "Lord Gibson

removed the note from inside the case and passed it on to the appropriate authority. I called on him this morning."

All the colour drained from Lily's face. She glanced back over her shoulder and then cocked the pistol and aimed at Daphne's head.

"There is little point firing at Mrs Chambers," Daniel said, edging further away. "The note was written in code, and I am the only one who knows what it says."

"In code," Lily echoed. "Does it implicate me?"

"Your name is mentioned, but Lord Gibson did not give me the chance to read more than a few words."

Lily's lips curled up into an evil grin. "Then with you out of the way, Gibson will have no hope of discovering what it says. I'll be free to leave for France with no fear of reprisal."

Fear gripped Daphne by the throat. Lily would shoot. She was convinced of it.

"You should have kept the watch when you pulled it from Thomas' body," Daniel said, seemingly unperturbed by the threat to his life. "Had you bothered to examine it, none of this would have been necessary."

Yes, but a traitor would have been free to roam in their midst, causing untold havoc.

"My mistake was trying to save Thomas by grabbing his waistcoat," Lily said coldly. "The watch snapped from the chain as he fell. Had it ended up in the water, no one would have been able to read the note."

Daniel muttered a curse under his breath. "What motivates a woman to kill a man she professed to care for?"

"Money, Mr Thorpe." Lily snorted. "I'd prefer a comfortable life in France than to rot away in the back streets of Wapping. When the *Carron* leaves again, I plan to sail away never to return." She turned the pistol on Daniel. "I would have suggested you come with me. But as you've admitted you're the only person who can read the code, I've no option but to kill you. This time I'll not miss."

The click of the hammer falling sent a bolt of fear straight to Daphne's heart. The puff of white smoke wafted up into the cool night air. It took a second or two for the bang to reach her ears.

"Daniel!" Daphne cried as she watched him fall back, watched the cream waistcoat turn crimson with blood. With cuffed wrists, Daphne struggled to clutch her stomach as a searing pain ripped through her body. Tears burst from her eyes as she glared at Lily's indifferent expression. "How could you?"

Without a thought for her own safety, Daphne rushed forward and dropped to her knees at Daniel's side. She touched the back of her shackled hand to his waistcoat to find it saturated with blood.

"Oh, Lord. No!" The tears fell so hard they bubbled in the back of her throat. "Please, Daniel. Open your eyes. Don't leave me." She looked up and scanned the deserted wharf. "Help! Someone, help me!" Surely someone would have heard the shot.

"There is no need to cry," Lily said, "as you are about to join him. Only a fool would leave a witness alive."

Lily aimed at Daphne.

Daphne sucked in a breath, bent down and kissed Daniel on the forehead. "I love you," she whispered, determined she would own the words in this life as well as the next.

The loud crack of the ball as Lily discharged it from the pistol exploded in her ears. Daphne put her head on Daniel's shoulder and closed her eyes, waited for the sharp pain to hit her in the back.

When a woman's shrill cry filled the air, Daphne glanced up to see Lily lying in a heap on the ground. With eyes cold, wide and vacant, it was evident she was dead.

Two figures appeared in the distance. The smaller one carried a pistol. The larger one ran towards her.

"Thorpe!" Bostock cried as he fell to his knees at his friend's side.

"He's gone, Mr Bostock." Daphne's voice sounded fractured, croaky. She stared at the ugly burgundy stain on Daniel's chest. Why was life so cruel? Just when she'd glimpsed true happiness. Just when she'd found someone to love. "There's nothing we can do."

Bostock leant forward, ripped Daniel's waistcoat open, sent the button's scattering across the wharf. "He's not dead, Mrs Chambers. Least I hope not." Bostock tore at the linen shirt to reveal a strange contraption beneath.

"What's that strapped to his chest?"

"Two metal plates with padding in between," Bostock said, slapping Daniel around the face. He touched a point on Daniel's neck. "Oh, he's alive all right. Probably the shock that caused him to black out that's all."

"It … it has nothing to do with the shock," Daniel muttered as he opened his eyes.

Daphne's head felt suddenly light. "You're alive!" The pressure of grief pressing down on her heart, lifted.

Daniel groaned. "I'm alive, but the impact may have cracked a rib."

"But I saw the blood." Daphne shook her head. "I saw the ball hit you in the chest."

Bostock tugged the material bag attached to the metal plate. "Betsy made a pouch. I won't tell you what she used for the lining. We filled it with pig's blood. Thorpe wanted Lily to think he was dead so that he might have an opportunity to rescue you if need be."

"But I'm not dead, Bostock." Daniel winced as he touched his chest. "And I am capable of speaking for myself."

"I trust the ball hit the breastplate?" the other gentleman said as he stepped closer.

"Yes, my lord," Bostock replied. "He's damn lucky she didn't aim for his head."

Daniel came up to a sitting position. "It's a matter of mind manipulation. With my hands raised, my chest was an open target. I more or less told her to shoot me in the heart."

Daphne sat back on her knees and glared at Daniel. She didn't know whether to laugh or cry, whether to slap him or kiss him. "If my hands were free, I'd punch you so hard I'd be sure to break your nose."

"Then perhaps I should lie back and close my eyes and wait for you to tell me you love me again."

He'd heard her!

Bostock cleared his throat. "There'll be time for that later. We need to get those shackles off your wrists, Mrs Chambers, and get Thorpe to his feet. And no doubt Betsy will be out of her mind with worry."

"I've sent my man to find a constable," the lord said, looking back at Lily's lifeless body. "I'll deal with things here. But I shall need your testimony to satisfy the powers that be."

"Thank you, Lord Gibson," Daniel said. "I shall call on you tomorrow and will provide whatever you need."

Lord Gibson? Heavens, Daniel had achieved more in the few hours working alone than they had in days.

Finding the key to the shackles in Lily's satchel, Daphne spent five minutes massaging the marks on her wrists where the metal had dug into her skin. Bostock removed the odd contraption strapped to Daniel's chest. The lead ball had dented the first sheet of metal. Daniel shrugged into his coat. Despite her anger, Daphne had to admit there was something quite fetching about a bare-chested man wearing nothing but outdoor clothing.

"You still haven't explained why you risked your life when there were a hundred other ways to deal with Lily," she said.

They walked along the wharf toward Lower Shadwell. Bostock had hurried ahead to find Murphy. Daphne's heart was still racing. The memory of Daniel falling to the ground would never leave her.

"I needed to distract Lily long enough for Gibson to get close. And I needed you out of harm's way. Gibson wouldn't take the shot until Lily fired first and I couldn't take the chance she might hurt you."

"So you risked your life for me?" she said, anger surfacing again. "What if she'd hit you in the neck? What if she'd missed your stupid metal vest? What then?"

Daniel stopped walking, grabbed her arm and turned her to face him. "Then my only regret would be that I'd not told you I love you."

She was silent for a moment as the words seeped into her mind.

"You do?" The warm feeling in her chest banished the anger and fear. "You're not just saying that because I said those same words to you?"

He laughed. "For heaven's sake, Daphne. You're supposed to be a skilled enquiry agent. How can you not know that I've loved you since the day I met you?"

Daphne blinked. "Since when?" Her stomach did a little flip.

"Since the night at the opera."

"But in recent years you've been so distant."

Daniel raised a brow. "As I'm sure you're aware, I have never been good at dealing with rejection. My way of coping with emotion is to ignore it."

His comment brought to mind all she'd learned from Lavinia. "Is that why you refuse to accept who you truly are?"

His gaze dropped, and he shrugged. "Perhaps." He took her hand, and they continued walking. "We should go home and get some rest. With this case solved we must turn our attention to more pressing matters?"

"Do you mean what we should do now we have both declared our true feelings?"

"Indeed," Daniel nodded. "We must decide what we want to do now. Where we go from here."

CHAPTER 25

AFTER SPENDING THE MORNING WITH LORD GIBSON, GIVING HIM a full statement of events leading up to the death of Lily Lawson, Daniel made his way to Hyde Park. Daphne had asked to meet him away from New Bond Street. The bridge leading to Apsley House was a short distance from the main thoroughfare, but it was quiet, secluded.

He arrived ten minutes early. Despite Daphne's insistence she take a hackney, he'd not risk her waiting alone in such a sheltered spot. The time gave him a moment to reflect on the events of the last few days.

So much had happened. So much had changed.

The overwhelming feelings that consumed him made everyday tasks more difficult. It had taken him over an hour to eat breakfast, for his mind continually wandered back to Daphne. It had taken three attempts to tie his cravat. How was he to focus on a new case when seducing the woman he loved was his only priority?

The faint rustle of silk captured his attention.

Daphne walked towards him wearing an emerald-green pelisse that matched the colour of her eyes to perfection. A few ebony curls framed her face though the rest of her hair was hidden beneath her bonnet. His gaze fell to the velvet reticule, and he wondered if she carried a weapon, imagined running his hand under her skirt to see if she had one strapped to her thigh.

"Daniel," she smiled as his name left her lips. Had they been alone in her private parlour, he would have taken her in his arms and kissed her. "I trust things went well with Lord Gibson."

"Gibson was more than happy to accept your written statement," he said, bringing her gloved hand to his lips and brushing a kiss over her knuckles. "I promised to take it to him within the next few days."

"I'll have it finished this evening." She gestured to the path. "Shall we walk?"

A sense of foreboding settled over him. He cast her a sidelong glance as she threaded her arm through his. The shadows beneath her eyes suggested a lack of sleep. Her tightly drawn lips were a sign of anxiety.

"Have you spoken to Mr Bostock this morning?" she continued. "I assume you've heard the news."

Daniel nodded. "He came to tell me that he plans to wed Betsy." The conversation had been awkward. Bostock's incessant mumbling had made it difficult to understand his meaning. "I got the sense he thinks he's abandoning me. But I'm happy he's found love."

"Well, you've worked together for so long perhaps he's scared of change." She stared at the row of trees lining the walkway. "Will he still assist on your cases?"

"We've not spoken at length about it. But I'm to meet a prospective client later this afternoon and so no doubt we'll discuss it then." Taking another case was the only way to settle his mind. In truth, he felt nothing like himself. An uncomfortable feeling lingered in his chest, one of uncertainty and fear.

"You plan to take another case so quickly?" There was a hesitance in her voice that worried him.

"A man must work" was his only defence.

Daphne sighed. "But you do not need to work, at least not like this. Why pay a man to manage your estate when you're capable of running it yourself?"

He'd been expecting to have a conversation about Rainham Hall. "What is this really about?" He stopped walking and turned to face her. "Why are we meeting in the park and not at the modiste shop?"

She bit down on her bottom lip, struggled to hold his gaze. "Because I am not strong enough to fight my feelings for you when we are alone together. If we were in my parlour you would try to kiss away my fears, but you would only succeed in suppressing them."

His heart pounded as his mind tried to ascertain her meaning. "Why would you want to fight your feelings?"

"You cannot know the pain I felt when I saw you lying on the wharf." She closed her eyes for a moment. "I thought you were dead, Daniel."

"But I have explained why I felt the deception was necessary."

"Can you not imagine how it felt to witness such a thing?" She swallowed deeply. "Do I need to tell you how much you mean to me? Do I need to tell you that I love you so much I spend every minute wondering how I'll cope if I lose you?"

He stepped closer. "Daphne, there is nothing to fear for I have no intention of ever letting you go."

"But you insist on working these dangerous streets." Her voice was fractured. "Putting yourself in life-threatening situations."

"We both do." He shrugged, not knowing where the conversation was leading.

"There is no comparison. The cases you take are nothing like mine. You storm a building full of smugglers while I search for the person who stole a hat pin. You risk your life every day."

245

"But this is who I am." He placed his hand on his chest. "You've always known that."

"No," she insisted. "It's what you do, Daniel, not who you are."

For a man with a logical mind, he was struggling to understand what she was saying. "What is your point, Daphne?"

There was a tense moment of silence.

"I can't be the one who sits at home waiting, hoping you're still alive." A tear trickled down her cheek, and he wiped it away with his thumb. "I can't live my life always fearing the worst."

"Are you saying you don't want me?"

"I have never wanted anything more in my entire life."

Damnation. Why were women so confounding?

"But I am leaving London," she said with renewed resolve.

"Leaving?" How ironic that the one thing he'd always wanted for her was now the last thing he wanted to hear. "Where will you go?"

"To a place where the air is clean. Where the life is not squeezed from my soul day by day."

Lord help him. It felt as though the devil had punched a hole in his chest and ripped out his heart. "And what about me?"

"I am a hindrance to your work, Daniel. It was my fault you almost died in the alley, my fault I'd gone into a book shop and not stayed with Bostock as I was told." She touched him lightly on the cheek before pulling her hand away. "If I stay here, you'll feel bound to protect me. How can you be mindful of your safety if you're always worrying about me?"

Daniel dragged his hand down his face. The painful knots in his stomach made it difficult to stand straight. "I can't let you go."

"And I can't stay." She glanced left and right along the deserted path, leant forward and kissed him softly on the lips.

Her touch soothed the pain, and he wrapped his arm around her and deepened the kiss.

When she broke contact on a ragged breath, tears were streaming down her face. "I love you," she whispered. "But you must let me go." She stepped away from him.

"Wait." The word was but a whisper.

He stood like a fool and watched her hurry along the path. The back of his throat was tight, his tongue too thick and heavy to call out. Rather than a hundred thoughts filling his head, his mind was empty. He was nothing but a hollow shell. The lady had captured his heart and soul and spirited them away.

Time passed in a blur.

He had no recollection of how long he'd stood there staring at the trees, no recollection of how he'd walked from the bridge to his carriage.

Having failed to arrive for his appointment, he spent the time in Church Street, tidying the rooms and putting the books on the shelves in alphabetical order.

It was seven o'clock when Bostock arrived.

"Should you not be celebrating with your betrothed?" Daniel said, dropping into the chair in the study. The words carried a hint of bitterness which in no way reflected his true feelings. "What I meant to say is Miss Betsy deserves your full attention."

Bostock sat in the seat opposite. "Betsy says Mrs Chambers is leaving London. That she's going to apply for a job as a governess for a widower. The man has three children and has not long lost his wife."

"And what will she teach them?" Daniel snorted. "How to wield a pistol? How to lie and make it look convincing?"

Bostock frowned. "You sound like the old Thorpe. The man who cares for no one but himself. The man who likes to hide his feelings rather than show others he's weak."

Daniel rolled his eyes. "Love makes you talk in riddles, Bostock."

"And love is the only thing that can save you but you're too stubborn to see it."

247

Bostock had never spoken so openly to him before. "Did Mrs Chambers send you here to rub salt in my wounds?"

"Mrs Chambers has not left her bedchamber since she came home from meeting you in the park. Betsy went to check on her, but she wouldn't open the door."

A sharp pain shot through his heart. "Perhaps she's packing."

Bostock fell silent. When Daniel was in a cynical mood, his friend knew not to press him.

"Did you meet your new client?" Bostock asked, changing the subject.

"No."

Bostock appeared surprised. "It's not like you to miss an appointment."

"Things change." The truth was he could barely recall his own name let alone hold a lengthy conversation or appear remotely interested in other people's affairs.

Bostock stood abruptly. "I'd best be going."

"Murphy will take you back to New Bond Street."

"Then I'll say one more thing before I go." His friend hesitated. "Betsy said fate has a strange way of working its magic. That night I helped you fight those men in the street, no one would have thought I'd grow to care for you like a brother."

"You know how I despise sentiment." Well, he used to shy away from all emotion. Now he was able to acknowledge his feelings for the man standing before him. "You have been my friend and constant companion all these years. I would not be here today without your support."

Bostock stepped forward and gripped his shoulder. "Both our lives changed the day we met. Both our lives changed the day we walked into the modiste shop. We can't fight it. We can't run away from what's meant to be."

"It seems love has turned you into a philosopher as well."

Bostock gave a weak smile. "Don't you want to marry Mrs Chambers?"

Marry her? Was it a trick question? "Bostock, I would have married the woman years ago. But she rejected me then, and she has rejected me now." Just saying the words caused a tightening in his chest.

"I used to say you were the cleverest man in all of London."

"Used to?"

"Only a fool could be so blind as to miss what's so obvious."

Daniel was too tired to offer a rebuke. "Then tell me, Bostock. Tell me what a wise man would do?"

Bostock straightened. "First, he would stop moping about like a ninny. Then he would stop running and catch his breath. He would forget about the past, not care about the future. He would understand that the present is all that matters. A man's worth is measured by those who love him and those he loves in return. Not by the power he has over other men."

"I did not realise you had such strong feelings on the matter."

"Make a new life," Bostock said, undeterred. "One worthy of the great man you are."

"Without me, what would you do to earn a living?"

Bostock shrugged. "Though these hands are too big to grasp a needle, turns out I've got an eye for detail. Betsy's thinking of opening a new shop. A gentleman's tailors. I'd hire people to do the measuring and sewing, but the designs would be my own."

Daniel stared at his friend. To say he was flabbergasted was an understatement.

"So nothing is stopping doing the same," Bostock continued.

"I have no interest in gentlemen's fashion."

Bostock huffed. "I've seen how you are with Mrs Chambers. If you let her go, then there's no hope for you. Look at you. You've never missed an appointment in all the years I've known you."

"I'll admit, I've no mind for work at the moment."

Despite trying to fight his feelings, Daniel knew his old life was no longer a good fit. Outwitting peers had lost its appeal. He cared nothing for other people's problems.

So what was it that scared him?

Certainly not his love for Daphne. He would give his life for her. The thought forced him to question his logic. If he was prepared to make the ultimate sacrifice, then why not abandon his work and embrace a new life with the woman he loved?

But what would he do in the country?

Perhaps land management could become his new hobby.

"I've always known you were the brains of this operation," Daniel said as a sudden feeling of hope sprung to life in his chest. "Tell Murphy I'm in need of his services once he's taken you home."

"You're in no mood to work tonight," Bostock said nervously.

"I'm not going to work, my friend. I'm going to Rainham Hall."

CHAPTER 26

Two days had passed since Daphne had run away from Daniel on the bridge in Hyde Park, but the pain in her chest could not be tempered. Love, it seemed, could render a person helpless.

Seduction proved simple.

Love was a baffling conundrum of emotions, something far too complicated to define. To save the man she loved, she'd let him go. It seemed the only logical course of action. So why did she want to curl up into a ball and die?

A sudden rap on the door brought Betsy, who rushed into the parlour in an excited frenzy.

"Quick, where's your pelisse?" Betsy rummaged through the garments on the coat stand. "That pretty green one that enhances the colour of your eyes."

"It's in the bedchamber." Daphne didn't have the heart to ask why. "Borrow it if you wish, but it will be far too long on you."

"I'm not the one in need of it." Betsy raced over to the window. "Mr Thorpe's carriage is waiting outside, and it will be too cold to travel without one."

"Mr Thorpe!" Daphne jumped off the chair as though the pad

had caught fire. She hurried to the window and noted the black conveyance parked across the road. "What does he want?" Her heart lurched at the prospect of seeing Daniel again.

"Mr Thorpe isn't here. The carriage is for you."

"Betsy, you're not making any sense."

Mr Bostock appeared at the parlour door and cleared his throat. "Mr Thorpe would like to know if you'd be interested in taking a tour of Rainham Hall?"

"Rainham Hall?" Daphne's stomach performed a flip. She'd love nothing more than to see the house where his parents had celebrated their love. "Will Mr Thorpe be joining me?"

"Mr Thorpe is already there. Murphy will drive you to meet him."

"How far is it?" Oh, it was foolish to even think of meeting Daniel when the wound to her heart was still fresh, so raw. But her inquisitive mind insisted she go. Nothing could be worse than the pain she felt already.

Bostock frowned.

"Will I be returning this evening?" Daphne clarified.

"That I can't say."

"Best take a change of clothes," Betsy said. "Just in case."

Before Daphne's mind could catch up with her movements, she was sitting in Thorpe's carriage and rattling along the road on her way to Rainham Hall. Murphy had informed her the journey would take a little over two hours, and they would be heading west out of London towards High Wycombe.

She spent the journey wondering about Daniel's motives for bringing her to a place he'd always avoided. How had he fared in the two days since their last meeting? Did he in any way feel the same overwhelming sense of despair?

Rainham Hall sat nestled at the foot of a hill, amid a vibrant canopy of green fields. A small wood to the north offered protection from the wind sweeping down into the valley. The drive up to the house took her through a tunnel of trees. The sun shone.

The birds sang. Love filled her heart as she recalled what the place had meant to Daniel's parents.

Murphy drew the carriage to a halt outside the large oak front door. Daphne held her breath while she waited for Daniel to appear and was surprised when a woman in a plain grey dress exited the house.

Murphy climbed down from his box seat and helped Daphne alight.

"I'm Mrs Barton, the housekeeper." The middle-aged woman stood before Daphne and curtsied. "We've been expecting you. You'll find the master down by the fountain." She pointed to a gravel path on the left. "Follow the path across the lawn and past the pagoda. It will be clear where you need to go."

"Thank you, Mrs Barton."

"I told the master you'd be hungry after your journey, but he insists on speaking to you before you sit down to eat."

Food was the last thing on her mind. Daphne put her hand to her stomach. "I can wait a little longer."

Mrs Barton smiled. "There's no rush. As it's such a nice day, I can make a basket if you'd prefer. Come and find me once you've made a decision." The woman inclined her head and went inside.

Nerves held Daphne immobile for a moment. Then the urge to see Daniel took hold, and she hurried along the path.

While the grounds lacked the grandeur of Elton Park, there was something intimate about the space, something warm and welcoming that soothed the soul. If Daphne owned such a special place, she would never leave.

The pagoda was more a circular Roman-inspired temple. From there, she could see the elaborate fountain made up of statues of bare-breasted women cradling cherubs. She saw him then. Seated on a bench.

Daphne's heart fluttered up to her throat.

It took a tremendous effort not to pick up her skirt and run.

But she was not sure why he'd called her to the house and could not presume it was good news.

Hearing her approach, he jumped to his feet. Even though she could remember every line on his face, nothing her mind conjured compared to how wonderful it was to see him in the flesh.

"You came." He stepped forward and took hold of her hands by way of a greeting. "I wasn't sure you would."

"Regardless of what I told you in Hyde Park, I am always available should you need me." She wanted to kiss him, to take him in her arms, hold him tight and never let go.

"I've made a mess of things," he said solemnly. "With you. With this house. I turned my back on everything that mattered. This house was once filled with love. One only has to walk through the gardens to see the evidence of it."

"I feel nothing but love as I stand here admiring the spectacular view," she said softly, her gaze fixed on him.

A smile touched his lips. "My mother's inability to cope with the pain of loss turned it into a house of despair. A place where I was encouraged to strive to be that which I am not."

Daphne wanted to understand him. "Do you speak of her need to prove your legitimacy?"

He seemed shocked at the depth of her knowledge. "One cannot fight the truth. My parents were not married. No amount of cajoling and persuading will ever change that. My father's family follow a rigid set of rules. Other than a striking similarity to the man my mother insists is my father, there is no proof to support her claim."

"Is that why you stay away? Why you spend your life solving other people's problems, finding other people's proof?"

He shrugged. "Perhaps. But I am only just learning to process thoughts I've long since buried."

Daphne scanned the breathtaking panorama and inhaled the smell of freshly cut grass. "Do you think you might stay here from time to time? A spell in the country is like a rejuvenating tonic. And it's so beautiful here, so clean and quiet."

"That all depends."

"On what?" Her heart was beating so fast it echoed in her ears.

"On you." Daniel stepped closer. "Stay here with me. I can't do this alone. I can't do this without you."

Tears welled in her eyes. To build a life with this man was the only thing she wanted. "What of your work in London? Will you not take another case?"

"I could not give up my work completely." He smiled. "I have decided to become a farmer. Someone has to help find the lost lambs."

She doubted she could love him any more than she did at that moment. "I'm sure there are terrible crimes committed in rural areas. I hear the locals are still trying to determine who left mud in the pew last Sunday."

Daniel laughed, but then his smile faded. "I have loved you from the moment I met you. I once asked you to marry me without giving the matter much thought, but I'll not make that mistake again."

Daphne inhaled sharply.

"So now I am asking you to be my wife," he continued. "To lie with me at night, to be my constant companion. I am asking you to love me and in return know that I will love, honour and protect you until the day I die."

Joy burst forth in a torrent of tears. She flung her arms around his neck and kissed him deeply.

"Does that mean you accept?" he said, dragging his mouth away.

"Of course I accept." She kissed him once again just for good measure, told him she loved him ten times or more. "It will mean mastering a new weapon, though I doubt a scythe is as deadly as a blade."

"You once told me your weapon of choice is your mouth. I'd consider mastering that before moving on to anything else." A wicked grin formed on his lips. "I'm more than happy to offer myself as your tutor."

"And are your hands not said to be your greatest asset? If we work together I feel we shall make an excellent team."

EPILOGUE

RAINHAM HALL, BUCKINGHAMSHIRE
TWO YEARS LATER

"Don't pull the lamb's tail, George," Helena called to her son from the terrace as she cradled her daughter, Olivia.

"He's stroking the tail not pulling it," Lucas called back from their spot on the grass. He turned to Daniel. "I don't know why she's so worried. When I was a boy, I would have tried to climb on its back and ride it around the grounds."

Holding his son, Tobias, in his arms, Daniel knelt down to let the boy pet the lamb. The one-year-old had no concept of stroking and slapped the animal numerous times on the back.

"I think that's enough for today," Daphne said as she came to stand with them on the lawn. "Return the lamb to Mr Davies so he may reunite it with its mother. I'd hate for him to think it's missing."

There was something different about his wife today, Daniel thought. Her green eyes were overly bright. And the wide smile gracing her lips hadn't faltered in days.

"Why do mothers spoil all the fun?" Lucas teased. "Say goodbye to the lamb, George." Lucas took the boy's hand and escorted him back to Helena.

"Do you have something to tell me, Daphne?" Daniel said as

soon as Lucas was out of earshot. He stepped closer. The urge to kiss her took hold, and he bent his head and pressed his lips to hers before anyone noticed.

"Is it so obvious?" A giggle escaped from her lips as she struggled to hide her excitement.

"I am extremely skilled when it comes to reading the language of your body."

She took hold of his hand. "Then you should not be surprised to discover that I am with child."

His heart swelled. "You're certain?"

"Of course," she said, leaning forward to stroke Tobias' head. "As we both know what it's like to have no siblings, it's important Tobias has someone special in his life other than his parents."

Without a care for who saw them, he kissed her again. The need to demonstrate his love for her proved overwhelming. "Is that why you were awake for hours last night? As I recall, the last time you struggled to sleep you were worried about the intruder."

"With you by my side I have nothing to fear," she said, squeezing his hand. "I trust you're pleased with the news."

"Pleased? I could not be any happier." He suddenly wished they were alone so he could worship her as he wanted to.

"Perhaps we might celebrate our good fortune later this evening," she said in the seductive lilt he so loved.

"I shall look forward to it. Indeed, I shall think of nothing else for the rest of the day."

Daphne took Tobias in her arms. "The children need to rest. Return the lamb to Davies and then come and eat."

"Well, have you decided?" Lucas said, coming to stand at their side.

Daniel frowned, curious as to Lucas' meaning. "Decided what?"

"Which one of us is carrying the lamb?" Lucas brushed the

sleeves of his coat. "That is unless it's trained to follow your heel, and then it can trot along behind."

"I'll carry it," Daniel said with a chuckle. "I can see you're wearing a new coat."

Lucas raised a brow. "Ah, your eye for detail is as sharp as ever."

Daphne shook her head. "I shall leave you gentlemen to your duties."

Daniel stood in awe and watched Daphne walk across the lawn. Love burned so fiercely in his chest it was often difficult to breathe. Sometimes he'd wake at night in a cold sweat, believing his new life was but a dream. But then Daphne would wrap her warm arms around him and soothe away his fears.

His mind drifted back to the bleak day in Hyde Park when his world came crashing down around him. What if he'd let her go? What if Bostock hadn't come to offer a logical alternative to chasing criminals through the back streets of London?

"If you're sulking because you want me to carry the lamb then you only have to say." Lucas' comical tone disturbed Daniel's reverie.

"I'll carry the lamb," Daniel said. Thank the Lord no one else was party to their ridiculous conversation. "I was just thinking about Bostock."

"You were watching your wife while thinking of your associate?" Lucas grinned. "How interesting."

Daniel rolled his eyes. "I remember a time when you had a face of stone and growled at everyone who glanced your way." The lamb bleated as he picked it up. "Now, you appear to find the slightest thing amusing."

Lucas gave him a friendly slap on the upper arm, and Daniel nearly dropped the animal. "I think it's fair to say we were both angry with the world. I recall you being equally miserable. And now look at you—hugging a lamb as though you're its surrogate mother."

"Love has changed us both it seems."

"And for the better," Lucas said. "The sight of you in that billowing coat was enough to frighten the Devil."

Daniel laughed. "Fate is a funny thing. Had your brother not hired me to solve your case, I doubt I would be on speaking terms with Daphne."

"Then you owe him a debt so large it can never be repaid." Lucas stopped walking and glanced at the lush green fields. "You belong here. You belong with Daphne."

Daniel knew how fortunate he was. Every day, he counted his blessings.

"Bostock tells me you own a textile company and donated reams of fabric so he could make clothes for the poor."

Lucas shrugged. "One has to admire your man's efforts," he said modestly. "If you ever find land management tiring, I could always use a business partner."

"I shall bear that in mind should I ever break my crook."

Lucas chuckled. "Do you ever miss your work as an enquiry agent?"

Daniel considered the question. "I miss the thrill of the chase. The satisfaction gleaned from solving a case. But my life is richer now in so many ways."

"I understand. But one never knows what the future holds. Tobias and Olivia are the same age. Perhaps one day they might fall in love, and some dastardly devil will seek to cause havoc with their plans. In their desperate hour of need, we may be called upon to save the day."

"Our children are barely a year old, and already you're planning their future."

"There is one problem. Daphne and Helena love solving mysteries. We'd have a hell of a game trying to keep them in tow."

Lucas' imagination was running away with him.

"I have no desire to dwell on what might be," Daniel said,

desperate to deliver the lamb and return to the terrace in the hope of stealing another kiss from Daphne. "It's called the present for a reason. The gift of today is all that should concern us. Bostock taught me that."

Lucas brushed his hand through his hair. "You're just saying that because in twenty years you know I'll still be as handsome as ever and you'll be bald or grey."

Daniel shrugged. "Still, I have nothing to fear. According to Mrs Bostock there is a man on Mill Street who makes accessories for gentlemen who are follicly challenged."

"Ah, so that's how you managed to grow such an impressive beard."

The End

Thank you for reading
A Simple Case of Seduction.

You can read Anthony and Sarah's story in
The Secret To Your Surrender

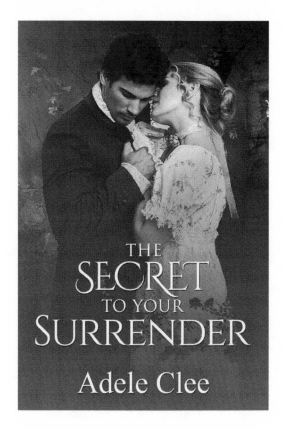

Made in the USA
Middletown, DE
25 January 2024

48463164R00161